BURIED LIGHT

Dear Sue,

I'm honored to be your friend. One are definitely not whose light is buried!

Dianne

BURIED LIGHT

DIANE DÁVALOS BEALE

ISBN: 978-1-976322-12-9

This book is dedicated to my beloved husband, Bob Beale, my partner on this amazing journey, unwavering supporter, love of my life, and best friend.

Dear Diane,

Thank you so much for your WONDERFUL book! I am blessed by it in so many ways. The history, the suspense, the love story, and the ending which answered all my lingering questions. What a gifted writer you are!! I had no idea.

I found myself reading many pages, when I began, but I slowed myself down and only allowed a certain number of pages to be read at night before going to bed: I just didn't want the story and the information and the beauty of the writing to end! You kept me on the edge of my seat throughout the book. I always left off reading when there was a cliff-hanger, so I would be even more excited to get back to the story.

What a gift you have given me! I am spreading the word, and hope I can get all my friends to read this awesome book. Thank you so much.

Much love to you, and thank you again,

Rev. Dr. Myron McClellan,
Theologian, Mystic, Teacher

ACKNOWLEDGEMENTS

My heartfelt gratitude goes out to the many people who with care, patience, talent, and honesty critiqued this book and gave invaluable feedback. They include Pat Bill, Allyn Breech, Dianna Butler, Theresa Byrne, Rudite Jaunarajs, Susan Norman, Lynda Parker, Cherie Peterson, and many teachers and students of Lighthouse Writers Workshop.

Thank you so very much!

AUTHOR'S NOTE

I hope this book entertains, informs, and persuades, as good fiction must. My main intent was to offer a picture of life that is much, much larger than most of us have imagined. Certainly way larger than I could have imagined before I delved into these topics five years ago—and I now believe that even these are tiny compared to what is really out there.

Readers have said to me, "Wait a minute. Which parts of this are fact and which are made up?"

Fair enough.

The facts are: The Ica Stones and the doctor who collected them, Dr. Javier Cabrera; Caral; the Nazca lines; the Pisco holes; the elongated skulls; the so-called *candelabro* in Peru; as well as the tunnels under Peru, Bolivia, and Ecuador. Also historical facts are the existence of Father Carlo Crespi, the treasures he was given by the Wari Indians, and the sad ending to his story. The information in the Hall of Records is accurate to the best of my knowledge. The existence of the Black Hand, or the dark cabal (Illuminati), is also true.

These are certainly controversial: the existence of Atlantis, Lemuria, inhabitants of both the inner earth and other planets, and Reptilians. Legends all over the world speak of the great Amaru Meru and his consort Amara.

All of this fascinated me and inspired me to create a story around them. So of course the story is fictional—as are the main characters Pleija and Zamayo, Sofía and Rogelio; and the minor characters including Padre Anselmo, Cafre, the children of Dr. Cabrera, and Shelaya and the other inhabitants of New Lemuria.

Enjoy.

PREFACE

Back before the annals of time, forgotten by nearly all of humanity, there was a place inhabited, as the legends say, by the Children of the Sun.

This land was a veritable paradise where war, disease, hunger and strife were unknown. The lakes, rivers and waterfalls sparkled like crystals. Vegetables grew lush and the fruits were succulent. Nature offered these freely generously from her abundant bosom.

The luminous beings who inhabited this land were intelligent and graceful. In their hearts they held deep love for each other, for all sentient beings, and especially for Creator/Source, which they called the Great Central Sun. Ceremonies and celebrations in the sacred temples expressing gratitude for Life were offered often, but most fully on the yearly solstices and equinoxes.

This 'garden of Eden' was known as Lemuria. Some dismiss it as pure fantasy. Others insist that it really existed.

CONTENTS

PROLOGUE: THE LAST DAYS OF LEMURIA

Raj Haroon, Lemuria
APPROXIMATELY 50,000 YEARS AGO

The harmonious and complex songs of doves and nightingales gently broke Pleija's dreams. In that semi-somnolent state where insights often graced her consciousness, she sensed that today would be a special day indeed.

A rare black mamo bird flew by her window and as she looked out to admire him she noticed that both moons were still out, but it was starting to get light.

Shala 'am, Play zshah. "Good morning, Pleija." The words drifted behind her.

She looked over to see her beloved mate smiling at her. *Shala 'am, wale iho*, "Good morning, soul of my love," she said softly. Even after nearly 200 years together the sight of Zamayo made her a bit dizzy. He was nearly eight feet tall, had the muscular physique, and the wisdom and kindness of Muras, his forefather and the founder of Lemuria. He was every cubit priest and spiritual warrior, beautiful in body, mind and soul. She kissed him on the back of his head and he began caressing her.

"Oh dear. How could I have forgotten?" she said suddenly. "This is the solstice. The sun is almost up. I must begin my prayers and prepare for the children's initiation."

"Stay," he urged. He kissed her neck, knowing that usually was enough to make her forget everything else.

"No, really, I have to go," she said, pulling her hips away from him.

"Now?"

Hurrying out of the room she called back to him, "Yes, now. I'll see you at the council meeting."

Was there a trace of concern on his face? Or was it just disappointment? *Shala 'am. Shala 'am.*

Pleija went out to the baths and immersed her tall, graceful, nearly translucent blue-copper body in the fountain. She drank the vril-infused water from the exquisitely grained mahogany bowl that her mother had given her. From out of nowhere a surprising thought came to her, *I have the feeling I'm going to need some extra life force today.* So she took an extra sip then donned her white ceremonial robe, braided her golden red hair with pearls and white daisies, and carefully placed her sacred lapis lazuli necklace around her neck. Before she left the complex she placed one hand on the golden disc that hung over the portico and the other on the image of her hand painted in red on the wall.

She walked the marble path, grateful for the deep blue sky and the lemon-scented breeze. The summer solstice was her favorite day of the year, not only for the birds' morning serenade and for the flowers bursting forth a kaleidoscope of colors, but because this was such a special day for the seven-year-old children. It was, essentially, a new year for them and the opening of a new world. Today they would learn the magnificent and astounding history of their people and begin to take on the responsibilities and the pride of being a Lemurian citizen.

Pleija breathed deeply as she passed the orchards of papayas, mangos, passion fruit, and pineapples. She pulled off a bright yellow carambola from a nearby tree and let its crisp sweet-sour juice run down her mouth. Passing a macadamia tree, she thought, these nuts have never been so healthy. They're as big as oranges.

She passed a few houses, all made of a white marble, decorated with amethyst and jade in patterns of sacred geometry or the popular motif of a triangle within a circle. Children were dancing in the rays of the rising sun. Adults were tending their gardens, playing musical instruments, painting, or carving stones. They all waved to Pleija. *Shala 'am,* she called out in her melodious lilt.

As she neared the temple her step quickened in anticipation. Though she didn't see how her joy and serenity could be any greater, her hour of meditation in this most sacred of places invariably took her to a place of ecstasy.

The temple was actually a pyramid, built to raise vibrations and enhance connection with Spirit. Inside was a giant altar hewn out of one block of blue chalcedony. Both the gold altar and silver walls were adorned with gems placed to form mystical symbols. Carved stones and paintings depicted the vast history of their race.

Pleija was surprised to see others already deep in meditation, so she decided to go to a tiny side chamber where she could be alone. The gold walls of this room were covered in artistically fashioned *bas reliefs* of birds, animals and fish.

Holding her lapis stone to her heart, she began by sending prayers of gratitude to the Great Central Sun. Soon she was deep in meditation.

Two hours passed.

"Pleija! Pleija!" Her wise old friend Ranu was shaking her. "What happened to you? Everyone is waiting for you to begin the council meeting. Ah! By the powers of our Mother/Father Creator! You are ashen! What did you see?"

"Dearest Ranu," she replied. "I cannot now speak of the vision I had."

AT THE COUNCIL MEETING

Ranu and Pleija entered to find the other members in a rare argument. All twelve were dressed in robes of rich colors, the hems adorned with images of snakes, suns, and moons.

Selat, the most advanced in years and spiritual gifts, stood up slowly and with authority. Her mature beauty and wise counsel had always had a calming effect on the citizens of Raj Haroon. But today her words pierced. "In my meditation this morning I saw that the Atlanteans have made a new breakthrough in thermo magnetic power and that they plan to harness a nearby astroid and use it as a space station in order to 'monitor' our entire planet."

Zamayo was incredulous. "But that technology is totally untested— as is the safety of thermo magnetic power itself. Surely they wouldn't risk destroying their own islands in their attempt to control all of blessed Terra."

Yelala stood, her smoky hazel eyes moist. "Lord Aramu believes they would. That's why he is urging all citizens to consider leaving for safe haven."

Pleija looked up at the sun. "The timing is now that I must go to the children and prepare for their initiation. I propose we call an extra session of the council tomorrow and discuss this further."

Ranu murmured, "That is good."

The rest of the council responded in unison, "So be it. *Shala 'am.*"

Pleija took some comfort in experiencing the vibration of that phrase. It not only meant 'Good morning,' 'Hello,' and 'Goodbye,' but 'We are of One Heart.'

She hurried to the edge of the river to meet the nine children who turned seven years old this year. Pleija smiled to herself on seeing them waiting patiently, their faces glowing with anticipation. How she loved these beautiful souls. Every one of these children was smart, loving, earnest, and creative—each with a specific gift. For instance, Lelila was a talented water-color artist, Wonee was fascinated with science, Saluya wrote charming, funny stories, and Maila was a natural athlete.

Pleija began, "Let's sit in a circle where I'll explain what we'll do today." Her eyes glistened as she watched them eagerly gather around her. "First we'll take this canoe up the river, then follow a path to the highest point on the mountain. There I'll tell you the history of Lemuria and teach you how to meditate. Afterwards we'll have our initiation ceremony. When we're finished, you will have completed Level One on your way to becoming fully conscious and true Lemurian citizens. Then we'll have a big celebration! Do you understand?"

"Yes, Mother! Let's go!"

The canoe has been prepared earlier and was waiting just down river. It was made of birch bark with gracefully curved ends and was big enough for all ten of them. Pleija guided them effortlessly through the crystal water. The children squealed in delight at the fish, turtles, tiny flowers, and strangely shaped colored rocks that glistened like gems against the emerald green riverbed. Along the shore, thousands of wild flowers in varying shades of blues and purples were interwoven with yellow and white fragrant wild *ui,* which would later be known as honeysuckle vines.

After some time they arrived at their destination, disembarked, and sat to rest on a bed of cool green moss. A grove of bristlecone pine trees fanned out over the mountain all around them.

"Take a deep breath, now, and enjoy the invigorating smell of pine. Excellent. Now I want you to try something different. Smell the sky. Listen to the flowers. Taste the breeze. We'll be practicing this art all throughout your initiation. It's called synesthesia—can you say that? Synesthesia means mixing up sight, sound, touch, smell, and taste. By practicing this, your senses will become sharper and you'll be able to notice things you didn't notice before."

Pleija stopped speaking for just a split second as she seemed to be looking at something in the far distance, but quickly regained her composure.

"Your life will become much richer."

The children enjoyed this new game and became remarkably good at it in a short time.

"Now it's time to continue our journey. If you look up this way, you'll see some trees with fluttery leaves mixed in with the pines. These are called hemlocks. Can you see the thin silver path winding through them? We'll be walking up that path, so have a drink of river water and we'll begin."

Though the path was steep, the children, energized by their excitement, had little difficulty climbing it.

At the end of the path, Pleija said, "This, my beloved children, is the Universal Temple. Please enter in single file and in silence."

The temple was made of chestnut trees that wound among themselves to form an enclosure. The trunks formed columns along the sides and the branches were interwoven at the top. Inside, stone benches were placed in a circle, leaving spaces for the invigorating mountain air to enter and providing a stunning view over the vast continent and emerald sea.

The initiates all sat in silence for some time. Their faces reflected awe and reverence.

Then Pleija spoke. "And now you shall hear the story of Lemuria, the grandest civilization that ever graced our dear Terra.

"For millions of years there were wars throughout the galaxy. Some planets, like Maldek, were totally destroyed. Others, like Mars, became so cold and dry that nothing could live there anymore. Apparently the different races didn't know how to do anything except fight and kill each other."

Lelila's liquid brown eyes widened, "Why did they do that, Mother?"

Looking tenderly at the girl, she answered, "Because they had forgotten the Light and Love from whence we were all born."

Focusing her attention on the entire group once more, Pleija resumed her story. "They chose greed and revenge over forgiveness. And they continued fighting. Finally, after millions of years, a great leader named Atlas decided to travel to a new place and start over. His ships wandered through the galaxy until they came to our solar system. When he saw our golden sun, blue lands, and waters swimming with life, Atlas decided to colonize here on Terra.

"Now this great leader had a daughter who became his successor. She was called Pleija…"

"Like you!" several children cried in joy.

"Yes, I was named after her. When she became queen she changed the name of their home star system to the Pleiades."

"Which we can still see in the sky!" exclaimed Wonee, the budding astronomer.

"Right. Well, Atlas returned with his wife Pleione, thousands of crafts, and millions of people and started a whole new way to live. They built a society of splendor, glory, beauty, and peace upon this planet. Since the father of Atlas' wife was called Muras, they decided to name this golden, magical home…"

"Lemuria!" shouted all the children.

"Yes, our beloved Lemuria. Now this all happened a long, long time ago. Over that time many people came here to live. Beings from the star system Orion came. Arcturians came. Lyrians came. Pleiadeans came. And they often married each other and had children, so you can see that you are all a mixture of many races, right? Some of you have red or dark hair, some are blond, some have black, green, or turquoise eyes. Some of you are taller or have larger heads.

"Anyway, for all this time the people lived in peace and in harmony with each other and with nature. This was because they were guided by the Great Central Sun, the Source of all."

Wonee's huge gray eyes were moist. "May I ask a question?"

"Yes, of course."

"My cousin tells me that there are bad people out there who want to hurt us. Is that true?"

Pleija looked out over the ocean.

She hesitated for several heartbeats, her thoughts not in the past now, but in the future. At last, she answered, "Perhaps he's talking about our younger brothers and sisters who live far away, over the sea. Their land is called Atlantis. Atlantis was formed much later than Lemuria, and over the years the two civilizations became the greatest on planet Terra."

Pleija did her best to explain to the children that in the beginning they were quite alike but gradually developed different ways of looking at life. Lemurians believed in living simply with respect for all and in harmony with the laws of the Great Central Sun. Atlanteans had developed a great technology and they believed that science could solve all problems. Lemurians believed that the other continents should be left alone to develop at their own speed. Atlanteans, however, believed that since their technology was more advanced they should control and teach the others.

Daniel interrupted, "My mother says that we have something even better than science."

"What is that, my love?"

"She says that many of us, especially you, can see with an inner eye. That you know everything—even what's going to happen in the future."

Pleija touched his face softly, straining to hold back tears. Her heart was breaking. She quickly changed the subject.

"You're going to love the next part of our adventure! First we're going to have a picnic. Will you help me carry the bundles from the canoe?"

"Oh, yes, Mother!"

They scampered over to her, gave her big hugs, then ran to the canoe and came back with a rolled blanket of llama wool and bundle after bundle of fruits, nuts, vegetables, breads, jams, and chocolates. After they had placed the blanket on a mossy patch of ground and put all the food in the middle, she asked the children to hold hands and give thanks to their great Mother/Father for all their blessings.

The sun shone brightly through the trees, warming and energizing them. A gentle breeze filled the air with the scent of earth and pine. The sky was the color of blue jays. As Pleija watched the children giggling and enjoying their picnic, she almost succeeded in convincing herself that her premonition had been wrong. How could anything destroy this bucolic life?

"Let's play the game you learned earlier," she suggested. "Do you remember what it's called?"

Several of the children gave their best guess.

"Sin-tease-ya?"

"Santasia?"

"Sun is Pleija?"

Pleija smiled broadly. "Pretty close. It's synesthesia."

The children were very creative and took immense delight in closing their eyes, picking up a nut, or a gourd, or quinoa seeds and saying, "This sounds like the buzzing of a bee." Or, "This feels like yellow." Or, "This tastes sweet and sour at the same time."

"Beautiful my darlings! Now it's time for our next surprise. Let's gather our things and store them in the canoe. Then we'll climb to the very tippy top of the mountain."

The sun was directly overhead as they began climbing up the mountain. The ground was now uneven with branches and rocks on the path.

"Be careful, children!" Pleija's warning was just an eye blink too late. Maila had run ahead, twisted her foot on an exposed tree root, fallen down hard on a sharp-edged rock, and badly gashed her knee. She was crying when Pleija and the others caught up to her.

Blood was running freely down her leg and her knee was swollen and turning black and blue.

"Oh, my sweet baby!" Pleija held and soothed her. "Leilila, please run to the stream and bring some water. Wonee, see if you can find a tavari plant and bring back some leaves."

Leilila rushed back with water in a coconut shell and Pleija washed the wound. The children instinctively gathered around Maila, raised their palms to face her, and silently sent healing energies to her.

Soon Wonee returned with the tavari leaves. Pleija tore one in half and squeezed the sap over Maila's wound as the children continued to send healing thoughts to their friend. After a while Maila smiled. The bleeding had stopped.

"It doesn't hurt anymore! Let's keep going. I want to see the surprise ahead."

"Are you sure?" Pleija was hesitant, but she knew that Maila was strong and just a tad stubborn, so she gave in.

It took quite some time to reach their destination, but they finally came to the last curve in the path. Then they arrived at a flattened area.

They had been walking with their heads down, careful not to fall as Maila had.

"Now look up!"

"Wow!"

"Amazing"

"I don't believe it!"

"Incredible!"

"We must be dreaming!"

"Oh, my gosh!"

What the children saw as they gazed toward the sky was a sight that defied description. There were hundreds of stone statues of giants twenty times their own height. Their huge heads looked out over the land.

"Ooh. They look so serious!"

"Look at those eyes!"

"Yeah. They sparkle like black diamonds or something."

"Ha. What funny long ears!"

"These statues are very special," Pleija told them. "They're called *Matakiterani*—'Eye turned to the sky.' Go have a closer look, but please don't try to climb on them."

When none of the children were in view, Pleija had an inspiration. She walked to one of the unfinished statues, picked up an obsidian tool lying nearby, and sketched the image of a ship on the back of one.

Then she sat alone on a grassy knoll. Absolute despair was fighting in her with an instinctive desire to protect these innocent little ones. Since she was the age of these children and had had her first initiation, these sacred statues had been a comfort and an inspiration to her. They had also been a source of comfort and inspiration for sea and space travelers since time out of mind. They held the highest vibration and also served as a testament to the immortality of Lemuria.

It's impossible that all this could end…

When the children came back she asked them to sit around her.

"What do you think?" she asked.

"They're amazing," Loni cried. "They almost seem alive even though they're so huge. What's that in their eyes?"

"The artists put pieces of shiny obsidian or cowry shells so it seems like they're really looking out over the horizon.

"Did you notice anything else?"

"Yes," answered Leilila. "They're all facing the setting sun."

"Very good." Pleija smiled. "Do you suppose they're always facing the setting sun?"

"No," responded Wonee. "Since the earth turns, the sun doesn't always set in the same place. I bet it's because today is the solstice."

"Excellent! You get a gold star."

"How come the workers aren't here today?" Leilila asked.

Her mind a cauldron and her soul seared, Pleija thought, *The workers aren't here today because, like everyone else, they're preparing for a possible imminent disaster.*

How could she tell the truth? How could she lie? In desperation she chose the latter.

"It's a holiday because of the solstice."

"OK," Wonee wondered aloud. "But how do they lift those huge statues and get them into place on top of those big platforms?"

"Wow, you ask hard questions," Pleija gave him a fake frown. "Those platforms are called *ahu's*. The artisans have learned over the millennia to develop very strong minds. When they're ready to lift a statue onto the *ahu* they gather around it, focus their minds, begin chanting, and the stones lift and float up right onto the *ahu*. Our scientists call it anti-gravity. It's been known by many civilizations for eons of time."

"Wow! Amazing!"

"Yes, very amazing," Pleija replied. "But it's getting late and we need to start walking down the mountain before it gets dark."

"Mother, how did they learn to use their minds like that? Do you think I could learn?" Maila asked softly.

As they walked down the mountain, Pleija answered more of their questions.

"My dear, dear children. Let's gather in a close circle, hold hands, and sing a song. Do you all know I will remember you?"

Pleija gazed for a moment at each child, a thorn in her heart. For the first time in her life, it was difficult to sing the familiar lament. But she started, and the chorus of sopranos joined in with gusto.

Shama 'an lu.	*I will remember you.*
Sama ama lu.	*I will always love you.*
Jaya salamajaree.	*I hold the light of the*
Lee sol zaru.	*Sun in my heart.*
Acharaya lu.	*No matter what happens.*
Achar Raj Haroon.	*Even if I leave our Motherland*
Sama ama lu.	*I will always love you.*
Shama 'an lu.	*I will remember you.*

As they walked back down the mountain, Pleija told them another legend.

"A long, long time ago there lived a goddess named Oestre. She was magical. She could make dead things come back to life. Every morning she brought the Dawn. Every year she brought the Spring. She taught the people many things, including the limitless power of their thoughts. And, yes, she taught them how to move these giant statues with just their minds."

They returned just before sunset and the children's families were all waiting for them at the Illumination Temple.

After everyone had said 'thank you' and 'goodbye' and the children safely on their way, Pleija went home, collapsed in Zamayo's arms and sobbed.

The following morning the great Amaru Meru and Arama Mara, luminous and majestic, high priest and priestess and overseers of all the communities of Lemuria, presided over the emergency council meeting. Pleija and Zamayo represented Raj Haroon and six other couples came from all corners of the continent. Atlas III, the current king of Atlantis, was sent a special invitation as well. He did not respond.

After everyone had gathered in the golden Illumination Temple and sat in silence for a few moments, Pleija gave the opening invocation:

"We call to you today, oh Great Central Sun, Source of All, Light of Light, Mother/Father God. Guide us as we seek to determine the wisest course of action in the face of this monumental crisis. Impart your loving wisdom. Free us from fear and from all that is less than the highest light within us. Let the blue flame of Your Divine Love be a force field of protection. And, if it is in the highest good of all concerned, please protect us and our beloved Lemuria from harm. For all this and for so much more, we give our heartfelt deepest gratitude. And so be it."

In unison, the citizens responded, *Shala 'am.*

Then Amaru stood to speak. Though his title was 'High Priest,' the citizens considered him to be more like a god. His wisdom far surpassed any other (except Amara, his consort) and both of them had been leaders for as far as anyone could remember, never aging, never losing their powers.

"My sisters and brothers, this is the most dangerous moment that Lemuria has ever faced. I have received word from Sirius and Venus that the Atlanteans' plan to conduct their very risky experiment with the force of vril power is imminent. Apparently they really believe they can harness an astroid, bring it into Tera's orbit, and use it as a space station from which to control the whole planet. Our sister, Pleija, who is gifted with far sight, had a vision yesterday. Would you please describe what you saw, Pleija?"

Tears flowing, voice shaking, Pleija began.

"It was more like a dream than a vision, filled with potent symbols. I saw our temples become fluid, dripping, expanding and contracting like a bleeding heart. With great force, the Solar Disc rolled out toward the crimson ocean. Then the statues of gold and bronzed shattered, the pieces floating up to the sky—where they reassembled, reforming themselves into ghoulish figures. These shadowy figures danced with each other and then began kicking the Solar Disc in a bizarre ballgame. Then our homes, gardens, animals, and trees melted like ice sculptures in a tropical jungle, dripping white-gray flows of lava that rushed violently to the sea where they were greedily swallowed."

Pleija was now sobbing.

"That was followed by a misty image of our children and adults also disappearing into the sea.

"Time then moved forward hundreds of revolutions of the sun. In the distant future I sense that all that will be left of Lemuria will be soul memories in the hearts of certain humans… and the tip of our mountain with the *Matakiterani* statues half buried in the dirt. People will call it Easter Island. They will look up at those statues in awe with no clue as to how they got there… nor of our illustrious history."

Shaking violently, Pleija sat down.

The council members sat in silence, motionless.

Finally the priestess Amara stood, put her hand on Pleija's shoulder, and spoke.

"I know some of you don't believe that a disaster could happen; we've lived in peace and prosperity here for thousands of years. But we simply cannot ignore the possibility. Pleija's visions have been remarkably accurate and we're facing an aggressive and dangerous move on the part of the Atlanteans. We must make a decision about what to do, and then we must act… soon!

"Let us now enter the central nave of the temple where we might listen for a message from Source."

In silent procession, the council members walked through the large outer area of the temple and up the thirteen steps into the central sanctuary. Here the walls were lined with mother of pearl which mirrored the fountains of silver liquid light and brilliantly colored flowers glowing with a translucent mist. These flowers emitted not only an exotic spicy yet sweet scent, but also subtle harp melodies that filled the temple. In the center of the sanctuary was a golden chalice with an unfed flame representing the eternal nature of life and love. In a circle around the flame were sixteen chairs—one for each council member and two for the priests. The chairs were cushioned with lavender silk woven with threads of pure gold. On the wall behind the chalice was a *bas relief* image of a tree of life fashioned of ebony, gold, and emeralds. High above, over the flame, the domed ceiling opened to the sun.

Each person breathed in the beauty and the power of this most holy place. The comfort that they had always felt here, though, was nearly erased by fear that the unthinkable might happen: that this Temple of Light and Illumination may soon be no more.

"Before we enact our ritual and connect with the Cosmic Sun through our most sacred Solar Disc," Lord Amaru announced, "we would like to hear your thoughts about what may be happening and what your communities are feeling. Therefore, I shall pass around our 'talking stick' and allow all esteemed representatives to speak from their hearts."

He then passed around the amethyst studded silver and gold staff and listened intently as the representatives shared their opinions, fears, and suggestions.

"I truly doubt that Atlantis would be foolish enough to unleash untested nuclear power, especially since they would be placing their own lands in critical danger."

"I say we launch a preemptive strike before Atlantis wreaks havoc on us as well as a large part of the entire planet."

"The only way to truly secure our safety would be to board the Silver Fleet and flee earth, at least temporarily, and take safe haven on Venus or Sirius or the Pleiades."

"But that's insane. You know that the Silver Fleet can hold no more than ten per cent of our population."

"The wisest course of action would be to join Amaru and Amara and sail east to Itzla to start a new life."

"I say we do nothing—simply surrender to the will of Mother/ Father God, and trust that all will be well in the end."

"Thank you all for sharing from your hearts," Amaru stated. "And now we shall begin our Solar Disc ceremony, connect with the Cosmos, and collectively attempt to glimpse into our future."

He walked to a hidden door, which at his touch opened to a small enclosure. From there he pulled out a large bundle. It was an object wrapped in a cloth woven with symbols of the Language of Light. He placed the bundle next to the chalice in the center of the room and then slowly unwrapped it to reveal the most revered object ever to grace Tera: the Solar Disc. It was convex, measured one and a half cubits in diameter, and was made of a special type of highly polished transmuted gold. But it was more than an object. It had its own subtle consciousness. Its frequency was such that, when struck by a priest who could resonate with its energies, it would open his channels to receive information directly from the Great Central Sun.

The representatives gathered together that day knew that the Solar Disc had been with them since time out of mind, gifted by the Creator God when the planet was first seeded with humans. It had acted as a mechanism for healing, for spiritual upliftment, and as a kind of computer that offered the priests virtually any information that was needed for the betterment of the lives of the citizens. Today, however, its high frequency energy wouldn't be used for any of those purposes. It would be used as a cosmic mirror that reflected the future. At least that is what the tortured souls gathered together on that summer morning were praying for with every fiber of their being.

Lord Amaru then positioned the disc on the floor precisely so that a beam of sunlight coming through the dome would be reflected throughout the hall. He reached behind one of the fountains of light and brought out an obsidian and gold inlaid box. Inside was piled what appeared to be a white powder. Everyone present, however, knew that this substance was anything but a simple powder. It was the famed *mfktz*, made of monatomic gold, platinum, rhodium, iridium, and ruthenium that had been heated to a temperature approaching that of the sun. When ingested it would dramatically enhance psychic powers, intelligence, health, and longevity.

"I'm sure I don't need to remind you," Amaru noted, "that any thought or emotion will be immediately amplified in the presence of this powder. So take care to keep your thoughts pure and your emotions balanced."

He then offered everyone a small spoonful and invited them to meditate on the following syllables as the *mfktz* blossomed within them: AMMA RA HAR LOT NOK LAR.

Pleija gazed at the Solar Disc, silenced her mind and repeated the sacred syllables inwardly, anticipating yet terrified of what she might see. After a short time the polished surface began to reflect, not what was in the room, but images of Lemurian life. There were people going about their day in the gardens, temples, homes, schools, and enjoying family celebrations. She was just about to let out a sigh of relief when the images started to become blurry, then faded completely.

Without warning, the image of a blinding blaze filled the entire disc and she could actually hear the sound of a thousand thunderstorms and see citizens being thrown angrily to the ground. As Pleija continued to watch, she realized that it was exactly as she had feared: the asteroid would be hit with all the force of the atoms in the vril. She waited a second as it ricocheted back to earth.

It was then that she felt sure that both her premonition and her dream had been correct. The Atlanteans would attempt to bring the asteroid into earth's orbit—and fail dramatically and horrifically.

Everything went into slow motion for Pleija.

She looked across the temple and it was clear by everyone's expressions that they were watching the same scenario.

The Solar Disc now revealed another deafening explosion. And another. And another. The sky was a giant fireball. Brown particles blocked the sun. Volcanoes on land and under the ocean erupted violently in rapid succession. A thousand cubit wall of ocean water roared towards them. And then, just as she had seen yesterday, their beloved Lemuria was deluged, buried in fire and water. Mercifully, it only took only a short time for the continent to sink to its watery tomb on the ocean floor.

The Lemurians gathered on that fateful day continued to gaze at the Solar Disc in stunned silence.

Time stood still for Pleija. She thought she might lose consciousness.

Finally, Amaru spoke again. Very softly he said, "Please return now to your pods, tell the people of this prophecy, poll them to determine their wishes, and then return in two days to report. Then we can set about making plans."

After the other members of the council had departed in their crystal-powered crafts, Pleija and Zamayo were alone with Amaru and Arama.

And that's when Pleija broke down. Still crying, she spoke to the three people she loved and trusted more than any other.

"After my visions, my rational mind tried to tell me that what I saw was just a manifestation of fear. But when you spoke, Lord Amaru, of receiving information from the other systems about Atlantis' intentions, I knew I was probably seeing a picture of the future." She was uncontrollable now.

"Our blessed Lemuria destroyed! Thousands of years of developing our perfected way of life. Our brothers and sisters. The children. Our sacred mountains, lakes, trees, plants, our lovely temples, homes, our art, our brilliant technology. Our connection with Source. All to be destroyed? It simply can't be. Everything in me wants to try, somehow, to preserve what we can."

Zamayo, his tone low and somber, then spoke. "If this is truly to happen, then I, for once, would prefer to perish with our beloved Lemuria. I will go willingly into the abyss. I will experience, at last, Nagual—that place I've longed for. That place of 'no-thing.' I sense that it will be beautiful beyond our capacity to imagine. I want to merge with Universal Mind Source, be one with the Light, know Mother/Father God completely."

Pleija simply stared at him through her tears. Finally she spoke, almost imperceptibly. "You would stay? And die? Not struggle to survive? Just let go of everything we hold dear? Leave me? Allow our legacy to perish without a trace? Go willingly to an icy grave at the bottom of the sea?"

Zamayo could only hold her close. For the first time in their hundreds of years of divinely inspired marriage, he could think of nothing to say.

They all sat in silence for a long time, still gazing at the Solar Disc. Then Amara Mara spoke. "Beloved Zamayo and Pleija, you have both spoken wisely and from the depths of your hearts. My husband and I love you both totally, unconditionally. You are, in spirit, our children. And it pains me beyond words to see you so divided at this, the most important moment in your lives.

"Surely we don't need to remind you that you two are in a *hierogamos* marriage, an eternal commitment of mind, body, and spirit. You are soul mates, just as Amaru and I are. This makes it virtually impossible for any of us to make a choice separate from our partners—especially at a crucial time like this."

Amaru took both their hands before he spoke. "Amara and I, too, have struggled with this decision. We would have loved to return to the stars and live in joy with our True Family, so we empathize with Zamayo's longing to allow his soul's journey to be complete, to merge with the Light, and to enjoy peace and bliss. But we have been chosen to lead the people, help save those who decide to continue in this life stream, and attempt to preserve our legacy in the hope that some day, in the far distant future, people might know our great story and perhaps find the courage, strength, and wisdom to build a New Lemuria.

"And so we plan to travel to our colony across the great waters. We shall seek protection there from the cataclysm that will surely befall us. We shall take those pilgrims who wish to accompany us. And we shall take with us the holy Solar Disc and the most powerful of the other sacred objects for safekeeping, protection, and empowerment of ourselves and everyone we encounter."

"Well spoken, my beloved," said Amara. "Now we must leave you to make your own decisions and to begin preparing for our great journey."

Amaru and Amara spoke these ancient words in unison as they departed: *"Saman ama lu."* We will always love you.

Pleija and Zamayo responded, *"Jayan salamajaree. Lee sol zaru Acharaya lu."* We hold the light of love of the sun in our hearts.

That evening Pleija and Zamayo were alone in bed. Their love for each other burst through any constraints they might have felt and their burning passion could no longer be contained. Zamayo put his strong, protective arms around her. "Come to me now," he murmured.

"Yes," she whispered. "But first I need to tell you something. If you wish to stay and go down with Lemuria, I will stay with you. I love you more than life itself and could not bear to be without you."

"Oh, no, my life, my heart," he responded, kissing her all over. "You are right. And so are Amaru and Amara. We must leave. We must begin a new life. We must honor our commitment to the people made so long ago."

And with that, Zamayo and Pleija made love as they had never made love in all the millenia they had been together. All the passion, all the pent up desire that had been thwarted two days earlier came to a climax. Their anguished bodies, minds, and souls merged, and the explosion of the orgasmic moment felt to them both as though a Divine fire was thrust into them from Viracocha Himself. That violet fire burned away all their fear and all their indecision. At that precise moment they knew that their love was stronger than anything that might befall them. They were one. Totally and eternally.

Truth be told, they were one. And they were also three. For they both knew that at the second the violet flame came down upon them, that Pleija had been impregnated with the seed of her beloved Zamayo.

Two days later the representatives of the different provinces returned to Raj Haroom to report the wishes of their people. After they had tallied the results, Pleija invited them to enjoy their last meal together in the lavender orchid garden and then retire. They would gather the next morning at sunrise.

Pleija never voiced her thought to anyone—not even to Zamayo. *It would have been so much easier if we'd never known. The ache, the sense of impotence, the agony of losing everything we've cherished for eons. It's truly unbearable. I've always felt grateful for my gift of far seeing, but today it feels more like a curse. To look into the children's innocent eyes and realize that many of them will have their lives cut tragically short…*

At the appointed time and just as the sun was appearing over the horizon, Pleija greeted the gathered group in as steady a tone as she could muster.

"*Sala mat.* My dearest brothers and sisters, I'm going to be blunt. We don't know how soon the end will come, and we aren't even positive that Atlantis' plan will, indeed, go awry. But the fact that Atlas won't even communicate with us does not bode well. We believe they are already working on enhancing the power of the mother crystal so their 'experiment' could happen within one rotation of the earth around the sun. At any rate, here are the results of the surveys you have conducted with the citizens of your provinces. Zamayo and I have recorded the people's desires, and in general they don't differ from province to province: Approximately one fourth of you wants to journey to the lands to the east or the west; approximately one fourth wishes to return to the Pleiades or travel to another star system; one fourth will stay here, but remain in the fifth dimension, safe and separated from whatever might befall our continent; about 15% does not wish to travel—either because they want to go down with their beloved Lemuria or they are elderly; and approximately 10% plans to remain with those who stay in order to offer comfort and strength.

"We have arranged for all the groups to gather here again in three days to make the final preparations. Each group will be assigned several priests and priestesses to guide them."

There were 200,000 citizens who chose to travel. Half of them would head west to settle in what would later be known as Egypt and half would head east toward Itzla, later to be named Peru.

One avant guard ship would go ahead of the others to determine the course, ask permission of the natives to settle, assure them that their purpose was peaceful, and decide where to settle and begin preparing the land. It was determined that Lords Amaru and Amara and Pleija, because of her gift of far seeing, would go in the first ship headed east. Also in that first ship would be experts in all the required arts and sciences, potent plants and seeds, and the most important sacred objects.

Zamayo would stay with those coming later because a leader would be needed to build additional ships, see that the hundreds of details necessary for the journey were handled properly, and to lend his emotional strength to the frightened citizenry.

When the preparations were complete, the ships loaded with all necessary provisions, the prayers offered, and the sacred flames placed on the bows, Pleija and Zamayo had just a few minutes alone together.

"This is not the way I would have organized this," Zamayo murmured softly.

Pleija gently put her arms around him and tiptoed to whisper, "Nor I. The thought of being separated from you for only a few moons is the cruelest type of torture for me. But we must obey the wishes of Lord Amaru. Obviously, there's no one but you, my beloved, who has the strength, courage, and knowledge to lead the people in their preparations. And I suppose it makes sense that I go with the 'scout' ships, given my gifts."

Zamayo sighed. When Pleija stepped back to look at him, his eyes were moist, but he managed a slight smile. "I guess you're right. As you usually are. And it will be a constant comfort to know that our child will be growing in you while we're apart."

"Yes. I promise that she'll be well taken care of. She'll be loved, kept warm and safe and be cherished. Just think, by the time you arrive in Itzla you'll be able to feel her heart beat."

"Viracocha willing."

Pleija noticed that all the citizens were aboard the ship patiently waiting for her.

"I must go now. May Mother/Father god bless us all and keep us safe."

"*Shala 'am.*"

"*Shala 'am.*"

The ship was virtually a floating city, so there was much to organize and quite a bit of chaos at first. After a few days at sea, however, things settled into a routine and Pleija had time to allow her thoughts and emotions to surface.

Although missing Zamayo terribly, she managed to create a certain state of optimism. *What if nothing happens? Our prophecies have not always been correct—especially regarding the timing of events. If there is a cataclysm in our future, it might not happen for another thousand years. Maybe the Atlanteans will come to their senses and cancel this horrific project. Or maybe they'll be successful in harnessing the asteroid and bringing it into our orbit without doing any real harm. Who knows? We could receive good news and be able to turn around and head home before the others even embark.*

With those thoughts Pleija would go to sleep each evening feeling relatively content, resting her hands on her belly and smiling as she thought of their baby growing inside her womb.

But then she would sleep fitfully and the nightmares gave her no peace. So one night she got up, went to the upper deck and gazed out at the black calm sea. Above she could make out the Pleiades. She prayed that their Star Brothers and Sisters would be able to come to their aid in case of mortal danger.

If the worst were to happen, she thought, the most tragic part is that 50,000 years from now there would be no trace of the splendor that was Lemuria. Maybe there would be a faint memory in the collective consciousness, but no artifacts, no libraries, no remnants of our magnificent temples, gardens, art or music.

And that's when she was inspired to write down a description of their life. It took her nearly the entire two moons of the voyage to put her thoughts to paper. *After we're a little settled in Itzla,* she reasoned, *Zamayo and I can transcribe these ideas to stone or metal or some other durable medium and put them in a safe place for generations far into the future.*

When they were almost at their destination, Pleija had a terrible premonition which created an excruciating knot in her stomach. She went to the upper deck and looked up at the clear blue sky trying to quiet her mind. *I fear missing Zamayo so much has allowed my fears to eclipse everything else. I must remain calm for the sake of the people counting on me... and for the sake of the child I'm carrying.*

Then she saw something that looked like a giant comet soaring across the firmament. Everything seemed to happen in slow motion. She looked to the west and saw a fireball that seemed to rise from nowhere and suddenly fill the entire sky. The sea began to roil. There was a deafening explosion. And another. And another. Brown particles blocked the sun.

The swelling in the ocean nearly capsized their ship.

There's no way the other ships could have survived. Pleija's grief was more than her mind or body could take. *Shall I simply throw myself into the sea right now?*

She collapsed.

Because Peija was on the upper deck and everyone else had taken shelter from the explosion in the ship's hull, she wasn't found until the next morning.

1

THE BLACK HAND

The bus station in Lima smelled like the morning after a rowdy party: old beer, old tobacco, and old urine. There were soiled disposable diapers overflowing the trashcans. A faded, tattered poster of Machu Picchu alongside one of a llama next to a young Peruvian girl with a red and white embroidered blouse and gigantic sad black eyes were the only attempts to brighten the walls. Even the cracked wooden benches seemed forlorn.

Sofía desperately wished she'd listened to her doctor and stayed home. But now there was no turning back; she still had to face five aching hours to the certain-to-be God-forsaken Ica. She was exhausted. She had a headache and fever. She was jet lagged from her flight from Madrid and side trip to Caral. She was hot and dirty. Her joints were badly swollen. The acrid air of one of the world's most polluted cities burned her eyes and irritated the rash across her face. She just wanted to be left alone.

A voice from across the waiting bench broke the silence. "So you're going to Ica." Sofía looked over to see a slightly balding, paunchy, middle-aged man taking his last puffs on a cigarette butt.

"Yes," she replied.

"Bet you're going to see them stones the Cabreras have in that museum there."

Suddenly feeling even more tired, Sofía responded with irritation, "Yes, I am."

"Why?" he queried. "I can't understand why so many tourists take the trouble to visit those rocks. Everyone knows they're fakes, just carved a few years ago. Why, them two farmers even admitted to it. And, besides, only an idiot would think dinosaurs and humans lived at the same time, like the scratchings show."

"¡Atención! ¡Atención! Cruz del Sur passengers going to Arequipa with stops at Pisco, Ica, and Nazca. All aboard!"

Relieved that she didn't have to answer the man, Sofía turned her back to him and handed her suitcases to the attendant who stored them below. She stepped aboard and gave her ticket to the driver.

"That'll be on the second level, seat forty three. All the way to the back, on your left. You'll be next to the toilets."

Sofía went to her seat, which didn't recline. *How could this trip be more God awful?* she thought. The pain in her body was agonizing and her exhaustion was total.

After twenty minutes the heat and the smell of urine and cigarettes were making her nauseous. At the first stop she told the driver that she wasn't feeling well.

"Why don't you move to the first level? I think you'll be more comfortable there. Seat number ten is available. And I won't charge you extra."

He smiled at her in a way that Sofía felt to be slightly lecherous. Over the years Sofía had become used to men making passes at her. So she'd always done her best to hide her beauty. Her reddish blond hair was pulled into a bun at the nape of her neck and covered by a baseball cap. Her shirt and pants hung loose on her thin body. She wore no make up or jewelry. However, she couldn't quite hide her stunning turquoise eyes.

"Thank you." Sofía scowled.

After getting settled, she reached into her bag and pulled out a dog-eared paperback, *El Mensaje de las piedras grabadas de Ica.*

"Excuse me for interrupting," the man seated next to her said politely, "but I see you're reading *The Message of the Engraved Stones of Ica.* Interesting topic. And interesting, too, that you read Spanish. Pretty unusual for a blue-eyed blond. Are you going to Ica?"

He seemed genuinely curious, but Sofía was in no mood for chitchat.

Why won't these idiots leave me alone? Exasperated, she looked at him and said coldly, "Yes, I'm going to Ica. And, yes, I read Spanish. I'm from Spain. The blond hair comes from my mother, a German scientist." *From whom I apparently also inherited my disdain for men.* She continued reading. The man turned to look out the window.

Finally, the bus was quiet. Even the noise of the crying babies and disgruntled chickens settled down.

Sofía drifted off to a restless sleep.

A half hour later she was jolted awake by a loud popping sound. It seemed to come from the rear of the bus on the second level. The pungent smell of gunpowder filled the air as the bus screeched to a halt. People began screaming and scrambling for an exit. The driver got on the intercom, begged everyone to remain calm, and announced that they would all have to depart the bus while they inspected the damage.

Sofia sighed, picked up her purse, and reluctantly joined the other passengers who were jostling to get off the bus as quickly as possible.

Outside, everything was hot, dry and brittle. The land was flat and brown. The air crackled with snippets of tense conversation.

"Sounded like a car bomb."

"Bet it was the *Sendero Luminoso* again!"

"The Shining Path? Thought they disbanded after Guzmán was captured."

"Don't know. Heard they were back and active in cocaine smuggling in these parts."

"*¡Atención!*" the voice of the driver was barely comprehensible over the ancient loudspeaker. "Looks like the explosion was from a crudely made car bomb. It wasn't powerful, and luckily no one was hurt. But it's gonna take some time to check out the damage."

Many of the passengers, apparently just as tired as Sofía but with much more patience, sat impassively on a rock or the ground to wait.

Sofía paced the highway's shoulder.

After a very long hour of waiting in the dusty heat the muffled voice over the loudspeaker announced that they would have to bring in a new bus.

"It'll take several hours." Then he added helpfully, "There's a gas station, convenience store, and small cafe a half kilometer to the south if you'd like to wait there."

The man who had asked Sofía about the book she was reading invited her to join him to walk down the road to the cafe.

"You look like you could use a cup of coffee and maybe some food. At least we can get out of this scorching sun."

The pain was intensifying and Sofía didn't want to talk with anyone, but coffee and food sounded good. Wearily, she agreed.

Walking along the road, Rogelio seemed insistent on making conversation and Sofía finally allowed herself to be drawn in. *After all,*

I know no one in this country, which is presenting itself as a bit hostile. Maybe it would be good to have an acquaintance.

"So why are you interested in the Ica stones?" he asked.

"Well, I'm an archaeologist. I improved a method for dating artifacts called thermo luminescence. It works on substances such as rock that don't contain measurable organic material."

"Like the Ica stones?"

"Right."

"When carbon dating doesn't work?"

"Correct. Anyway, I got a bit of a reputation when I used my technique to help verify the age of the Chauvet Cave paintings in France. Then last month I received a letter from Elenia Cabrera begging me to come to Ica, test the stones, and, once and for all, determine their age." She turned to the man and, for the first time, really looked at him. He was tall, looked strong without being a body builder type, had dark curly hair, tourmaline eyes and a copper complexion. His features were slightly Peruvian but his clothes were definitely American.

"So how is it that you know about the stones and carbon dating and all?"

He laughed. "Because Elenia's my sister. I was born in Ica, became ordained as a new thought minister, then went to live and work in Los Angeles. This week there was a global conference for spiritual leaders in Lima, so I decided to attend and then come down to visit my family."

"A minister. Spiritual leaders?" Sofía stiffened.

When Rogelio grinned, his eyes reflected shades of brown, hazel, and amber. They made her uncomfortable.

"It's not as bad as you might think… Maybe we can discuss it some day. Oh, sorry, we haven't introduced ourselves. I'm Rogelio Cabrera Blanco."

She looked away. "I'm Sofía Cabeza de Vaca Weissmann."

"So, Señora Cabeza de Vaca, what did my sister say in her letter to convince you to come all this way to determine the age of the stones?"

If you only knew. This has nothing to do with the stones. This is about my entire career. My reputation could be restored with this study.

Aloud she said, "It's Señorita. Your sister is a very intelligent and persuasive woman, Señor Cabrera."

He grinned again, "Would Rogelio and Sofía work for you?"

"Sure." Sofía hadn't intended her tone to sound quite so sullen. "Look. I'm sorry I'm not in a better mood. I've been traveling for twenty four hours and that explosion shook me up pretty badly."

In the café Sofia and Rogelio mostly sat in silence.

Eventually, other passengers started straggling in. Someone mentioned he'd heard there wouldn't be another bus until tomorrow.

Rogelio sighed. "Look, we can't sit here all night. The seaside town of Paracas isn't far from here. What do you say we try to get a taxi and find a hotel there? Besides, as an archaeologist I think you'll find its artifacts quite interesting."

Sofía frowned and sighed. "OK. I suppose so. Frankly, I'm beyond exhausted and suffering terrible jet lag. Also, I'm very nervous about that bomb on the bus. You know, it exploded in the seat where I was originally assigned. I asked to switch because the first one was uncomfortable and the stench from the bathroom was unbearable. For some reason I have an extremely sensitive olfactory system."

"Do you think the bomb exploding there was more than a coincidence?" he asked.

"I have no idea."

After arranging for their luggage to be sent to his home, Rogelio took her to the Hotel Bahia Paracas and booked two rooms and two massages. After an early dinner they bid each other an awkward goodnight.

Sofía went to her room, collapsed on her bed, and immediately fell asleep fully clothed.

The next morning there was no word about a new bus so Rogelio asked if she'd like to go to the Paracas museum. She didn't want to. She still felt miserable, but there was nothing else to do while waiting for a bus so she reluctantly agreed. There they saw strangely elongated skulls.

Sofía shook her head. "Disgusting. I've read about this. In several cultures around the world they would tie boards to children's foreheads and force the poor things to endure pain to their soft skulls until they became formed like this." She shuddered.

The museum's director approached them. "Excuse me for interrupting, but I'd love to clarify for you. Many people believe as you do, and as I did. But we've learned that these skulls are not shaped like this by force. If you look carefully you'll see that these skulls have only two plates. A regular human skull has three. These also have twice the thickness, greater internal space, and a slight difference in the shape of the jaw and teeth."

Sofa rolled her eyes. "Are you suggesting that these skulls aren't human?"

"No. Not necessarily. I'm just saying they don't resemble skulls of any humanoid that we've known for the past 10,000 years."

She had nothing to say in reply.

"I think we could use some fresh air," Rogelio offered as a way of changing the subject. "Would you like to take a boat tour along the coast?"

Sofía nodded unenthusiastically and they boarded one of the tour boats docked nearby.

When they were twelve kilometers from the shore Rogelio pointed back to the coast. "That's the famous *candelabro*. It's carved two feet deep into the rock and stands 595 feet tall. The locals don't know who carved it or why. They simply shrug and say it's always been here. Does it look like a candlestick holder to you? To me it seems more like a cactus… or maybe a trident. I've always wondered who made it… and for what purpose."

"Who knows?"

"Sounds like you're not interested in these things. I wanted to hire a helicopter to show you the mysterious holes of Pisco. They're not too far from here. But we don't have to go sightseeing. We can just go back to the hotel and wait for the next bus that goes directly to Ica. I'm not going to trust that our original bus will be replaced any time this week."

"I'm sorry. I'm not feeling at all well. And I didn't come to Peru to see the sights. I just want to look at the stones, test them, verify the results, and go home." Her sharp tone startled Rogelio.

"I see. Well then let me check the bus schedule and get you to Ica as soon as possible."

On the long bus ride Sofía asked him about the Pisco holes.

"Are you really interested or are you just trying to make polite conversation?"

Sofía sighed, unable to hide her irritation. "You don't know me very well. I don't just make polite conversation. As a scientist, I have an inquiring mind."

"OK." Rogelio pulled out his phone, searched for a few moments, then showed her a photo.

"These are the Pisco holes. There are over 6000 of them carved into the barren rock in the mountains. They go on for over one and a half kilometers, are arranged in groupings, and range from one to seven meters in depth.

"No one knows who made them or why. The locals say they've always been there. But there are no artifacts, no bones, no carvings, no legends, myths, or stories about them."

"Just the holes?"

"Yep. They just sit there kind of mocking us with their secrets."

"It's been proven that they're manmade?" Sofía asked.

"Absolutely. Well, let me correct myself. They weren't made by nature."

"And they can only be seen from the air, I suppose."

"Correct."

"Hmm," was all that Sofía could offer before she fell into a pensive silence.

After a while she turned to him and asked, "Do you know anything about the archaeological site of Caral?"

"A little. Why?"

"Well, I made a side trip there after I arrived in Lima. I'd read that it's possibly the oldest site in South America and wanted to check it out as part of my research."

Rogelio looked at her. "Yeah. It's believed to be 17,000 years old. What did you think?"

"It's pretty impressive. But the part that confused me is that there are no relics of war or any kind of violence at all. Just artwork and hundreds of musical instruments, especially elaborately decorated flutes."

"I know. I've thought about that. Most historians claim that every culture has exhibited some kind of violence. But here we have indications of a very, very old civilization that apparently valued beauty and harmony over warfare."

"Strange," was all Sofía offered before falling into another long silence.

After a seemingly interminable bus ride and taxi from the station, Rogelio and Sofía finally arrived at the front door of the Cabrera family home. She commented briefly on the smell of cooking filling the evening air.

"Oh, I forgot to mention," Rogelio responded. "My sister's a world-class chef. She'll insist that you stay for dinner."

"I'm sorry. I really can't stay. My stomach is upset and I couldn't eat a thing."

"Well, then, let me at least show you the museum and give you a quick tour of the house."

As they waited at the door Rogelio continued, "Our home, which is connected to the museum, has hosted dinner parties and cultural events for fourteen generations. I hate to brag, but we're very proud of the heritage of the Cabrera family. For example, in 1563 Don Diego Carlos Cabrera y Santistevan immigrated from Spain, founded the town of Ica, acquired all this land, and built the house."

Sofía was numb from pain and exhaustion and could only think. *Will he never stop babbling?* But she forced a half smile when Elenia greeted them at the door.

"Oh!" was all Elenia could muster when she met Sofía.

"What's wrong?" Rogelio asked.

"Uh, nothing. It's just that I was expecting a rather plain-looking scientist…"

Rogelio laughed and quickly interrupted her. "Please forgive my sister, Elenia. She's never had a thought that didn't make its way to her mouth."

Elenia gave him a mock punch in the arm then hugged him effusively.

Rogelio apologized for being late, then introduced Sofía to everyone. His younger sister Elenia was tall and angular with warm brown eyes and Rogelio's dark curly hair. Maria de la Paz, better known as Mapi, wore an apron over her black religious habit that was only partially effective in protecting it from a generous dusting of flour. She was round, jovial, and apparently the oldest—wisps of gray hair escaped from the wimple under her black veil. Cafre, director of the museum, had a prominent chin, a tight jaw, and a somewhat pasty complexion. Padre Anselmo, who was wearing a black shirt with a clerical collar and a bronze cross around his neck, was thin and slightly stooped. A generous smile mostly camouflaged his shallow breathing.

Sister Mapi took Sofía's hand warmly. "Sofía, there are no words to express our gratitude for your coming. Please sit down and relax. May I offer you a pisco sour? Dinner's almost ready. Surely Rogelio invited you to eat with us?"

"Thank you. But I must admit I'm quite anxious to see the stones… and then get some rest."

Rogelio answered for his sister. "Of course. The museum is just through the passageway to the left. Come. I'll show you."

When Sofía opened the door to the museum, she was aghast. Here were thousands of stones, some the size of oranges, others resembling a boulder, piled helter-skelter over one another. She hadn't quite known what to expect, but it certainly wasn't this. The room was dusty and dry—and ugly like the stones.

The images etched into them were ridiculous: A man riding on the back of a dinosaur? Cavemen types looking through a telescope? Absurd.

I traveled all this way to view this nonsense? Especially feeling as god-awful as I do. And these people—so naively believing that these rocks are anything but the crude money making scheme of a couple of third-rate swindlers.

In his enthusiasm, Rogelio didn't read Sofía's face accurately. He went on explaining that their father, Doctor Javier Cabrera, had arranged this 'library' of information by topic, and, when appropriate, into series and sub-sections.

"But it was hard for him to keep up, as the supplier kept bringing more and more stones. So I'm afraid it's become a bit disorganized since his death. Why don't you look around a bit? Oh, and, truly, my sisters would be devastated if you didn't stay for dinner."

Sophia had to admit to herself that she was famished. And it would be rude to turn down this invitation. It looked as though Mapi had been cooking all day. "OK. I guess I can stay for a short while."

"Great. I'm going to help my sisters in the kitchen. Make yourself at home."

"Thanks." Sofía picked up a stone and was surprised by its weight, even though she had known that all these stones were made of extremely dense anthracite. She picked up and studied another and then turned to see Padre Anselmo behind her.

"Sorry to interrupt your reverie, but I was asked to tell you that dinner is almost ready. In your honor, Sister Mapi has prepared a meal of Peruvian specialties. She hopes you'll like it."

By now Sofía was so exhausted she wasn't sure she could make it to the dining room. Her joints were aching and her head was throbbing.

"Thank you very much, Padre. I'll be there in a minute."

"Esteemed Doctora Cabeza de Vaca," the priest continued, "if I may be so bold. Why are you interested in testing these stones? What possible good can it do to learn their age? Even if they are proven to be very old, that will simply confuse and upset the people."

"My dear Padre," she responded in an even a tone as she could muster, "I respect that you are an old friend of the Cabrera family. However, I am extremely uninterested in any repercussions of what I may or may not find. I am a scientist. My job is to discover the truth. What people decide to do with it is their business."

"Yes, my child, of course you're right." A curtain came down over his eyes. "Please forgive my impudence. Shall we proceed to dinner?"

As they were being seated at the table, Sofía asked, "What are these dishes? They look and smell quite good."

Rogelio grinned. "Now you've made Mapi's day. Even though she's a nun and is supposed to be without hubris, her weakness happens to be compliments on her cooking."

Mapi blushed. "These are *humitas*—fresh corn tamales. Those cactus-looking rolls are *yuquitas rellenos*—stuffed yucca. That is *tacu tacu*—a local dish of specially spiced steak with rice and beans. The bread is *pan de anis* and the dessert is *pastel de tres leches*—a pastry with three types of milk."

As the dinner was coming to a close, Sofía said, "Thank you so much for preparing such an outstanding meal… and for your hospitality to a stranger." She glanced at the door.

But Elenia was excited. "Please tell us more about your approach to determining the age of the stones."

Sofia tried to stifle a yawn. Then she quickly explained that technically she was a paleo archaeologist and that what she'll do while here is first take a few stones and test them with a portable device she brought, send a larger sample back to Spain for a more exhaustive test, then interview locals and, finally, visit some archeological sites to make geological and contextual comparisons.

At this point Rogelio interrupted to insist that Sofía be taken to her hotel.

"I'll borrow Cafre's car and take you now, if you'd like."

In front of the Hacienda Jazmín, Sofía shook Rogelio's hand awkwardly. "Thank you for all your courtesies. And I apologize for being so grumpy. Good night."

The receptionist checked her in, handed her the key, and, with it, an envelope. Inside her room Sofía collapsed on the bed and opened the envelope to find a note in a sloppily scrawled hand:

OLVÍDESE DE ESTE PROYECTO Y REGRESE INMEDIATAMENTE A ESPAÑA. SI NO LO HACE, LAS CONSECUENCIAS SERÁN FEAS.

There was no signature. Just the image of a black hand.

"Forget this project and return immediately to Spain? If you don't, the consequences will be ugly..."

Who could have written this? Why? Is this an empty threat or am I really in danger?

Being a strong, independent woman, Sofia didn't want to admit it, but she was scared.

2

THE ICA STONES

Though Sofía was beyond exhausted, she didn't sleep that night. *Who would send this? Why? Should I tell anyone? Who can I trust? Seems like that bomb on the bus wasn't courtesy of the Shining Path after all.*

She was in excruciating pain now. She thought back to the last few days in Madrid. A colleague had convinced her that this might be the opportunity she needed to prove herself and regain her reputation. She was already suffering a lot of pain, but had already booked her trip by the time she received the lupus diagnosis and, against the advice of her doctors, decided to go ahead. *Well, perhaps we'll get the results quickly and I can go home and continue with my treatment.*

Early the next day, Sofía took a taxi back to the museum.

"Good morning, Sofía," Rogelio greeted her. "You look tired."

"Just jet lag. Shall we get started looking at the stones?"

Elenia gushed, "Sofía, you need to know that your work is of crucial importance to us. In fact, it may be the most important event of

43

my life. If you can prove that the stones are ancient, it will vindicate my father's and my life's work. If not… but of course you mustn't…"

Padre Anselmo stepped forward and interrupted her.

"I hope you don't mind that I came over today. This is important to all of us. Poor, sweet Elenia, your loyalty to your father is touching. However, you must give up this wild goose chase and get a life."

Turning to Sofía, he added, "If you've done your homework, you'll know that a local farmer, Ishmael Negromonte, has admitted that he etched the stones himself. And that a Spanish investigator, Vicente Paris, declared after four years of investigation using microphotographs that the stones are a hoax. He found traces of modern paints and abrasives in the engravings and also noted that since most stones were found outside, the engravings should be eroded instead of being crisp. Indeed, every serious archaeologist and scientist has declared that these stones are fakes. Why, common sense alone tells us that it's absurd to think that dinosaurs and humans lived together."

"The good padre is a dear friend of ours… has been for decades," Elenia countered. "But he definitely has his opinions; some would say that he's rigid. The fact is that we believe that there are around 50,000 of these stones here and with collectors around the world. How could one peasant, even with help, have carved them all? And how would he know to depict images that are so far from his world? Besides that, similar designs were found in unearthed tombs hundreds of years old."

"Did you know," added Cafre, "that in the 1570's the Indian chronicler Juan de Santa Cruz wrote that many stones with strange animals carved on them were found in the Kingdom of Chinca, near here, and that some of them were taken back to Spain at that time."

"Besides all that," Mapi chimed in, "our grandfather, a cultural anthropologist, found hundreds of ceremonial burial stones in the sealed tombs of ancient Incas depicting things like dinosaurs and open-heart surgery."

"With all due respect, he claimed to have found them," the padre interjected. "The famous writer Erik von Daniken, author of Chariot of the Gods, has stated, 'Today many people still believe in the authenticity of the stones despite the fact that this authenticity has been disproven.'"

Elenia was now flushed and speaking loudly. "Barbara Hand Clow, researcher of pre-Incan civilizations and highly respected author, states, 'The Ica stones are ancient. They cannot possibly be fakes, and they are one of the most important archeological discoveries of all time.'"

"Whoa," said Padre Anselmo. "We've rehashed these arguments hundreds of times. Finally, we won't have to argue or wonder much longer. Dr. Cabeza de Vaca will give us the answers with this… what did you call it… thermo illumination? That is, if it's accurate."

Sofía's stare was frigid. "It's thermo luminescence and after the improvements I developed, it's been shown to be 99% accurate in blind trials. And may I ask why you're so anxious to prove the stones fakes?"

Rogelio interrupted, switching to a safer topic. "Can you give us a layman's description of how it works?"

"Yes. But I fear it would bore you."

"Not at all. We'd be fascinated," said Mapi.

"Well," Sofía began, "we learned that you can determine the age of inorganic materials by measuring the accumulated radiation dose of the time elapsed since they were either heated, as in lava or ceramics, or exposed to sunlight, as in sediments. As the material (in this case, a stone) is heated over time, thermo luminescence, a weak light signal, is emitted, proportional to the radiation dose absorbed by the stone. All crystalline materials contain imperfections that disturb the regularity of the electric field that holds the atoms together."

Sofía noticed that Mapi and Rogelio were shifting their weight, but she continued. "This leads to humps and dips in its electric potential. When this happens, a free electron can be tripped. Then the flux of ionizing radiation excites the electrons in the crystal into the conduction band where they can move freely. Most excited electrons will soon recombine with lattice ions, but some will be trapped, storing part of the energy. Depending on the depth of the traps, the storage time of trapped electrons will vary—some traps are sufficiently deep to store a charge for hundreds of thousands of years."

"I see," said Elenia. "Would you like some more coffee?"

Sofía scowled slightly. "I warned you. You wouldn't believe the number of people who simply walk away from me at cocktail parties."

Rogelio grinned. "It certainly sounds impressive. Now would you like to inspect the stones and choose the ones you want to send back to Spain? Afterwards, I suggest we make a surprise visit to the lovely home of Ishmael Negromonte."

"All right," Sofía answered. "Would you mind if I took along a few small stones? I'd like to compare them with what Negromonte shows us—assuming he'll let us in the door. Then tonight I'd like to take them to my hotel and do a small test on my portable device. It's not nearly as accurate as what we have in the lab, but we might get an initial idea. At any rate, it will take at least two weeks to get the results back from Madrid."

"Help yourself," Elenia offered.

Sofía chose a few small stones, examined them carefully, then put them in her pants pocket.

Negromonte's home was indeed beautiful. It was in a Spanish colonial style with courtyards, gardens, hand-painted tiles, and a huge flat screen TV. Dozens of children were running and playing and video games were blaring. Ishmael answered the door, seemed a little flustered at first, but soon regained his composure.

"Well, it's the Cabreras. What a surprise! It's been a long, long time. As you can see, I've gotten older… We now have ten grandchildren and four great grandchildren. And who is this beautiful woman? She doesn't look like she's from around here."

After introductions and a beer, Rogelio stated the purpose of their visit. "Ishmael, we know that you've been telling the authorities that you made the engravings yourself that you sold to our father. Would you be so gracious as to show us how you did it?"

"Certainly. Come with me to my shop."

In his shop Ishmael demonstrated his process. "You see, I take a stone—there are thousands of these anthracite stones still in the caves around here. I rub cow dung on it, bake it, rub in black shoe polish, then drill the design with this dentist's drill."

As he was proudly showing off his work, Sofía got up and inspected the stones he had on display. Holding up one depicting a 'tree of life' symbol with two reptiles intertwined around each other, she asked, "How do you get your inspiration for the designs?"

"Oh, that's easy. At first I copied pictures from matchboxes. Later I went to the library for ideas. Sometimes I just make them up." He puffed his chest out just a little.

Elenia said, "Ishmael, we appreciate your honesty. But how could you, in good conscience, make these and then sell them to our father, passing them off as ancient artifacts?"

"I never said to him that the carvings were ancient. I just said I found the stones in caves."

On the drive back Elenia couldn't contain her anger and frustration. "I just can't believe that man! Ten years ago he was put in jail for selling archeological treasures. After he convinced people that he had made them, the Peruvian government released him, said no more, and allowed him to continue selling the stones."

"Well, that didn't get us very far," mused Rogelio.

"That's for sure," Sofía muttered under her breath, feeling again that she probably had come all this way, living in pain every minute only to learn she had signed on for a fool's errand.

Aloud she said, "He was quite convincing, and it's hard to distinguish what he produced for us today from the stones in Dr. Cabrera's collection. And I just can't wrap my mind around the dinosaur thing. If 'gliptolithic' man, as Cabrera called the subjects of these stones, lived millions of years ago and interacted with dinosaurs, how did he survive the various earth cataclysms and the ice age? And if dinosaurs survived into relatively modern times, we'd be able to date that with the fossils we have."

"I don't know what to tell you," an exasperated Elenia stated, "except to say that if you've lived with these stones for as long as I have, you would know they're authentic."

Sofía was so frustrated and in so much pain now she almost allowed herself to say out loud the sarcastic comment she was thinking: *You would have made a great scientist, Elenia.*

When they arrived back home, Sofía asked if she could spend some time alone in the museum to further study the stones.

3

THE NAZCA LINES AND K'ANTU

The following day when Sofia arrived at the museum Rogelio asked her if she had results from her portable testing device.

"Yes, but they were disappointing. The results were so mixed that they were essentially useless. I'm going to have to rely on the lab in Spain."

Then she boxed thirty of the stones and sent them via DHL to Spain and explained to Rogelio that she'd like to visit Nazca to compare the famous lines there with the etchings on the stones since several were similar.

Rogelio looked at her thoughtfully. "You certainly are a focused person. But it's a tough trip to make alone. If you'd like, I'll drive you. My dad always believed that there were thousands more stones like the ones in his collection buried in the area of Nazca. Sadly, no one's been allowed to dig there since UNESCO declared it a World Heritage site. In fact, you can't even walk or drive in the area of the lines. Still we might learn something. Would you like to go as well, Padre, Elenia, and Mapi?"

Elenia was flushed. "This is so exciting! After all these years we're finally going to have an answer to our giant mystery. Wish I could join you, but I have to mind the museum. Cafre has been putting in a lot of hours here, and we don't want to take advantage of his kindness."

"I'd love to go, too," Mapi said. "But I have to teach tomorrow. Can't run out on my adorable little rug rats."

So Rogelio, Sofía, and Padre Anselmo drove to Nazca where they hired a helicopter and pilot/guide.

"Welcome to the world-famous Nazca lines and to their never-ending mysteries," he said by way of greeting as they settled in. They lifted and flew over the breathtaking 450 square kilometers expanse of lines and images.

Seeing these famous lines for the first time, Sofía was duly impressed, but totally flummoxed. "Who made these lines? How? When were they made? Why?"

"Bottom line, we don't have any idea who made them or how long they've been here," responded the guide. "Some archeologists say, based on pottery chards, that they were formed in the first century CE. But that doesn't make any sense to me. Just because they found and dated pottery, that doesn't mean that the lines were made at the same time. Other 'alternative' researchers say these lines probably go back many thousands of years."

"I'm sorry, but I can't agree." The padre's voice was confident if not arrogant. "The vast majority of respected archaeologists say these lines are no more than 2,000 years old. To suggest that they might go back 10,000 years or more contradicts science, common sense, and Holy Scripture."

Sofía gave the padre a stare that could have turned molten lava in hell to ice in half an instant.

The guide continued as though he were getting slightly bored. "You see how these lines crisscross and go toward the mountains? They've been measured carefully, and even though they traverse hills and uneven land, they are absolutely straight. And, as you probably know, they can only be seen from the air. That's why, regardless of how old they may be, they weren't discovered until 1930 when airplanes first flew over this area. They were etched into the land by clearing aside the grayish brown desert pampa to reveal the yellow sand just below. Since the weather is dry and stable here, we believe they've stayed pretty much the same all this time. The one question that's perplexed everyone—experts and amateurs alike—is how the lines could be made perfectly straight or even seen from the ground. One is 65 kilometers long, for goodness sake."

"Kind of begs the question," Rogelio added. "Could they have been made by people in flying machines thousands of years ago?"

The guide shrugged then shouted, "Look to your right on the side of the hill separate from the other images. There's the famous astronaut."

Rogelio said to Sofía, "Keep in mind that several of our stones show images of men flying or looking up at the stars through a telescope. I wonder why…"

"Hundreds of scholars and individuals have also wondered," the guide interrupted. "For example, one German lady, Maria Reiche, was so intrigued that she moved to Peru and studied the lines for 50 years. But she still didn't come up with an answer that satisfied everyone. Basically, she felt that they had something to do with the stars and planets. Others thought they were landing fields, a labyrinth to walk as a religious ritual, an indication of underground water, an attempt to call the gods back down, a celestial calendar, warnings of an imminent catastrophe, or just an expression of man's need to create art."

After several minutes of silence, the guide spoke again. "Now we're coming to the depictions of animals. Most scholars believe the straight lines that crisscross and form trapezoids were made first and these animals were drawn much later. On the left you can see the famous monkey with the spiral tail, the hummingbird, the lizard, which seems to point to both the east and west, the dog with its tail pointing straight up in the air, and a whale. By the way, we just discovered a new image. It's not as clear as the others, but there's definitely a 60-meter snake. Can you make it out way over to the left?

"Some of the animals depicted here are not native to the area and many, like the toxodon, are extinct. See that spider just below us? It's 45 meters long. Notice anything unusual about it?"

"Yes," Sofía answered. "It's called a 'Ricinulei' and is only found in remote and inaccessible parts of the Amazon jungle. One of its legs is longer, and that one also serves as its reproductive organ."

"Wow, Sofía," Rogelio exclaimed. "Where in the world do you get so much information?"

"Well. I read a lot while others spend their time on more superfluous activities. I also happen to have an eidetic memory." Sofía looked down.

After a somewhat uncomfortable silence, the guide continued. "We have no idea how the makers of these lines could have known about a spider that can only be found thousands of miles from here."

Rogelio added. "I've read that the spider image could be related to the constellation of Orion. It appears on one of our stones and also on many artifacts throughout Peru and Bolivia… and even at Giza in Egypt and at Teotihuacan in Mexico."

"Yes," the guide said. "That's one belief. It's been so frustrating that, over all these years and all this research, there are so many conflicting theories. We seem to know less for sure than when the lines were first discovered."

Sofía was quiet for a few moments. When she spoke, the sharpness in her voice surprised even herself. "This is all quite interesting, but I'm not sure how this is helping us determine the authenticity of the stones."

Anselmo's voice was barely audible. "Weren't you the one who wanted to come?"

Rogelio glanced at Anselmo then said, "Seems like it has to mean something that several images on the stones match those in the lines. Besides the method of etching is the same."

"I'm really sorry to be such a skeptic," Sofía said. "But of course the stones are the same. It's obvious that andesite is prevalent throughout this whole area, so that's what they would work with. And what would prevent a hoaxer from simply copying the images on the Nazca lines and then burying the stones?"

"Simply the fact that many of the stones were found in this Nazca region far from Ica and long before any of the so-called hoaxers were even born," Rogelio replied just a bit testily.

"Well, that's about it," announced the guide. "Time to head back… unless you'd like me to swing around so that you can see a particular image again."

"No, that's fine," responded Rogelio. "We've seen enough."

Sofía's entire body was now wracked in pain, but she was glad she'd decided not to say anything to Rogelio or the padre.

They landed, thanked and tipped the guide, and walked back to their car.

"Oh my God!" Sofía gasped. Then she broke down crying.

A brightly colored desert coral snake was wound around each of the slashed tires. The dashboard window was smashed, and the outline of a hand was smeared on the hood.

"Are they alive?" Sofia had a mortal fear of snakes.

"Let me check. No they're dead."

A woman who had been selling crystals near the entrance to Nazca heard Sofía, rushed over, and said something to them in a strange language. She had black braids down to her waist, a bowler hat, a brightly embroidered blouse, and a wrinkled face the color of the landscape.

"I'm sorry," Rogelio said in a halting Quechua, "we don't know your language. Do you speak Spanish?"

"Yes. A little. My name K'antu. Perhaps I can to help you?"

At this kindness Sofía broke down even more. "I can't stay in Peru any longer. Someone, or many people, want to hurt me, and I can't take this pain!" She doubled over in agony.

"What's wrong?" Rogelio asked, but Sofía was now sobbing so hard she couldn't speak.

K'antu held Sofía and put her hand on her forehead. "This woman very sick," she explained.

"What are you talking about?" Rogelio demanded.

"We discuss later. For now, please trust me. Look, it getting dark and no one can to fix car tonight. It close here soon and no way get to hotel. Please. You come to my hut. I make you something to eat, the lady sleep on my cot. Tomorrow you fix car. Come. Follow me. Señorita, can you walk a little?"

"Yes," Sofía responded weakly.

As they walked, Rogelio introduced everyone then added, "But I don't understand. What do you mean, Sofía is very sick? How do you know?"

"I just know. Something attacking whole body. Very serious."

"But how…"

"I am *curandera*."

"What's a *curandera*?" Sofía wanted to know.

"It's person who heals—body, mind, and spirit. We come from very, very long tradition. We use energy, stones, crystals, herbs, and intention. You trust me. I can help."

No one but the *curandera* noticed Sofía rolling her eyes.

At the hut K'antu offered broth and bread to everyone. Then she instructed Sofía to lie down on the cot, went to a corner, pulled out and unwrapped a threadbare cloth with the faint image of a red hand and some strange-looking hieroglyphics woven into it. Searching through many objects wrapped in the cloth, she found a stone that looked similar to those in the Cabrera collection, though in the dim light no one could quite be sure.

K'antu began boiling water and gathering little packets.

"What are you making?" Sofia was concerned that whatever 'potion' K'antu was preparing might counteract with the medications she was taking.

"Not to worry, señorita. These all natural. You see, I mix with the water lemon, coconut oil, turmeric, cayenne and black pepper. Then I add pure honey." She poured the mixture into a small cup and offered it to Sofia.

"Sip slowly."

K'antu then placed the stone on Sofía's stomach, wrapped a blanket around her, held her hands over her body, and murmured some undecipherable syllables for several minutes.

"Good. Now to relax. Breathe."

"This is ridiculous," Anselmo interrupted. "What she needs is prayers from a real priest. Please allow me to lead us in addressing our Savior, Jesus Christ."

After Anselmo's prayer, K'antu gently explained that *curanderos* believe that disease can be caused by resentment, anger, fear, or an ancient grief.

"You carry resentment, my child?"

Sofia could feel her spine stiffen. *Resentment? What did this woman know about how she was feeling?*

For Sofia, sharing this kind of personal information had always been impossible. But then she found herself too exhausted and in too much pain to protest.

"Well, yes… maybe." Sofía whispered.

"Be very good if you talk me about it."

Sofía sighed. "I guess you're right." Turning to Rogelio and the padre she said, "You can listen, too, if you'd like.

"You all may be familiar with the Chauvet Cave in the Ardeche Valley in southern France? There was a movie about it called The Cave of Forgotten Dreams. It was discovered in 1994. It's huge and has exquisitely crafted and well-preserved paintings throughout. There are domestic, wild, and long-extinct animals, a depiction of a part-human, part-animal creature, a wolf, handprints and a footprint of a child. The problem was that the paintings appeared to be very, very old, but it just didn't make sense in terms of our evolutionary paradigms. For example, there's a painting of a group of horses that's so beautifully crafted it looks as if it were drawn by a very accomplished modern artist.

"All the paintings show accurate detail, depth, and emotion. Cave paintings are supposed to be rather crude, yet, based on research, these were estimated to be 20,000-30,000 years old. So they asked me to come and verify the age with my thermo luminescence technique."

K'antu asked quietly. "You sure you strong enough to continue? Could to finish story in the morning."

"No, I actually feel better now. To be brief, I went to France five years ago and spent two weeks with two French paleo-archaeologists, one of whom I was dating. We tested the pigmentation, fossils, and soot in the cave, being very careful to follow scientific protocol. In the end, we determined that these paintings were at least 30,000 years old. I wrote an exhaustive article for the prestigious, peer reviewed Archaeology magazine and generously allowed all three of our names to be listed as authors. When the article was published, I was astounded to see that the other two men had changed the date from 30,000 to 10,000 years, that Jean-Marie Chauvet was listed as the lead author, and that my name had been completely removed as a coauthor. Neither Chauvet nor the man I was dating answered my calls or emails. They had suddenly turned on me like a pack of wolves!

"Well, anyway, later they wrote a terrible article about me, saying that my methodology was sloppy and that I had such a vested interest in those paintings being really old that I had fudged the results. They said that we all know that if humans had lived that long ago, they certainly wouldn't have been sophisticated enough to produce those kinds of drawings. This article was circulated throughout our profession, and was even presented at our annual conference in Paris."

Sofía looked pale, but she seemed intent on continuing.

"As you can imagine, I was devastated. If I am anything, I am a rigorous scientist and would never, ever fudge results. As it turned out, ten years later it was verified that the paintings were at least 30,000 years old. But by that time, my reputation was ruined. I lost my university position, and I'm afraid I've lost my health as well."

Rogelio took her hand. "I'm so sorry this happened to you. I don't know what to say."

K'antu added, "*Sí, mi hija.* Yes, my child. Very bad thing. But you must to forgive. This anger hurting yourself. Very interesting that 'wolf' is one animal painted on cave. Brother Wolf is powerful totem. Is no accident that your condition called 'lupus,' mean wolf. Start with others attacking you. But now your own body attacking itself. But OK now. Can teach you a lot. Know yourself, must die to old self, be reborn new self.

"Now breathe. Deep. Bring in love with air. Breathe out. Let go."

Soon Sofía was asleep. K'antu lay down on the floor next to the cot. Rogelio and Padre Anselmo insisted on sleeping outside the door as a protection against any future uninvited visitors.

The next morning over a breakfast of beans and coffee K'antu asked Sofía how she felt.

"Well, I'm still pretty exhausted." She hesitated. "Actually better, though. The swelling in my joints is down. The rash on my body has definitely improved. And somehow the stone felt good on my stomach. Thank you."

"You're welcome. You must to know, though, that you not completely healed. Remember. This take time. Time and forgiveness. Must give up the anger and the fighting inside you."

K'antu paused for a moment. Then she continued, "Now I want you should know my story. Help you understand yours.

"As I told, I come from long line of *curanderos*. We have special gift… being link between spirit and physical world. We can to connect with Great Central Sun and heal. But many in Catholic Church believe we are of the devil. Say we practice savage magic, we make people to act against their own will. Say we sell our soul to demons. All crazy."

K'antu wiped her eyes with the cloth and continued.

"So two years ago my family here in prayer. Men in dark robes and hoods burst in. Such a rage! Like madmen! They throw our sacred objects around. Then, suddenly, they go crazy. They pull guns from under their robes. They scream 'ungodly demons!' They shoot and kill my mother, my husband, and my little girl. Then they hold up big crucifix and run away."

No one's expression of shock and disbelief was greater than the padre's.

After a long silence, K'antu continued, "I don't tell this so you feel sorry. Or make anyone guilty. I don't have words to describe my agony."

She paused and her eyes watered again.

"After long, long time I am able to forgive. Finally then I find peace."

"Thank you for sharing that with us," breathed Sofía. "We're all so very sorry this happened to you… and… I never thought I'd use these words, but I believe that you are a deeply spiritual woman and a healer. Honestly, I feel much better now."

Sofía was pensive for a moment. Then she added, "I must apologize to all of you. I'm afraid my physical pain and my resentment have made me quite difficult to be around."

K'antu said, "No. You are fine. But please keep practicing what I taught you… breathe deeply, feel love, try to forgive. Trust."

"I will. I promise."

Rogelio smiled warmly at Sofía. Then he turned to K'antu. "You are a very kind and wise woman. Would you be willing to answer some questions for me?"

"*Sí*. What question?"

"Well, first, would you mind if we looked again at the cloth you use to wrap the herbs and the stone?"

"*No problema.*" She removed the objects and carefully laid open the fabric.

"Why is there a red hand woven into the material?"

"Is ancient symbol of our people."

"Thanks. And the hieroglyphs?"

"Sorry. Cannot say you now."

Rogelio continued calmly. "Well, somehow I feel that I know what it says: 'Children of the Law of One.' Is that right?"

K'antu's voice was shaky. "*¡Sí! ¡Sí! Es correcto.* Cannot believe it!" She became excited and began speaking very quickly. "You the first person… Must be the one!"

"The one?" Rogelio was baffled.

"What do you mean?" Padre Anselmo asked.

"The one!" K'antu repeated. "Our legend say one day come person not of our tribe. He understand hieroglyphs. He fulfill our destiny!"

"Oh no," Rogelio protested. "I'm not the one. I'm just a simple minister from Ica who works in the U.S. and is now searching for the truth about the stones my father collected."

K'antu's ancient eyes sparkled. "OK, I see. Anyway, you must to go to Lake Titicaca and Tiajuanaco. There you see real things that seem impossible. And you see things impossible that seem real. Ask native there about the portal of Amaru Meru. Even maybe you have interest in caves in Ecuador near Peru. Go to *Las Cuevas de Tayos*. Lead to tunnels with treasures and secret information. We call them Hall of Records of the Ancients. Part of puzzle of the stones."

Now even more animated, K'antu continued. "You get to caves, main entrance is blocked. Go around to west and you see what seem like two other entrances. They lead to nowhere. But between them is flat surface. As sun sets it shine on that surface. You see pictographs carved into it. If you can read them, they tell you how to get into tunnels."

Rogelio wasn't sure whether to take her seriously or not.

His face flushed, but he tried to remain calm. "OK. We'll keep that in mind... and... K'antu, I do have another question: Do you have any idea of who might have vandalized our car?"

"No. Cannot say you who did this awful thing. But they don't like what you do. Certain they telling you they're with Black Hand."

"The Black Hand?" the padre asked.

"Yes. Some people in the world love and help others. They are Sons of Law of One. Others follow Lucifer. They called Sons of Belial or dark cabal. They hold back light and truth from the people. They worship themselves, power, and money. They sometimes draw black hand as signature."

Sofía's face was still pale, but her eyes reflected intensity and she let out a gasp. "Excuse me for interrupting, but there's something I haven't told any of you. When I first arrived in Ica and went to my hotel, there was a letter waiting for me. It warned me to stop this investigation and return home. It was signed with the image of a black hand."

K'antu's face went white. "Oh dear. Let me explain a little more so you understand. Many years, people who are of light often draw red hand. People not so much light draw black hand."

"I remember reading about that," Rogelio interjected. "And those hands can be found all over the world. For example, in Indonesia they've found images of a red hand that's been dated as 40,000 years old. And right here in South America—in Argentina–there is an underwater series of twenty limestone caves with images of black hands. It's known as *Las Cuevas de las manos.*"

"I never heard of the Cave of the Hands. That's fascinating," said Sofía. "At Chauvet Cave there was an imprint of a red hand. Archaeologists couldn't figure out what it meant, so they determined it was just the artist doodling."

"Now you know those artists connected with good people," K'antu offered.

Sofía was both excited and scared. "So these 'signatures' of a black hand mean that whoever left them believe that what we're doing will hurt their interests?"

K'antu looked worried. "Yes. And Sons of Belial can be cruel. No care about destroying people who get in their way. Just be careful. But remember you always have protection."

Rogelio whistled under his breath, then spoke. "Thanks for everything, K'antu. I wish we could stay here for days, but we have to get going soon. So please be so kind as to answer my last question: Can you give us any insights as to what the lines of Nazca mean and who made them?"

"Yes, of course. Straight lines are… how you call it…? Synchronic… or ley lines. They show us where is energy. Is sad people no longer allowed to walk on them. Were put there to help us."

"Help us?" asked Sofía.

"Yes. Help us to see, to hear, to feel, and to know. And to help us heal. This area very powerful. Lake Titicaca and Tiajuanaco, too, places of great power. But then Sons of Belial learn they can control others by keeping information secret. Or say sacred places are evil. Many years go by, people lose understanding of power spots. Political leaders become more greedy for power and money. Sometimes they build churches."

Sofía couldn't quite stifle a yawn.

"Well, enough for tonight. You need to rest." K'antu bid them dream with the angels. *"Sueñen con los ángeles."*

In fact, neither Sofía, nor Rogelio, nor Anselmo slept well. All three had had their belief systems seriously challenged that day and spent most of the night trying to make sense of what they had just experienced.

The next morning it was time to bid this remarkable *curandera* a tender farewell.

"I feel so much better now," Sofía exclaimed.

"You look much better, too," Anselmo offered. "Did you realize that the rash has disappeared from your face?"

Instinctively, Sofía reached up to touch her face. "No, I didn't. There's no mirror here."

K'antu reached behind a curtain in the corner of the hut, produced a piece of highly polished obsidian, and held in front of Sofía's face. "Look."

"Oh my gosh!" Her eyes were moist. "How can we ever thank you, K'antu, for your warm hospitality and for healing me?"

"Please do what we do. Pass on favor to a stranger."

"We will definitely do that." Sofía took her hand and Rogelio and Anselmo hugged her profusely.

"But remember, you're not all healed yet. Complete healing will take time."

"Yes, we understand," Rogelio said. "And thank you again!"

As they began walking back towards their car, K'antu waved and said, *"Tari Pei Pacha!"*

"Excuse me?"

"Oh, just saying of ours. About return of Golden Age… the Age of Meeting Ourselves Again."

K'antu smiled as the three walked away perplexed.

It took most of that day to repair the car, but finally they were on the road. The drive back to Ica went quickly as they had so much to ponder and discuss.

"That was weird that you were able to read those hieroglyphs," Anselmo said to Rogelio. "How did you do it?"

"I have no idea," he replied. "When I looked at that cloth, the symbols looked familiar, as though I've always known how to read them. And how interesting the words: 'Children of the Law of One.' What's even weirder is K'antu saying that I'm the one to fulfill their prophecy."

"I don't think it's so weird," Sofía commented. "You've been telling us about your interest in the concept of oneness and your fascination with languages. Maybe they're somehow related."

"I don't know," Rogelio answered. "Also, I wonder what in the world she was talking about—treasures and information hidden in tunnels."

"I can help you with that," Anselmo offered. "But it's a very long story. If you come to the rectory tomorrow, I'll show you some letters that you'll find quite intriguing. And, Sofía, my friend, what are you thinking about all this?"

After a few moments of awkward silence, she answered, "To tell the truth, I was inclined to believe the stones were a hoax. Now I'm not so sure. When we get back, I'd love to stop in the museum to have another look (and maybe get a better feel) for those stones." Sofía looked a little sheepish. But Rogelio just grinned at her.

She turned to Anselmo. "And what about you, Padre? How do you feel about all this? You seem somehow softer now. Did K'antu's story affect you?"

"I'm afraid it did. You know how I love the Church and have always been loyal to my superiors, but all this has me wondering."

"Did your bishop instruct you to say the stones were fakes?" Rogelio was just teasing, but the good padre blushed deeply.

When they arrived in Ica, Anselmo went back to the rectory. Rogelio offered to drive Sofía to her hotel, but she said she'd like some time alone in the museum. So it was arranged that she'd borrow a car and drive herself back

When Sofía approached the museum she noticed that just one dim light was on but the door was unlocked. So she slowly started to let herself in and was startled to see Cafre behind the counter and Negromonte placing about a dozen stones in front of him. Cafre quickly sorted them, pulled out a roll of cash, and gave it to Negromonte who quickly departed through a side door.

Then Cafre carefully studied those stones, placing four of them in his briefcase and the rest on an already crowded shelf.

He, too, quickly slid out the side door.

4

FIRST MEETING OF PEDRO JIMENEZ AND CARLO CRESPI

March 3, 1955
Cuenca, Ecuador

Pedro Jimenez, a slight young man of barely twenty, was a seminarian in the Salesian Order of the Catholic Church in a small village in northern Peru.

The Order's emphasis on simple living, charity, and on Christianity as the only path to salvation appealed to the kind-hearted, earnest Pedro. He was also very interested in ancient history. So one day he took the five-hour bus trip from his village in El Alto to Cuenca, Ecuador to visit the Salesian priest, Father Carlo Crespi. He wanted to ask him questions about what a life of chastity, poverty, and service would really be like. And, if he were to be totally honest with himself, he was dying to see Crespi's puzzling yet reputedly dazzling collection of artifacts from ancient and pre-historic civilizations.

On arrival at the Church of Maria Auxiliadora, which the good father shepherded, the shy Pedro was relieved to find that Father Crespi greeted him warmly with profuse thanks for his coming.

"*¡Bienvenido, mi amigo!*" The 65-year-old priest had white hair but the gait of a young man. His twinkling eyes and strong embrace immediately put Pedro at ease.

"*Muchas gracias, Padre Crespi.* I'm so grateful that you've allowed me to visit."

"The pleasure is mine. And please call me Carlo."

Pedro stuttered, "Oh I couldn't call you Carlo. Would 'Father' be OK?"

"Of course, my son."

"Thank you. As you know, Father, I'm a Salesian seminarian. They're very strict and only allowed me one day away from my studies, so I'm afraid I have to catch the return bus in just a few hours. But I'm very interested in learning what you can teach me about the life of a Salesian priest and…"

The kindly priest laughed. "Yes, I know. Your formation director is a friend of mine. He called to tell me that you also have a passion for ancient history."

After a brief conversation about the simple life of those who followed the way of St. Frances de Sales–one of humility, prayer, helping the poor, and the renunciation of material goods–it seemed a bit incongruous to Pedro when Father Crespi suddenly exclaimed, "And now you must see my treasures! Come, follow me."

Carlo led Pedro next door to the College of Salesino School and to a giant storage room. Then he turned a key, entered, touched two wires together, and light illumined thousands of objects in gold, silver, bronze, wood, and aluminum, all piled randomly up to the five-meter ceiling. This collection would have made King Midas look like a pauper.

"Ah!!!!!!" was all that Pedro could utter. And, finally, "Where did you get all this?"

"That's a question that will be answered in due time. But first allow me to show you some of my favorite pieces."

Father Crespi proceeded to pull out treasures of incalculable value both monetarily and archeologically.

Pedro exclaimed. "Father, this is absolutely astounding. These things simply shouldn't have found their way to South America. And there are so many!"

"Right. I now have over 2,000 pieces. As you can see, there's no longer room here at the school to house them all. So I've written to Rome to ask permission to build a museum."

Pedro saw pieces that appeared to be of Egyptian, Phoenician, Abyssinian, Babylonian, and African origin. There were golden mummy cases, gold ceremonial armor, beaten gold Chaldean-style helmets, and golden inscribed plaques with unknown hieroglyphics on them. There were European musical instruments, gold and silver decorated enclosures similar to the Hebrew Ark of the Covenant with carrying poles and hinged doors bearing images of elephants, hippopotami (which don't exist in South America), brontosaurs, extinct toxodons, crocodiles, and llamas.

There were stone and copper mechanical devices with circular rollers, thousands of pounds of bronze air pipes, stone corn mills, crowns of gold, images of pyramids, suns, and reptiles, statues of Assyrian Nisrochs apparently of Hindi/Tibetan origin, 'wallpaper' of an aluminum-like alloy beaten into abstract patterns. There were wooden statues carved in the Pacific Oceanic island style depicting Negroid men and women, images of people with Semitic features and beards, a plaque with the image of a Caucasian man writing linear script with a quill pen.

Father Crespi was beyond excited to show off his treasures.

"I believe there are thousands more items like these," he exclaimed. Pedro Jimenez was speechless.

"They come from all over the world. Most of them pre-date Christ and many of the symbols and pre-historic representations are believed to be antediluvian."

"You mean, they date from before the flood? According to the Bible, that's more than 6000 years ago!"

"Way more than that, in my opinion. And I believe they've been here long before historians claim there was global travel and trade."

"But how...? Who...? I don't understand."

"Oh, there's much to explain. We will, I believe, have a long and fruitful relationship and much opportunity to discuss all this. No one knows how these treasures came to be here in Ecuador. And I am sworn to secrecy as to how they happened to come to me. Perhaps in due time that, too, can be revealed." His deep hazel eyes twinkled.

"When it is, the world will be shocked."

"Wow. Well, what do you plan to do next?" Pedro Jimenez was very excited but was trying hard to maintain a calm exterior.

"Once we create the museum, I expect people from all over the world will come, appreciate the beauty and remarkable craftsmanship of these artworks and perhaps add to our knowledge so that one day the secrets these objects hold will be revealed.

"And I hope you'll return often, especially after you've become a priest. Then we can spend more time discussing the legacy of the great St. Frances de Sales and you can have a chance to see my treasures once they are cleaned, organized, and catalogued."

"This I promise," responded the eager Pedro. And then, hesitantly, "I'm an amateur photographer, and I have a new camera that takes pictures in color. Would you mind if I captured the images of some of your pieces?"

"Be my guest," responded the priest with a wide smile.

For the next two hours Father Crespi pulled out priceless artifact after priceless artifact while Pedro took pictures. Finally, Pedro said, "Unfortunately, we've barely scratched the surface, but I've run out of film, and I must hurry to catch the last bus back to El Alto. Father, will you write to me? I truly need spiritual guidance and I would love to stay in touch and learn more about your treasures."

"Absolutely, my dear boy. It will be my great pleasure."

And so the old priest and the young seminarian began a friendship that would last until Father Crespi's death in 1982.

5

CORRESPONDENCE BETWEEN THE TWO SALESIAN PRIESTS

THE PRESENT TIME
ICA, PERU

The morning after their return from Nazca, Rogelio knocked on the rectory door.

"Well, my friend," Anselmo teased him, "you're here ahead of the sun. Looks like you're pretty excited to learn about the tunnels and treasures."

Rogelio feigned exasperation. "My dear Padre, you know this is a pretty big deal for me. Please save the wisecracks."

"Is that showing proper respect for your priest? Well, anyway, I've told you about my friendship with a certain Father Crespi from Cuenca. But I haven't shared too many details. It's quite a fascinating story and, I think, best told through our correspondence over the years. So why don't you sit down, make yourself comfortable, and I'll bring you the

71

first stack along with a cup of tea. The correspondence started just after my first visit to him when I was a young seminarian in 1955 and continued until his death. Please enjoy and let me know what you think.

Rogelio sat down and began reading.

June 1, 1955
Esteemed Father Crespi:

I fear that I don't have the proper words to thank you for your kind hospitality, the time you spent away from your parishioners, and your generosity in allowing me to begin photographing your amazing collection. Please let me express a simple 'thank you' by sending copies of some of the pictures I took (including a couple of you).

I'm very grateful that you are taking me under your wing, so to speak, as I begin the daunting journey from first year seminarian through ordination. I feel that becoming a priest is challenge enough, but becoming a Salesian priest with its additional requirements will take much courage, strength and perseverance on my part.

Looking forward to your reply, I remain

Your humble servant,
Pedro Jimenez

June 10, 1955

My dear Pedro,

It was, indeed, a joy to meet you, and I'm so grateful for the photos you sent. However, I wonder about the accuracy of your new camera that takes pictures in color. I couldn't possibly look that old!

At any rate, I very much look forward to our continued correspondence.

I trust your studies are going well?

I'm happy to report that I have received permission from our blessed Pope, so I will begin construction on the museum immediately. The works of art continue to accumulate, and though I'm grateful for these beautiful and priceless gifts, and certainly don't want to tell the generous people of Cuenca to stop bringing them, I must say that there is not now one centimeter of extra space for more.

Oh, yes, forgive me, I haven't told you yet about the Waris and how I came to have in my possession this amazing collection of treasures. I promised you that I would tell you in good time, and I believe this is as good a time as any.

As you know, in 1930 I was sent to Cuenca from Milan. At first I thought this mission would be impossible as the people in my district were not Catholic—heck, not even Christian—and they didn't speak any of the languages I know. (My studies in Latin and Greek certainly didn't prepare me for communicating in Quechua!)

So for the first couple of years I wondered if I would survive here. But I persevered, and little by little I learned their language and customs. Actually, trying to get into their minds was the hardest part. As you may know, this tribe was famous for shrinking the heads of their enemies. They believed that way the spirit of those they conquered couldn't come back for revenge. And, believe me, warring, avenging, taking the spirit from the conquered, and fiercely defending their property was (and still is) of the highest priority. To tell you the truth, I was quite frightened of them at first—especially when they would paint their faces with scary designs, beat the war drum, and chant and dance the entire night before going into battle.

Christ's teachings to forgive, strive for inner peace, and love and live in harmony with our neighbors were the furthest things from their minds.

I guess they saw something in me because gradually as I learned their language and customs, they would come with their problems and I was able to help them. Then I started to slip in a bit of the gospel here and there. They were very happy with those words! Eventually, most of them converted to Catholicism. After I baptized, married, and buried them, they wanted to pay me. But they didn't have any money. So they offered these works of art in gold and silver and bronze. When they realized that I have a deep interest in archaeology and ancient history, they started bringing me more and more items. When I asked where they came from, they simply said, "Oh, the caves and tunnels and jungle-covered pyramids in the Amazon." I truly believe they have no idea of where they came from originally, and, of course, they have no use for any of these items.

The only thing I have been able to determine is that these objects had been hidden for thousands of years near Tayos, at the confluence of the Santiago and Morona rivers in the Ecuadorian jungle. But their origin and how they got there remain a mystery.

Well, that's enough for now.

I close with an affectionate embrace and, as always, prayers for your wellbeing.

In Christ,
Father Carlo Crespi

May 15, 1956

Dear Father Crespi,

Please forgive the lapse in time since I last wrote. My studies and the obligations here at the seminary require an immense amount of time, and I'm generally too exhausted at the end of the day to do anything but collapse on my cot.

I found your description of the Wari Indians and how you came to be in possession of the amazing treasures extremely fascinating.

And... if I am to be totally honest... a bit troubling. I told my rector about your situation, and I must say, I was totally unprepared for his reaction. He said these objects were stolen or else they are frauds, and in either case, he would advise you to turn them over to the bishop and tell the Indians that they must not give you any more presents.

Concerned for you,
Pedro Jimenez

July 31, 1956

My Son,

If we are to have an honest friendship, I must ask you to keep our correspondence confidential. The fact of these 'out of place artifacts' is obviously a huge unsolved mystery. There will be detractors, naysayers, conspiracy theorists, and angry people. All this leaves me in a quite vulnerable position.

I beg you that in the future you not conjecture about the artifacts' authenticity, my motivations, or those of my indigenous friends. And you will certainly not divulge what I've shared with you with your rector.

If I can learn to trust you again, we may continue our correspondence (which, by the way, I have greatly valued).

¿Comprendes?
Father Crespi

August 1, 1956

Father:

A thousand apologies. I cannot express how truly sorry I am to have compromised your confidence and pray that you will forgive me so that we may continue our friendship.

In a feeble way to try to explain, I entreat you to remember that the seminary allows for no privacy, no secrets, and complete obeisance to the Order and to our superiors. Not only in the confessional, but in everyday life, we are taught to be ever humble, transparent, and obedient.

And thus I feel torn in half between my loyalty to you (whom I consider my good friend and closest confidant) and the Salesian Order (to which I have pledged total loyalty).

I feel that I need to take some time to go inside and consult with my heart.

Would you be willing for us to have a hiatus in our correspondence until I can sort this out?

Painfully,
Pedro

Sept 2, 1957

My dear Pedro,

Thank you for sharing from your heart.

Believe me, I have deep compassion for your dilemma, as I have been there myself.

At this point, I'm not going to give you advice, as this is a decision you must make after going inside and conferring with your God.

However, I would like to respond to your rector's accusations of robbery or fraud.

Stolen? How? The Wari tribes never leave their land here around Cuenca. They have no motivation and no means. Even if they did, from whom could they have stolen thousands of items?

Frauds? Who would make frauds out of gold or silver? And, if they did, why in the world would they hide them in tunnels for thousands of years and then give them to me? Yes, a few are not real ancient artifacts. These come from some of my very poor parishioners who don't have access to the tunnels, but wanted to give me something. I buy them occasionally to save their dignity.

By the way, the museum is coming along nicely. And the gifts keep coming in. This week I received several plaques with strange hieroglyphs on them. I'm sending them to the linguistics department at the University of Guayaquil to see if they can give me any information.

Until our next correspondence, know that I deeply respect you, have the highest regard for you, and pray that all will be well with your soul.

Peace be with you,
Carlo

P.S. How I love these Waris! In fact, I'm making a movie about them. It will be called "The Invincibles" because they are such fierce warriors. Did you know that they were the only group in all of South America who never succumbed to the cruel invasion of the Spaniards? And yet they can be so gentle and so loving...

February 10, 1959

Dearest Father,

Again I must apologize for taking so long to respond. It has been very difficult for me over the past several months.

In addition to wrestling with my dilemma regarding loyalty to the Order or continuing my most precious friendship with you and what I consider a high truth, another issue has come up.

Have you heard about the scandals regarding sexual abuse by the Salesian priests? Well, it's happening right here at our seminary.

Even the rector, whom I mentioned earlier, is being accused. And I know the accusations are true, as he has approached me.

What to do? If I testify against him he'll probably find an excuse to throw me out just before ordination.

If I say nothing, I don't know if I can live with my conscience.

Help please!

Your faithful protegé,
Pedro

March 17, 1960

My dearest Pedro,

This is, indeed, a most difficult quandary. I, too, have witnessed such things, and, to be truthful, it's one of the reasons I left Italy.

In my opinion, scandals of sexual impropriety will escalate in the next decades. It is, after all, unnatural to impose celibacy upon a young, healthy man. And since we Salesians work a lot with boys, it's only to be expected that there will be some bad things that happen.

I would suggest that you contact both the Vatican and the International Society for the Prevention of Child Abuse and Neglect. In both cases you can make an anonymous report.

Further, I would advise that you keep detailed records and release them to both church and government watchdog agencies after you're ordained.

I pray that these moves will be beneficial to all concerned.

And after your ordination why don't you plan to come visit our new museum? It will be a wonderful reunion and you'll be amazed at the new pieces I've received.

May the peace of Mary be with you,
Carlo

May 19, 1960

Dearest Father,

Thank you so much for your advice. I will take it.

And if all goes well I'll be ordained in two years and will have a sabbatical before I'm assigned to a parish. Thank you for your kind invitation to visit. I would love to come for a somewhat extended stay about two years from now if that works for you.

Regarding your earlier question about how all your artifacts, apparently coming from around the ancient world,
happened to find their way to South America, I have a thought.

I took a class last semester called "Are You Sure?" from a
priest who is brilliant, a little strange, but not afraid to consider
alternative ways of looking at history. I found it fascinating.
He presented many theories, such as the Mormon's belief that
Jesus came to the new world after his resurrection, that there
is quite a bit of evidence that the continents of Atlantis and
Lemuria actually existed, and that there is an ancient map
called the 'Piri Reis.' Have you heard of it?

Let me know if you're interested in learning more, and I'll
send you the details.

Until then, I remain your devoted
Pedro

November, 20, 1960

Dear Pedro,

No, I haven't heard about the Piri Reiss map. Please tell me
what you've learned.

And just to update you on the scandal, I'm dismayed that not a word
has been said to the public. I fear that this whole affair is going to go down
in history as the biggest cover-up ever by the Catholic Church.

Please pray that this matter will be resolved in a fair and open
manner and that justice will be served.

The blessings of Jesus,
Carlo

December 8, 1960

My dearest Father Crespi,

First, may I take this opportunity to wish you a blessed day of the Immaculate Conception of our Mother Mary. I imagine that since your church is named for her, that the whole congregation celebrates wildly.

So, here is a brief summary of the map. Piri Reis was a 16th century navigator who drew a remarkably accurate world map. It shows a circumference that's within 50 miles of being accurate. It was one of the first to show correct latitudes of the North and South American coastlines. And quite incredibly, it shows Antarctica 200 years before it was allegedly discovered. At first people thought Antarctica was drawn quite inaccurately, but recently it's been discovered that it is actually an accurate depiction of the continent before it was covered in ice. Reis wrote on the map that he had drawn it based on several earlier maps. One of these is said to come from the time of Alexander the Great, 332 B.C.

So I'm wondering if the history we've been taught about the age and relative advancement of earlier civilizations might not be quite wrong. Perhaps some of the ancient cultures such as the Sumerians, Babylonians, Syrians, and Egyptians did travel the world and enjoyed a robust trade industry. That would certainly explain how your objects came to be found in the new world. Since we know that the Spaniards stole everything of value, it would make sense that valuable objects were hidden in tunnels by the Waris for safe-keeping.

Now how the web of tunnels that apparently crisscrosses Peru, Ecuador, and Bolivia got there in the first place—seems no one has figured that one out yet.

So there is much to ponder.

Looking forward to seeing you soon.

Your humble servant,
Pedro

February 15, 1961

My dearest Pedro,

Thank you for the information on the Piri Reis map. It certainly provides food for thought and early global travel is definitely one theory as to how these thousands of objects came to be here in Ecuador. Let's discuss it more thoroughly when you come to visit.

One thing that puzzles me is why the vast majority of the objects have reptiles all over them. And many depict the sun—not in the sky—but over the heads of people.

Ah, so many mysteries.

The objects keep coming. I must admit that I continue to purchase some from the natives as they so desperately need money, and this allows them to keep their dignity. As I mentioned, some of them are fabricating 'ancient' objects. I chide them for this, but don't have the heart to turn them away. They are very good people. And they are beginning to know and love Jesus and have stopped their abhorrent practice of shrinking the heads of their enemies.

Wishing you good luck on your exams,
Carlo

November 29, 1961

My dear Pedro,

I haven't heard from you in a long time. Are you OK?

Just wanted to let you know that my museum is growing. It's beautiful. Many people come to visit and they marvel at the precious art, scrolls, machinery, crowns, and rolls of 'wallpaper.' When they ask where it all comes from, I just smile, shake my head, and say, "No one knows."

But now perhaps I'm coming a little closer to the truth. Today I finally received notification from the university. They verified that the writings on the plaques are classic Egyptian, Celti-Iberian, and Punic (a latter a form of Phoenician). Whew! This is exciting news!

I've felt for quite some time that many of the items came from ancient Egypt, Greece, the Mideast, Babylonia, Syria, and Tibet. This information will go a long way in authenticating the objects.

Something that I'm increasingly noticing is the recurrence of themes. Certain images on the plaques appear over and over again: snakes, suns, reptilian-looking humanoids, and pyramids. Perhaps we can both be considering this and, together, come up with an explanation of why those particular images?

But the huge question remains: How did these untold thousands of items get here? And how is it that the Wari tribe gained access to them?

Praying that you're doing well,
Carlo

December 22, 1961

My dear Father Carlo,

Again, I must beg forgiveness for taking so long to respond. Preparing for the final exams along with all the other obligations here and preparing for Christmas have kept me burning the midnight oil.

But the end is in sight, and I'm so looking forward to seeing you!

I promise to write more next time.

Yours,
Pedro

March 1, 1962

My dear Pedro,

Someone has burned my treasures!!!! A fire started in the middle of the night! I raced to the museum to save some pieces while fire fighters managed to put out the blaze.

The experts suspect arson. But who??? And why??? I just cannot believe it.

Of course all the wooden items were destroyed, but I was able to salvage one full room of the treasures, and I hope that the metal pieces can be cleaned.

I am beyond distraught. I feel that my soul has been singed; my heart torched.

The questions of who would do this and why will haunt me, I fear, till the day I die.

I'm sorry. I must close now. I simply can't carry on writing.

Carlo

6

TRAGEDY AT LAKE TITICACA

As Rogelio was finishing the letter about the arson, Sofía arrived at the rectory and stood at the doorway hesitantly.

"Oh, here you are. I've been looking all over for you."

"Sofía, I'm happy you want to see me. I hope it's personal…"

"Actually, it's business. Sorry, am I interrupting you?"

"No. Not at all. What's on your mind?"

Sofía spoke slowly. "Well, I've been thinking about K'antu's suggestion that we go to Lake Titicaca and Tiajuanaco. She seemed pretty adamant, and it's clear she knows what she's talking about."

"How 'bout that?" Rogelio exclaimed with a grin. "I've just finished reading some of the padre's correspondence with Father Crespi. They mention tunnels that apparently run for hundreds of miles under Ecuador, Bolivia, and Peru and the treasures that are still hidden there. Maybe we could plan a field trip to Titicaca, Tiajuanaco, and then perhaps try to find the tunnels.

"Well," Sofía added shyly, "it's clear that you have some pronounced gifts. And according to K'antu, this is your destiny. Frankly, I can't decide whether to keep my skeptical attitude and make fun of all this… or to get really excited."

"Why don't you hold them both until we know more. Skepticism and enthusiasm are both charming on you."

So they made plans. Just as they were about to leave for Lake Titicaca, the museum's employee Cafre showed up and begged to accompany them.

"Please, may I tag along? I've been working so many hours I'm close to burnout and it's quite a lonely job. Besides, I love Titicaca. Haven't been there in years."

Sofía tried to signal to Rogelio that she thought this was a bad idea, but he didn't notice and it was agreed Cafre would join them.

Along the drive, Sofía suddenly turned to Rogelio and said, "Rogelio, when we met on the bus you mentioned that you were very interested in The Law of One and had, in fact, just returned from a conference on Oneness. Can you tell me a little more about it?"

"Sure. Didn't think you were interested."

"Well, a lot has changed for me since I arrived in Peru," she responded. "Anyway, could you define Oneness for me? Also, is it related to what K'antu was telling us about the Sons of the Law of One?"

Rogelio beamed. "Let me answer by first asking you a question. Is it true that you don't believe in God?"

"No. I certainly don't believe in an old man in the sky who hands down judgments and punishes the wicked. And we as scientists know that he didn't create the world—at least not in seven days. I've always based my world view on hard science, on facts that can be proven or refuted." She hesitated. "But after our experience with K'antu, I've been considering re-considering."

Cafre's eyes drifted downward, then he spoke. "Well, I believe in God. And I believe in the Catholic Church. It's quite comforting to know that we can go to confession, have our transgressions forgiven, and look forward to everlasting life in heaven."

"Both of those belief systems are very popular," Rogelio responded. "I'm afraid mine is a little harder to articulate, though at its essence, it's quite simple. In a word, I believe in Infinity. That means there was no beginning and there will be no end. That which is infinite cannot be many, because many-ness is a finite concept. So to believe in an infinite Creator, there is only unity. There is only one of us here. All that we experience, all the people, objects, nature, emotions, events are all part of this Infinity. You are unity. You are love/light. You are. Ultimately what we think we see as polarities, good and evil, for instance, is an illusion. Once we see that, there is no more sorrow, guilt, anger, or need for revenge. It's easy to forgive. The trick, of course, is, as they say, 'To be in the world, but not of it.' In other words, I try to live my life with intensity and with unconditional love, knowing all the while that it's all a dream.

"I think that's what K'antu was trying to show us. You see, when we realize that there is just one energy, it's not that difficult to tap into that energy, harmonize with it, if you will, and elicit so-called magic."

"Is that how K'antu was able to help me?" Sofía asked.

Rogelio gave her a huge grin. "Yes. I believe it is."

Cafre chuckled to himself. "You are me and I am you? Patently absurd, if you ask me. Are you trying to tell us that…"

Cafre was interrupted by the sudden appearance of a roadblock and three men in uniform motioning them to pull off to the side of the road.

One of the patrol guards with acne, a gold incisor, greasy black hair, and smelling of rancid pisco stuck his head in the open window.

"Welcome to Bolivia. Park your car right over there and get out. We need to fumigate it... inside and out."

Sofía was appalled and began to speak, but Rogelio motioned her to stay quiet.

"I need to see everyone's passports!" shouted the second guard. He roughly grabbed the offered passports and walked with them into a tiny office just off the road.

"What the...?" Sofía whispered.

Rogelio explained to her that this is how things are done down here. "It's not like Spain. We've learned to just let them go through with their nonsense. Otherwise, it can get messy. In fact, if you have a sense of humor about it all, it helps."

"Oookay." Sofía laughed hesitantly.

The guard returned with everyone's passport except Sofía's. "What's so funny? Señorita, you're on a travel watch. You won't be able to enter the country."

"What? Why not?"

"I'm sorry, I'm not at liberty to say. Now do the rest of you want to go ahead and let this young lady wait here with us? We'll take good care of her," he added with a lascivious smile. "Or do you want to turn back?"

Rogelio got out of the car and walked toward the office. Sofía noticed that Cafre was staring at her. *This is all so creepy, she thought. I wonder if I should say something to Rogelio. Hang on. Get a grip. Don't let this situation toy with your sanity.*

In a couple of minutes Rogelio returned to the car and started the engine. The guard waved them through.

"How much did it cost you?" Cafre wanted to know.

"Cafre, are you becoming a cynic after all these years?" Rogelio flashed a mock frown. "Just for being so nosey I'm not going to tell you. I'll just say that no price is too great for keeping Sofía safe."

It was just before dusk when they finally arrived at Copacabana on the shore of Lake Titicaca. As they looked over the majestic but mysterious lake, a strange blue light emanated from it.

"What's that?" Sofía asked.

"No one knows for sure," Rogelio answered. "But the natives believe that this lake is magical somehow."

"Yep," Cafre chimed in. "There are many fairy tales surrounding Lake Titicaca…"

Cafre was interrupted by a middle-aged indigenous man with a knitted cap, a multi-colored tunic, black pants that came to just below the knees, and sandals made from car tires. He asked them if they'd like to book a private boat tour to the Isla del Sol and Isla de la Luna for the next day.

They decided this would be fun, so Cafre negotiated the price and they met their guide, Chuy, the next morning at nine.

The four of them stepped into Chuy's totara reed canoe and headed toward the Islands of the Sun and the Moon. As if on signal, Chuy began telling them about the lake.

"Did you know this is the highest navigable lake in the world? And though it's 12,507 feet above sea level and far from the ocean, it's composed of salt water. Seashells and seahorses are in abundance."

"How could that be?" Sofía asked.

"Well, our best understanding is that the archaeological site of Tiajuanaco, which is fifteen miles from here, once was a port, and that with earth changes over thousands of years and the lowering of water levels, this 'sea lake' was formed. We consider it sacred because the first humans, Manco Kápaq and Mama Ocllo rose out of these waters."

"Really?" Cafre made no attempt to hide his disdain.

Ignoring him, Chuy continued. "Occasionally people see a blue light coming from the lake."

"Yes!" Rogelio exclaimed. "We saw it when we first arrived yesterday."

"That's very interesting. We've noticed that most people in your culture need to see something to believe. In ours we say you need to believe to see. Therefore tourists seldom see it. The blue light is pointing to the location of the Solar Disc."

"The Solar Disc?" Sofía asked.

"Legend has it," Chuy explained, "that a disc made of a special translucent gold with powers to connect priests to the Universal Mind Source was important to Lemuria, a civilization that has long ago disappeared. This Solar Disc also gave their citizens perfect health, longevity, psychic gifts, and protected them from harm. Until the final disaster, of course. Anyway, the story goes that the priest and priestess Amaru Meru and Amara Meru knew that their continent was going to sink, so they brought the disc to what is now Peru for safekeeping. For thousands of years it hung in front of the Coricancha Temple in Cuzco. It is said that the gold of the Solar Disc and the gold-covered walls of the courtyard glowed magnificently in the reflection of the setting sun. The Spanish looters wrote in their journals that the beauty was beyond anything in the known world. But Amaru knew that they would soon destroy the temple and steal all the gold, so they took the disc to Lake Titicaca and hid it. We believe that it's still in or around the lake and now that we're in the ninth Pachakuti, we will retrieve it and enjoy the return of peace and harmony to our people."

Cafre chuckled again.

At the Island of the Sun they marveled at stone structures, temples, pathways, and what appeared to be ancient ceremonial sites. Sofía asked for more details, but Chuy didn't seem to know how long they'd been there or who built them.

"Archaeologists have different opinions," he explained. "But our people believe that these structures were made by the Ancient Builder Race, who came from the stars."

On the return trip over the lake, Chuy continued his commentary. "Before we return to Copacabana I'd like to show you Huiñamarka, an island on what we call *el lago menor,* or the smaller lake."

He carefully maneuvered his light but agile boat through a narrow strait.

"Do you see the slight difference in the water's surface in the smaller part of the lake to the south? That's coming from the remains of a lost city that we call Wanaku. It was believed for a long time that there were ruins under this lake, but since it's so deep, no one had been able to find anything. However, in August of 2000, divers learned how to navigate diving in such high altitudes and were able to go deep enough to see and photograph the remains. They found a 660 foot by 160 foot temple, a terrace for crops, a 2600 foot containing wall, and a pre-Incan road."

Sofía felt a deep emotional tug on hearing of this buried city. "Can they be seen from the surface?" she asked Chuy.

"Not unless it's a really clear day and you have an extremely high-powered magnifying lens."

"As a matter of fact, I have a high-powered camera," Cafre announced. "My latest hobby is aerial photography, so I bought this beauty and brought it along just in case we might have a use for it. What would you two think of hiring a helicopter and pilot tomorrow and flying over the lake? Maybe we could get a glimpse (or even a photo) of this buried city."

Rogelio wasn't pleased as he was hoping to spend the day alone with Sofía. But there was no way to refuse this invitation gracefully.

The following day was sunny and mild with just a trace of clouds.

"Perfect day for an adventure over the lake," Cafre noted as the helicopter lifted off.

Soon they were flying low over the area where Chuy had told them the buried city was located.

Rogelio had borrowed the camera and was leaning far out over the side opening, concentrating hard on getting a glimpse and a photo of the underground city.

To Sofía, Cafre's next words had an exaggerated theatrical tone.

"We're going to need a stronger zoom lens if we hope to see anything."

He reached down for his camera bag and unzipped it. But what he pulled out of the bag was not a zoom lens.

It was a Glock handgun. He pointed it at Sofía.

"OK. Get over by the opening next to Rogelio!"

Sofía was speechless for a moment.

Then she demanded, "What the hell are you doing, Cafre?"

"Shut up! I know you saw me buying authentic stones from Negromonte in the museum. You were told not to be snooping around there without permission. So now it's time for you to have a real close look at this buried city. Don't worry. It'll be over fast. Now move it!"

Then he shouted to the pilot, "Don't look back. Just keep circling over the lake."

Rogelio said in an even tone, "But Cafre, you've been a loyal employee and friend of the Cabrera family for fifteen years!"

"Yes, long enough to amass a fortune from your silly stones."

"What?"

"I suspect Sofía has already guessed at the truth. But since you're a little slow, Rogelio, I'll need to explain why your final resting place will be under the waters in the buried city. You see, Negromonte would come by when I was working alone in the museum and sell me stones for a pittance. I put the fakes and lower quality authentic ones on the museum shelves, kept the best ones, then sold them to collectors on the internet for hundreds of times that amount."

"How many did you sell?" Sofía asked.

"That's none of your business, bitch. But let's just say more than there are in the museum… and they were of exquisite quality. You'd be surprised what was drawn on them. Poor Javier. It pretty much broke his heart when he learned. But enough…"

Rogelio's voice was barely audible "That's what caused my dad's heart attack?"

Suddenly Sofía shouted to the pilot, pointing to a place on the lake behind Cafre. *"¡Señor, cuidado!"* Cafre, distracted, turned to look behind him. In a nanosecond Rogelio reached over to grab the gun from him. They struggled, but Cafre had the better leverage and pushed Rogelio out the opening.

A shot rang out. Rogelio started to fall, but was able to grab onto the frame of the side door. Cafre's look of astonishment quickly turned to agony and terror as he fell backwards. In a bizarre head over heels acrobat stunt in slow motion, and still clutching the gun, he fell into the vast lake below.

Time froze.

Sofia was in a state of total, absolute shock. She couldn't move. For a moment she simply stared at Rogelio hanging from the helicopter's opening. Then two realizations overtook her. One: Rogelio wouldn't be able to hold on much longer and would probably fall into the lake along with Cafre. And two: she cared about this man. Jolted into action, she rushed to the edge, wedged her foot against the wall, grabbed his wrist, and pulled with a strength she didn't know she had. Slowly, slowly she gained enough leverage to pull him over the ledge where he was able to get his footing and pull himself up and into the cabin.

But then the helicopter, which was already flying dangerously close to the water, started veering to the right and losing altitude. The pilot tightened his grip on the the controls and as Sofia and Rogelio watched in amazement, he put in the left pedal and pulled in some collective. The chopper acted as though it had suddenly come to its senses. It lifted straight up, and like a hummingbird, poised in midair. Then it reversed direction and headed back towards the landing pad.

Sofía, still white and semi-paralyzed, was staring out at the lake and shivering like a tiny bird in a blizzard. Wordlessly, Rogelio put his arm around her.

The pilot then reached behind him, grabbed Cafre's camera and bag, and forcefully threw them out the opening.

After they had landed, but before they disembarked, the pilot shut off the engine and turned to face Rogelio and Sofía.

"You were brilliant!" Sofia blurted out before he could speak. "Not only did you save Rogelio's life, you maneuvered this thing beautifully."

"Yes!" Rogelio added. "I'd say you saved my life twice! How can we ever repay you?"

"You can repay me by not saying anything to anyone. I couldn't see exactly what happened, but of course I heard the shot and then saw your friend fall into the lake…"

"Let me explain," Rogelio began.

The pilot put his fingers to his lips. "*No, Señor.* I don't want to know what happened. Let me tell you something about my country. If we try to explain the circumstances here, the case will go to trial, court and lawyer fees will cost a fortune, there will be no justice, and we could all end up in jail for decades. Trust me, you don't want to spend even a day in a Bolivian jail."

He paused for a breath then went on. "So, here's what happened: your friend thought he saw something interesting under the waters. Fascinated and focusing his camera lens, he leaned over too far. Since the lake is 1000 meters deep at that spot, there's no way we could have retrieved him. It was a tragic drowning accident. Just leave it to me. I'll handle everything when we speak to the officials. *¿Comprendido?*"

"Yes, we understand," Rogelio said softly. He tipped the nervous pilot generously before shaking his hand and taking leave.

Back in the hotel room, Sofía and Rogelio were still trembling.

"I can't believe what just happened," Sofía said through her tears. "That was a horrible, horrible thing Cafre did, but still it doesn't feel right that he's at the bottom of the lake. I wonder if anyone will miss him, file a report, and start a search."

Rogelio put his hand on hers. "Don't worry, Sofía. That man was a loner. He really didn't have any family or friends so sadly no one will miss him. The pilot will swear it was an accident. Case closed. But I simply can't believe how naive we all were. Imagine trusting that man implicitly for fifteen years. We never once doubted his honesty."

"To be frank, I'd say your whole family is a bit naïve… but in a very endearing way. I, on the other hand, am a bit of a cynic."

Rogelio said softly, "I don't believe you were ever basically a cynic. You're a good, caring person who has been burned. If you hadn't been a little suspicious you probably wouldn't have been able to think and act so quickly."

Sofía laughed. "Well, that verifies the old Spanish folk saying, *'No hay mal que por bien no venga.'*"

Rogelio sighed. "I guess you're right. There's nothing so bad that something good doesn't come from it. At least now that we know the truth, we'll be able to keep the newly acquired stones in the museum, and the thievery will stop."

"In view of what happened," Rogelio asked her later, "are you still up for going to Tiajuanaco?"

"I think we owe it to your dad… and maybe even to the memory of Cafre."

7

TIAJUANACO

Driving to Tiajuanaco both Rogelio and Sofía were lost in thought.

After some time Sofía broke the silence. "You never finished telling me about Oneness before we were stopped trying to enter Bolivia."

Sofía noticed that when Rogelio grinned his eyes lit up in a rather charming way. "So you're really interested?"

"It's such an odd philosophy. I guess I'd say intrigued more than anything."

"Well, that's good enough. As I was starting to say, the concept of Oneness is that we're living in an illusion. We seem to be separate beings, but that's not true. We're all part of the One Mind.

"Further, free will gives us the opportunity to make choices and learn from those choices. So the earth is a school for our spiritual growth. Our experiences here are about the Creator knowing Itself. Since we're part of the Creator, all the power in the universe is ours. But we've been taught by the Sons of Belial that we're powerless because they seek control over us. However, they don't understand that when people infringe on the rights of others, they're only hurting themselves. There really is such a thing as karma, so that sooner or later, those who hurt others will themselves be hurt."

"Whoa," Sofía interrupted. "That's a little too much for this agnostic scientist. Could you just simplify, please?"

"Of course. Basically, I believe in One Creator, in myself as part of that creator, in love, service to others, and the importance of forgiveness of self and others. In contrast, the Sons of Belial worship Lucifer and focus on service to self and on gaining obscene amounts of wealth and power over others.

"And, by the way, this philosophy isn't just part of our Unity Church community. It's ancient."

"I see," Sofía mused. "That sounds a lot like what K'antu was telling us. Also sounds like maybe the red and black hands are different names for the same concept."

"I think they probably are," Rogelio answered. "In fact, there are plenty of names used to describe these bad actors, including the dark cabal, the Annunaki, the Illuminati, and the Red Shield (Rothchild)…

"Oh, here's the entrance to Tiajuanaco. I think you'll find it amazing and surprising. It's been a long time since I was here, so I'm kind of excited, too."

The gargantuan Gate of the Sun loomed before them.

"Oh my God," gasped Sofía. "This is awesome!"

Rogelio grinned again. "Glad to hear that God has slipped into your vocabulary. But you're right. The locals say this was built by an ancient giant race, what we might call the Titans. As you can see, this portal has cracked over the millennia. But originally it was carved from a single block of stone weighing 15 tons. You see the sun god with rays coming from its head and holding something that looks like two staffs?"

"Yes. Looks like he's crying. I wonder why."

"No one really knows for sure," Rogelio said. "But let's hire a guide and see what he has to say."

Cauac, a young man who grew up in nearby Copacabana, was very enthusiastic about his job as official guide and seemed happy to tell them everything he knew about this mysterious place.

"Before we start the tour," Rogelio asked, "could you tell us what these images on the portal mean?"

"Well, it's quite controversial. Some people believe the figure in the middle is the sun god. Some believe it's a representation of the Venusian calendar. And some say it's an astronaut with helmet and a space suit. What experts do agree on, though, is that the staffs in each hand are power objects and that the images of birds along the sides are important. Before we started counting time there was an extremely advanced group called the Bird Tribe, which later evolved into the worship of Quetzalcoatl, the Mayan god who was part bird and part serpent. But let's start walking and I'll give you some history and an overview.

"Tiajuanaco probably represents the greatest ancient civilization that most people have never heard of. This region is currently populated by my people, the Aymara. Our life is simple. We live on maize, potatoes, and chicha, a fermented alcoholic beverage made of cornmeal. But it wasn't always like this. We believe that in the distant past Tiajuanaco was a flourishing port at the edge of Lake Titicaca with around 40,000 inhabitants. Here's an artist's drawing of how this site might have looked at the height of its glory."

Cauac pulled out a sheet from his backpack and showed them a drawing.

"All around this magnificent building was water, so that it appeared to be an island. In fact, the original name of Tiajuanaco means 'stone in the center of water.' We believe that it was not only a sacred ceremonial center, but was considered to be the center of the entire universe.

"A 16ᵗʰ century Spaniard named Pedro Cieza de León was clearly astounded when he came across Tiajuanaco. He wrote in his diary, 'I asked the natives whether these edifices were built in the time of the Inca. They laughed at the question, affirming that they were made long before the Inca. In fact, they had heard from their forebears that everything to be seen there appeared suddenly in the course of a single night.'

"Today there are many stories of lost civilizations constructed by people of giant stature. Tiajuanaco, Giza, Easter Island, Teotihuacan, and Edfu are rich in these legends. In fact, the initiates at Edfu were instructed to 'stand with the Ahau' ('Gods who stand up') who measured 10 to 14 feet tall.

"It's believed that the Ahau were what we know as the Elders. It's also believed, by the way, that the Mayans received their world-view from the same very early source and thus their sacred Tzolkin calendar contains 'Ahau' as the Creator God, symbol of union, light, and love.

"Please take your time and drink plenty of water as we walk. It's easy to get dehydrated at this altitude."

"Thanks, we will," said Rogelio, pulling out a water bottle from his backpack and offering it to Sofía.

"How high are we?" she asked.

"We're at 13,300 feet, about 800 feet above Lake Titicaca. Our people believe these structures were toppled by some natural catastrophe, such as the eruption of the Andes mountain chain or a massive flood."

Cauac made a slight left turn, motioned them to follow, and continued.

"The main structures here are the Akapana pyramid, the Kalasasaya platform, the Subterranean Temple, the palace, and Puma Punku.

"Let's walk over to the south now where we can see the Akapana pyramid," Cauac continued. "It's also called 'Sacred Mountain.' It measures

200 meters on each side, is 17 meters tall, and has seven layers. Keep in mind, please, that only about 3% of this complex has been excavated so far, so much must be left to the imagination—at least for now. The major structures are all oriented to the cardinal directions. As you can see, beautifully cut and precisely joined blocks form the three major structures—which originally had panels covered with metal plaques, carvings, and paintings. Are you up for climbing to the top?"

Rogelio answered, "I don't know. Sofía's been sick and she's still pretty weak."

"Oh, I'm fine. There's something about this place that seems to give me energy."

On the top of the pyramid they found themselves in a small, sunken courtyard laid out in the form of a square superimposed over a perfect cross.

"Under our feet is a huge system of interlinked surface and underground channels. They carried water collected on the summit down and through the levels, where it merged with a major subterranean drainage system underneath and ultimately flowed into Lake Titicaca.

"Besides their genius in understanding engineering, among other sciences, these builders were obviously knowledgeable about metaphysics. However, experts still aren't in agreement about the deeper meaning of the seven layers, the appearance of an island and mountain on a sacred lake, and the orientation to the cardinal directions and to star constellations. I'll let you ponder that one.

"Now please follow me. I'd like to show you the stelae over in the corner. This is the largest one. It's called the Pachama Monolith and is 7.3 meters tall and weighs 20 tons. Look closely at the lower half of its body. It's covered with fish-scales or fish heads."

"Reminds me," Rogelio said, "of Oannes, the Mesopotamian deity who was half man, half fish who conveyed mystical knowledge to ancient peoples. He was part of a trinity of Mesopotamian gods, together with Enlil and Anu—believed to be originators of the now infamous Annunaki."

"Yes, replied Cauac. "Some of the other stelae are now missing, but originally many gods as well as all the races of mankind were represented here—even people with elongated skulls, people wearing turbans, people with broad noses, people with thin noses, people with thick lips, people with thin lips. You name it."

"You know what's really fascinating?" Rogelio asked. "I took a trip to Easter Island several years ago with some friends from our church. And these statues eerily resemble those on Easter Island—particularly the giant size, the square heads, the huge eyes, the elongated ears, and the hat or topknot, or whatever it is. And the stances are astonishingly similar."

"That's true," Cauac responded. "And there are many other odd coincidences, especially given that Easter Island is over a thousand miles away. The Incas around here say that those characteristics were inherited from their divine ancestors. And a well-known legend says that a long time ago Easter Island was part of a larger country. But because of the sins of the people, the god Uoke broke it up, and most of the continent sank into the ocean."

Rogelio was excited. "When I was studying ancient languages in graduate school, one bizarre fact stuck in my head. A Russian expert, J. V. Knorozov, discovered that Rongo Rongo, the language of Easter Island, was written in a style called 'boustrophedon,' in which every other line is upside down. After much research he learned that that style was only found in two places in the world: Easter Island and Peru!"

"Let me chime in," Sofía said. "A man named Erik Thorsby from the University of Oslo collected blood samples from Easter Island's inhabitants whose ancestors hadn't interbred. He studied their unique

HLA genes and learned that they were identical to the pre-Incas in South America! And if that's not enough, they've discovered chicken bones in Chile that come from Easter Island!"

"You continue to amaze me," Rogelio said to Sofía. "You seem to have a voracious appetite for knowledge. And don't you ever forget anything?"

She smiled timidly. "Well, I was once on Jeopardy in Spain. I was the champion for three days." She added wryly, "my big claim to fame."

Cauac said, "I don't know what 'Jeopardy' is, but it sounds impressive. Did you know that the explorer Thor Heyerdahl wondered if it were possible to sail from Easter Island to Peru. He accomplished that and wrote about it in a book called Kon Tiki. He also discovered an area called Orongo on the island that had holes bored into it to indicate the position of the sun on the summer solstice. Furthermore, there's a legend that says that King Hotu Matua's country, whose real name was Rapa Nui before explorers changed it to Easter Island, was located on a continent called "Hiva.' As you may know, another name for the Waris in this region is the 'Hivaros' or 'Jivaros.' The continent was destroyed, according to the locals, by a tsunami, leaving only the very tip above the waters."

"Maybe Easter Island is called that because of the connections with the goddess Oestre rather than that it was 'discovered' on Easter Sunday," Sofía ventured.

"Could be," Cauac said. "Anyway, when Captain Cook arrived at the island in 1774 he asked the locals how the giant stones could have been moved into place on top of the *ahu's*, he was told they were moved by mind power aided by a substance called 'manna' and a golden object called *te pito kura*, also known as the golden navel.

"I hope this information awakens your curiosity and gives you something to contemplate over the next few days. But we must continue with our tour.

"Let's walk over towards those enormous monolithic stone blocks. That's the famous Puma Punku."

"Those stones are among the largest on the planet, measuring up to 26 feet long and weighing more than 100 tons each. Please look at them carefully and you'll see some intricate stonework, as though the builders used machine tools or even lasers. And notice how most of these stones have perfect right angles and they're as smooth as glass. Not only that, but these massive stones were hewn at quarries over ten miles away. I ask you, how could 'primitive man' have accomplished that?"

"Impressive indeed. When was this place built?"

"Well," responded Cauac, "that's another question that's very controversial. There are, of course, layers of civilization built on top of the original one, so it's hard to date. Some archaeologists and historians say that it was built in about the year 1200. But many, including my people's oral tradition and some researchers, including Arthur Posnansky, Graham Hancock, Zecharia Sitchin and Ivar Zapp, believe that it is much, much older. Posnansky, a German-Bolivian scholar, studied Tiahuanaco for almost fifty years. Based on the orientation of the structures to the planets as they would have been positioned thousands of years ago, he dated it to 17,000 years ago. We believe that before the flood it was probably a port that allowed hundreds of huge seafaring vessels to dock. One of the construction blocks from which the pier was fashioned weighs an estimated 440 tons (equal to nearly 600 full-size cars) and several other blocks are between 100 and 150 tons! Although many western scientists dismiss these beliefs and date Tiajuanaco to around 900 AD, our people do not. There is no known technology in the ancient Andean world that could have transported stones of such massive weight and size. The Andean people of 900 AD, with their simple reed boats, could certainly not have moved them. Even today, with modern advances in engineering and mathematics, builders couldn't create such a massive structure. So the question remains: How were these monstrous stones moved and what was their purpose?

"Archeologists have found fossils, including of toxodons believed to have become extinct thousands of years ago, as well as utensils, pottery, and tools in the deepest layers of flood alluvia. Many of them believe that they are from before the great flood of 10,000-12,000 years ago.

"Our people not only believe that Tiajuanaco was built by people whose motherland was destroyed in a great deluge, but that that great civilization enjoyed world trade thousands of years before Columbus 'discovered' America."

"Ah. That could solve the mystery of Father Crespi's treasures," Rogelio said softly to Sofía.

"Are you getting tired?" Cauac asked.

"Oh, no," Sofía responded for both of them. "This is fascinating. The place is absolutely mind-boggling."

"I'm glad you're enjoying it. Look at the excavation that's in progress here. At this altitude some of the remains are found at a level six feet below the earth's surface. The mountain range that surrounds the area isn't high enough to permit sufficient runoff of water or wind erosion to have covered the ruins to such a depth. So this is another argument for a great flood or other cataclysm."

Sofía commented, "Considering the original size and scope of this site, what we see here seems like a small percentage of the stones that must have been used. Where are the rest of the blocks of stone?"

"Sadly, all the treasures and transportable materials have been removed—first by the Spanish conquerors, then looters, then 500 train loads were removed to build the Guipui-La Paz railroad. So a huge amount of information is lost forever. If the government can find the money and the will to continue excavating, I believe people will be astonished at what they learn. Of course, many authorities simply don't want to learn the truth—especially when it contradicts their beliefs.

"Well, we're coming to the end of the tour. I hope I've been able to give you an idea of the beauty and wonder of what Tiajuanaco must have been like. But it's difficult to describe in words, so I suggest you go to the Visitor's Center and view a film as well as having a look at the few artifacts that remain. Be sure to check out the famous ceramic Fuente Magna bowl with its Sumerian cuneiform and Proto-Sumerian hieroglyphics."

"Thank you," Rogelio said. "May I ask a favor?"

"Of course."

"Before we go, may we see some of the hieroglyphics carved into the stone here on site?" Rogelio asked.

"Yes, of course. Perhaps the clearest one would be the inscription over the Gateway to the Sun. I'm sure you saw it when you entered."

"Yes, but I'd love to see it again."

When they went back to look at it, Rogelio stared at the inscription for a long time. "Do you know what it means?" he asked.

"No," replied Cauac. "No one has been able to decipher the text."

"Would you like to know?"

"What?!"

"It says, 'Taypikhala is going to be destroyed by a cataclysm which will raise the land to the heavens, create a giant lake, and cause the death of nearly every living being.'"

"How could you possibly know that?"

Rogelio was feeling a little sheepish. "I know it sounds bizarre, but sometimes strange symbols just impart their message to me. I have no clue as to how or why."

Cauac and Sofía looked at Rogelio with a mixture of disbelief, awe, and respect. "Actually," Cauac stammered, "Taypikhala *is* the ancient name for this area. And that would certainly explain why the Sun seems to be crying."

Sofía said. "This is all so amazing! And I have another question for you, Cauac. Do you know anything about tunnels that supposedly crisscross Peru, Ecuador, and Bolivia?"

"Well, yes, as a matter of fact, both oral history and written records speak of them. In 1882, the Spanish historian Fernando Montesinos wrote *Memorias antiguas, historiales, y politicas del Peru.*"

Cauac reached into his bag and pulled out a well-worn book. "Here, let me read a passage to you."

> *Cusco and the city of ruins, Tiwanaku, are connected by a gigantic subterranean road. The Incas do not know who built it. They know nothing about the inhabitants of Tiwanaku. In their opinion, it was built by a very ancient people who later on retreated into the jungle of the Amazon.*

"And of course every Peruvian school child knows the story of Pizarro and the Inca King Atahuelpa. After Atahuelpa had greeted the Spanish warmly, offered dazzling gifts, jewels, and gold, Pizarro's men took him prisoner and promised to free him once he revealed where even more gold and riches were stored. The Inca never revealed this because the priestesses of the Sun God had prophetic powers and they knew that Pizarro would kill Atahuelpa whether or not he revealed the secrets. They were right, of course. Pizarro and his men sacked billions of soles worth of gold, melting down priceless artifacts and of course they did kill Atahuelpa. But they never found the true treasures—those that have been safely buried in the tunnels for hundreds of years."

Sofía asked if it's possible to visit the tunnels now.

"Oh, no," he responded. "As you can imagine, there are still untold treasures of gold, silver, and artworks from all over the world in those tunnels. Very possibly including the Solar Disc itself. But now my people are smarter. The toughest of our warriors guard the entrances. And no one is allowed in."

"I understand," Rogelio insisted. "But I would do anything to enter those tunnels. And it's not because of lust for wealth. We've heard that there are also plaques hidden deep within them—plaques that contain a sort of 'Hall of Records.' I'd love to find them and, given my ability to read ancient scripts, share this knowledge with the world."

"That is as I thought," responded Cauac. "You are an extraordinary person, and I wish you all success in your mission. I wish I could be of more help, but I'm afraid that I cannot."

"Thank you very much then. You've been an excellent guide and we are extremely grateful for all you've taught us," Sofía said.

After Rogelio and Sofía had visited the small and somewhat lackluster museum, they started their drive back to Ica.

After a few minutes on the road, Sofía suddenly turned to him and said, "Rogelio, there's something I really need to tell you."

8

THE UNREAD LETTERS BETWEEN ANSELMO AND CRESPI

March 12, 1962

Dear Carlo,

   The truth that someone has deliberately set fire to your treasures is beyond unbelievable. I don't know what to say. There simply are no words to comfort you after this terrible tragedy.

   At least we will be seeing each other soon, we can spend quality time together, and we can discuss the implications of this.

Until very soon
Pedro

June 10, 1963

My dear son,

Actually, I guess I should now address you as Padre Anselmo. And, again, congratulations on your ordination!

I find that I'm missing you desperately. The time we spent together was a balm for my soul and now that you're gone I'm feeling pretty empty.

Thank goodness I have my parishioners and my priceless treasures. I believe the Waris were so upset to see me so upset that they've redoubled their efforts to gift me. In fact, my museum is rapidly growing back to where it was before the fire!

They've brought statues resembling the Easter Island giant heads; a plaque of an Indian carrying the severed bearded head of a giant; a copper radiator; a golden tiara with undecipherable squares of symbolic writing; a baked clay rectangle leaf with a bas relief of a dinosaur and a worm (or perhaps sperm); a diorite slab inscribed with a Minoan-Cretan labyrinth; a bronze Phoenician calendar; a gold sheet with images of part human, part animal creatures; images that look like a Picasso inferno that include a Neanderthal attacking a prehistoric, now extinct crocodile; and a statue of an Assyrian five-legged winged bull with a human head. There are even images that look like space travelers. In truth, there seems to be no end to what my Wari friends bring me.

Can you believe it? I've now received over 5,000 items and they seem to come from an endless supply. I'm so grateful, but during all this time I still haven't been able to solve the mystery of their source or how they came to be buried in the tunnels, caves, and ancient pyramids hidden deep in the Amazon.

And, of course, the question of who would set fire to the museum and destroy these treasures plagues me every minute of my day.

I pray that before I die these colossal enigmas will be solved. For now, however, I wish you all the best in your new life. Have you received your assignment yet?

Yours always,
Carlo

August 13, 1963

My dearest Carlo,

I was so excited to hear about your recent acquisitions. This is amazing! As one of my fellow students exclaimed, "This is the biggest archaeological discovery since Troy!"

And I share with you the profound desire to get to the bottom of this mystery before too much more time has passed. You've been pondering the questions of who committed the arson and why in the world they did. I struggle with them daily as well.

Yes, I did receive my first assignment. I will be going to Ica, Peru to be the priest of one of the larger congregations there. It promises to be a demanding but fulfilling position and I look forward to moving there. The only downside is that we'll be even further apart. But I promise to stay in contact.

Take good care of yourself. It seems clear that there are those who wish you harm.

In Christ,
Pedro

Unfortunately, Pedro was unable to keep his promise to stay in close contact. His responsibilities at his new parish were very demanding—especially at first. And during this time Carlo Crespi was burdened by health problems on top of his job as priest of the community and 'curator' of the museum. Six years went by with little communication. Then one day Pedro was surprised to find a post from Father Crespi.

July 31, 1969

Dear Pedro,

I trust you have been well. Even though time has passed since we've written, I always feel that in Spirit we are not apart at all.

You will never believe what has happened!

One of our parishioners told me an outrageous story. At first I figured it was just a harmless rumor, but on investigation, I learned it was true.

A man by the name of Juan Moricz has filed a claim with the Ecuadorian government claiming ownership of the miles and miles of tunnels and all of their contents! Apparently he is of Hungarian descent and a naturalized Argentine citizen, a miner by trade, an opportunist by nature. One day he was mining near the Tayos River when he stumbled on an entrance to a tunnel. He went in, discovered hundreds of art works and plaques in gold and silver, and must have thought he had discovered El Dorado, or Paititi, legendary lost cities of gold.

Anyway, this clown filed a notarized claim deed to all the tunnels under Ecuador, Bolivia, and Peru and all their contents! This is what we know as cajones [balls].

Of course the Ecuadorian government totally ignored his claim. So then he went to the Argentine government offering to share the bounty

50-50 with them. Again ignored.

In a way this is comical, but I fear it might become a tragi-comedy because he'll undoubtedly stir up interest among adventurers and fortune seekers, and once that lid is blown off, there will be no peace or security for any of us. In fact, I hear that he's already trying to enlist people to fund and/or join him on an 'expedition.'

And then, naturally, there are still people claiming that all the treasures unearthed are frauds.

Who would have thought that my beautiful treasures would have stirred up so much trouble?

I thought you'd want to know and will keep you posted.

Your concerned friend,
Carlo

P.S. I haven't heard how life is for you in Ica. Please drop a line when you get a chance.

September 1, 1969

My friend,

I fear I'm building a reputation with you as a very poor correspondent. I'm sure you know, however, that you are always in my heart and mind.

Truly, it's amazing that this Moricz guy is claiming ownership of the tunnels and all their contents. I often marvel at some people's boundless arrogance.

As for my assignment in Ica, it is taking some time to feel comfortable here, but I have met some very nice families and I feel that, with time, this town will feel like home.

If you can find the time, I'd love for you to come for a visit. More later. Duties call.

Your loyal servant,
Pedro

February 3, 1970

Dear Pedro,

It is happening just as I feared. Moricz received a substantial amount of money from two men named Jasperson and Wells to lead them to the entrance of the tunnel that he found.

However, it seems there was a lack of trust all around. The two men had developed a secret code so that they could communicate with each other without Moricz' knowledge. But Moricz overheard them, discovered their plot, was furious, and then spent the following two weeks leading them in circles on a wild goose chase.

Needless to say, they all exhibited levels of distrust and rage. But, thank God, they never discovered the entrance to the tunnels!

Thank you for your kind invitation to visit you in Ica. For now, this doesn't seem feasible. As you know, Pedro, I am not a young man and I don't have the energy I used to. Sometimes I wonder where this will all end.

Do let me know how you're getting along.

Your trusted friend,
Carlo

June 6, 1971

My dear Carlo,

That story about Moricz is, indeed, interesting. I imagine that many others will attempt to access those tunnels as the years go by.

But my understanding is that ferocious head-shrinking natives guard those entrances with their lives. They are so fierce that no one has been able to access them, though many have tried. In fact, rumor has it that recently four men have died trying.

So, on a more pleasant topic, I am very much enjoying my parish here in Ica. The people are not wealthy at all, but they are earnest and hard working and love Jesus.

I must tell you about a family that I've become quite close to. With your interest in archaeology and mysteries I think you'll find this quite fascinating. The head of the family is named Dr. Javier Cabrera Darquea. He's a surgeon and quite respected in the community. Several years ago he was given as a birthday present a stone with an etching of an extinct fish. Fascinated, he began to learn that there are thousands such stones in the area and they were even mentioned in the journals of the 16th century Spanish 'conquistadores.' He began collecting these stones and has now opened a museum to display them.

So far no one has been able to date them accurately as there are only traces of organic material in them and carbon dating has produced mixed results. But Dr. Cabrera believes them to be at least several thousands of years old. He thinks they were etched by an advanced civilization, perhaps before the first flood, in order to leave a message for our times.

What I find interesting is that many of the images are similar to what you have on your artworks from the tunnels: Serpents, pyramids, the sun, and various animals, many of which are either extinct or are not to be found in the western hemisphere.

I don't have any idea what all this means, but I certainly enjoy stopping by the museum and chatting with Dr. Cabrera and his family.

Yours in Christ,
Pedro

Dec 2, 1972

My dear Padre Anselmo,

I read with absolute fascination the story of Dr. Cabrera's stones. What a huge boon to the study of the history of our race.

I'm still hoping that one day I might be able to travel to Ica. I'd love to see those stones for myself.

For now, my biggest news is that I've been receiving several visitors who, for a variety of reasons, have shown great interest in my collection. I have had explorers, curious students, conspiracy theorists. One gentleman in particular, a Richard Wingate, has come three times and has taken hundreds of photos, which he plans to publish in a book. And others have contacted me telling of plans to come and document my collection.

Although some of the visitors, especially accredited anthropologists and archaeologists, obviously want to prove this is all a hoax, in general I'm very happy. I love to see the excitement on people's faces, and I love the fact that as word gets out, serious research will surely follow.

I must leave to preside over a baptism, and so I bid you a fond adieu.

Carlo

March 15, 1973

Dear Pedro,

Oh my God! There's been another arson at the museum!

I am beside myself. I simply can't believe anyone would do this! At least if the items were stolen someone would reap the benefit.

But burned? Archaeological treasures that could change everything we thought we knew about our history as mankind? Priceless pieces that go back thousands of years and come from all over the world?

No one seems to have any clue as to who the arsonists might be. Both fires have started at night and local authorities don't seem to have found a clue.

By turns I move from rage to hopelessness. My life's work up in flames!

I know I must surrender to God. But how?

All I can do is cry out in anguish.

Help me!
Carlo

March 30, 1973

Dearest friend Carlo,

I have prayed to God to give me words to comfort you. But I fear all I can offer is that I share your outrage and distress.

We must figure out a way to keep your treasures (or what remains of them) secure in the future.

In the meantime, let's conjecture on who might have done this and what their motivation may have been. I see the possibilities as the following:

1   Hooligans, gangs of young people who get a kick out of destruction for its own sake.

2 A personal enemy you may have made along the way.
   (Although that seems unlikely as you've always been kind
   and generous to everyone and have devoted your life to serving others.)

3 The local government. (This, too, seems unlikely as one
   would think they'd be happy to have the increased tourism.)

4 The Church. (Of course this has to be impossible.) But I must
   say, and just thinking out loud here, they have the greatest
   motivation. I haven't mentioned this to you, but our bishop
   has come to me demanding that I renounce the authenticity of the Ica stones. When I asked why, he simply scowled
   and said, "Don't be stupid. If these stones really showed that
   there was an advanced civilization twenty or more thousand years ago that would destroy the validity of the Bible
   and many of the teachings of the Church. I don't know if
   these stones are authentic or not, and frankly, I don't care.
   But if you don't want to be defrocked, or worse, you will
   follow the instructions of our Holy Mother Church."

Now if the church feels that way about the stones, wouldn't
they feel the same about the treasures given to you by the natives?
These items are not fakes; they're made of gold and silver and
other precious metals and they've been authenticated as coming
from ancient Egypt, Babylonia, Syria, Persia, Polynesia, and
Africa. Doesn't this also suggest that there was an advanced
civilization in South America eons ago; in fact, so advanced
that they were seafaring, traded globally, and perhaps, given
the existence of the Nazca lines and some images on the stones,
even traveled into space?

I've thought long about all this, my friend, and I'm slowly

coming to the conclusion that we've been lied to about our history, and by implication, the very nature of who, as humans, we really are.

Sending my deepest condolences and anxiously awaiting your response,

Pedro

July 31, 1974

Padre Anselmo:

Perhaps you've deduced my displeasure by the delay in my response.

I am shocked and appalled by your implication that the Holy Catholic Church could have had anything to do with the fires. I thought I knew you well—as a fellow Salesian priest and as a friend.

Your lack of loyalty to Rome stuns me as much as the arson itself. (Or perhaps it wasn't arson after all, but merely an accident.)

At any rate, I beg you to remember that it was the Pope himself who gave me permission to build the museum in the first place.

Unfortunately, I feel obliged to cut off our correspondence, at least for the time being.

Regretfully,
Father Crespi

9

BETRAYAL

ICA, PERU, 1979

Five years passed with no correspondence between the two priests.

In 1979, Pedro Anselmo received a telegram from Carlo Crespi's housekeeper.

ESTEEMED PADRE ANSELMO
REGRET TO INFORM YOU FATHER CRESPI IS VERY ILL.
HE ASKS FOR YOU.

In an instant Pedro forgot about the rift in their relationship and rushed to Cuenca to see his dear old friend.

On arrival, Crespi's housekeeper explained that he was in the hospital in serious condition from complications following prostate cancer surgery.

When Pedro arrived at Carlo's bedside, the old man looked wizened and weak, but he smiled and reached out his frail arms toward his friend.

"Oh, my beloved Pedro. Thank you so much for coming. I fear I may be approaching the end soon. It has been a good life and I hope that I have helped some people. But my one regret is pushing you away. In spite of everything, you have been my best friend for decades and now I must pray that you'll forgive me. These past five years have been very difficult because even though my indigenous friends have shared their love and continued to bring me gifts, I am still deeply pained by the loss in the fires, and even more deeply, the rift in our friendship. I will regret until my last heartbeat having pushed you away—not once, but twice. I blame my impulsive erratic behavior on my Italian blood. But there's really no excuse. I should have…

"At this point I realize that I'll probably never know who set those fires. And it really doesn't matter. All that is called for now is for me to forgive… and to ask for forgiveness."

Pedro put his hand on the thin, trembling, veined hand of his friend.

"Shhh. Please don't try to speak. You must save your energy. I have loved you from the day of my first visit, and this silence from you has, indeed, been extremely painful. But, as you say, we'll probably never know the real truth about the fires, at least not until 'we shuffle off this mortal coil' as Hamlet said. We must surrender. And we must both forgive.

"But enough talk of this 'mortal coil.' You're not going to die. I can see from the twinkle that remains in your eye that you still have plenty of life force. Let's set about getting you well and back to the people who need you."

And so it was. Thanks to the love of Pedro, the ministrations of the nurses, and Carlo's will to live, he recovered in just three weeks. Just before Pedro was scheduled to return to his duties in Ica, Carlo asked to meet with him in private in his museum.

"Pedro," he began, "I've been thinking a lot about what you said over five years ago. I'm not going to live forever, and we must do what we can to preserve these thousands of treasures I now have from the tunnels. Eventually, they must be properly studied, catalogued, and dated. And the people of the world must learn about them.

"Despite our misunderstanding, for which, again, I deeply regret, you have been my most beloved and trusted friend. My intent is to will this museum with all its contents to you to ensure it remains intact. Your obligation would be to find an appropriate administrator, keep the museum open to the public, and, from time to time, visit it to be sure that everything is in order. Would you be willing to do that for me?"

"That, my good friend, would be a deep honor and my greatest pleasure."

And so Eduardo Rodriguez, the most respected attorney in Cuenca and member of Crespi's Maria Auxiliadora Church, had the necessary papers drawn up and signed.

Padre Anselmo had responsibilities in Ica and so the two sadly bid each other, not *adiós,* but *hasta luego*—'until we meet again.'

The years went by and the good Father Carlo Crespi went on ministering to his parishioners, receiving gifts, corresponding with Pedro, and pondering life's mysteries.

In April, 1982, when Carlo was 90, Pedro received a call from his housekeeper telling him that Father Crespi was extremely ill and not expected to live.

Again, Pedro dropped everything and took the next flight from Nazca to Cuenca. There was tremendous traffic between the airport and the museum so he arrived much later than he had hoped. When he finally got there, he was amazed to see a dozen trucks lined up along the street. Several men were loading the trucks with items from the museum.

"What's going on?" Pedro shouted to a person in clerical clothing who looked to be no older than a teenager.

The boy's expression carried a mixture of confusion, arrogance, and shame. "And who might you be?" he asked.

"I'm Padre Pedro Anselmo, a good friend of Father Crespi. Who are you?"

Just then everyone's attention was turned to a white-haired, white-faced old man running down the street in a hospital gown and screaming, "What are you doing with my things? Put them back! They belong to me! My will decrees they will soon belong to Padre Anselmo! Halt!"

How the old and dying man, his robes flying, his feet bare, found the strength to leave the hospital and run down the street can only be attributed to a mammoth adrenaline surge.

The workers, paralyzed, simply stared at the young priest.

Carlo spotted Pedro and ran to him.

Out of affection or perhaps fearing his collapse, Pedro wrapped his arms around his dear old friend. "What in the world are they doing?"

Carlo could only say, "My treasures! They're stealing my life's work. They're taking away the world's most valuable archaeological find! Stop them!"

"Unload those things right now!" Pedro yelled at the workers.

"Continue loading right now!" the young priest yelled.

"Wait a minute!" Pedro addressed the priest. "In the name of God, tell me what is going on!"

The young priest, gawky, with red splotches on his face, said he had been sent by Rome to replace Father Crespi.

He stuttered, "We thought he had died. I received a notice from Rome that we must sell these things to the church. They sent us a money order for $50,000 soles. See, it's right here." He pulled a paper from his pocket and thrust it in Pedro's face.

Pedro tried to keep his voice calm. "First of all, as you can see, Father Crespi is most definitely alive. Secondly, as he mentioned, he has bequeathed these items to me to assure that they remain intact and that the museum remain open. And, finally, even if he agreed to sell to the church, which he will not do, $50,000 is a joke. These treasures are worth tens of millions."

Father Crespi was extremely weak and his voice thin and halting but passionate. "Listen, this can be handled very quickly and efficiently. Padre Anselmo is right. I've hired a lawyer and had my will notarized to be sure everything is in order upon my demise. I can call him right now and he'll verify that I've left everything to Anselmo." He started moving toward the museum and a phone.

"That's just the problem," the young priest countered. "The word we got from the Vatican reminds both of you that Salesian clergy have taken a vow of poverty. You cannot own anything and therefore the museum and all its contents belong to the Supreme Pontiff. The $50,000 was not necessary; it was a generous gift to Maria Auxiliadora Church."

By virtue of the fact that Padre Anselmo was a priest, he was allowed to ride in the front seat of the ambulance. When they arrived at the hospital the exhausted Crespi was barely conscious and Pedro was taken to a waiting room while the anguished and dying priest was settled into his room.

When Pedro entered, however, Crespi was animated and coherent. "Come," he motioned to Pedro.

Pedro sat by the bedside and again put his hand on that of his beloved friend. "Don't try to talk, dearest Carlo. You need to rest."

"Ah, my son, this is precisely the time when I do need to talk. I know that my time is near and I have no illusions that my treasures will ever be retrieved. They're probably headed to the Vatican's vaults as we speak, never again to see the light of day. (That is, those that weren't stolen from the trucks.) I guess I underestimated the church's zealous commitment to keeping hidden information that would contradict their teachings. You were absolutely right and, again, I apologize. My life's work and passion are destroyed."

"Oh, dearest friend, I wish I had some words of consolation for you."

"I appreciate that very much, my beloved Pedro. But I have some words of consolation for you. I had a premonition years ago… after the second fire… that something like this might happen. Though I never learned who set the fires, it was clear that someone—or some group—was prepared to do whatever it took to prevent those artifacts from gaining worldwide exposure. So I took a couple dozen of the most historically intriguing and hid them in an obscure closet in the basement of the church.

"Since you're a priest, the maintenance people won't have any problem letting you enter. The key is here." He motioned to the drawer of the nightstand. "Go have a look. I think you'll find the contents fascinating."

Then the good shepherd closed his eyes, smiled slightly, and quietly expired.

Padre Pedro Anselmo sat motionless for a very long time holding the hand of the dearest friend he had had in this life.

The next day Pedro went to the closet in the church basement. There, wrapped in an altar cloth, he found an exquisitely carved statue of a strange-looking being. It was apparently half human and half reptilian.

What am I to do with this? he wondered.

Then he noticed a chalice that looked to be made of a transparent-looking gold. It reminded him of a chalice that he read about said to be 5000 years old and currently residing in a museum in Egypt. As he was admiring it and marveling at the unique type of gold, he put his hand inside and felt something. It was an envelope addressed to Padre Pedro Anselmo. Pedro could tell by the handwriting that it was from Carlo, and started to open it, but he had an insistent sensation that someone was watching him. So he quickly put the envelope in the pocket of his cassock, hurriedly replaced the chalice, locked the door, and headed toward the darkened back staircase.

A perfectly still and silent figure waited in the shadows. He held a heavy gold thurible high overhead and when Pedro approached the stairs, he let its full weight come crashing down on Pedro's head.

Padre Anselmo collapsed in a bloody heap.

The figure smiled slightly as he turned the body over, took the envelope from the cassock, replaced it with a folded paper, climbed the dark stairway, slid out the back door of the church, and disappeared in the Saturday afternoon crowd.

An hour later the young priest entered the sacristy to prepare for the following day's mass. When he reached into the tabernacle it was empty and he realized that the Eucharist had not been replenished. Muttering to himself about the inefficiency of the nuns in charge, he went to the supply room in the basement where additional hosts were stored.

He screamed in terror when he saw the body of Padre Anselmo lying in a pool of blood.

Then he ran upstairs for help and yelled at two very startled old women who were praying in the sanctuary.

"Quick! Call an ambulance! There's a priest on the floor in the basement. There's a lot of blood! I don't know if he's alive."

When Pedro was lifted to a stretcher a crumpled paper fell from the pocket of his cassock. The young priest picked it up and opened it.

Sloppily scrawled on the paper was nothing but the image of a hand… drawn in black ink.

Ah, just as the Vatican warned me. This man, along with his mentor Crespi and probably the pagan Indians as well, are all serving the dark side.

Meanwhile, the figure who had assaulted Anselmo and replaced the letter slid into a dark enclave on the outskirts of the city and read the letter from Father Crespi.

10

SOFÍA AND ROGELIO

PRESENT TIME

"Rogelio, there's something I really need to tell you," Sofía repeated as they were driving back to Ica.

"Go ahead."

"It just feels very important to be totally truthful with you. You and your family keep thanking me for coming to Peru to authenticate the stones and support their cause."

"That's because we're incredibly grateful for all you're doing to help us."

Sofía continued, "The truth is…" She hesitated for a good fifteen seconds. "I didn't come as a favor to you. I came because I thought I could use my thermo luminescence technique to prove that the stones were fakes. I had planned to return to Spain as soon as possible, document my results, publish them in a prestigious journal, and regain my reputation."

Rogelio was silent for a minute—which to Sofía seemed like an infinity. Then he said softly, "I see. Well, I appreciate your honesty.

Maybe by the time we get back to Ica the results from your lab will have arrived and you can go home and publish your article."

The Reverend Rogelio Cabrera stared straight ahead at the road.

Five minutes passed in a tense silence. Finally, Sofía put her hand on his arm. "Rogelio, I can't tell you how sorry I am. You… and your whole family… trusted me. And I was here under false pretenses."

Rogelio, stone-faced, glanced at her. "Well, again, I appreciate your honesty. And at any rate you'll be back in Madrid soon and can forget all about us."

Sofía looked over at him and thought she saw a slight quiver in his chest. "What I'm trying to say is that when I came to Peru, my only concern was for my career. Now, less than a month later, I hardly recognize that person I used to be. This is a little embarrassing to say, but when you touch my hand or hug me, I experience a totally new sensation. And I've been thinking about all we've experienced together, how you were consistently kind and gentle and patient with me—even when I was acting less than gracious."

"You've never been less than gracious."

Sofía smiled at him. "Please let me go on. So I've been thinking about all these things… and… I don't have the words… but I realize that I care for you. In fact… I've never felt this way before. I know it sounds crazy, but I don't want to go back to Spain right away. I want to spend more time with you. I want to help you find the entrance to the tunnels and retrieve the folios. And I want to help you and your family solve the mystery of the stones." Her eyes glistened as she spoke.

Rogelio turned to look at her. His cold face had softened to a warm glow.

Then he flashed that grin that melted Sofía, laughed, and squeezed her hand. "I forgive you! And actually, there's been something I've been wanting to say to you, too."

"What's that?"

Rogelio turned to look at her. She looked more beautiful than ever—her reddish blond hair now loose over her shoulders, her face and arms burnished by the Tiajuanaco sun, her aquamarine eyes earnest.

He suddenly swung the car to the right and exited the highway. In silence he drove for ten minutes on a back road until he came to a dead end.

There he stopped the car, got out, went around to the passenger door, helped her out, took her hand, and led her to an area of massive boulders. He put his jacket on the ground and motioned her to sit with him.

The silence of the desert was broken only by their breathing and a lone cricket apparently too impatient to wait for nightfall.

Rogelio put his arm around Sofía, tentatively first. Then he tenderly drew her close.

When she looked up into his eyes she had the sensation that she had known and loved him long before time began.

But then a strong reticence came over her. When he gently lifted her chin and bent to kiss her she gently pushed him away.

"What is it?"

Her long-lashed eyes filled with tears.

"I don't know. I guess I'm afraid. I feel this bigger-than-life pull towards you. And at the same time I feel that we're both north magnetic poles and the more I'm drawn to you the more some kind of cosmic force wants to push you away."

Rogelio's body slumped when she turned away from his kiss—and even more on hearing those words. "So you're repelled by me?"

"No! Yes! I don't know. As I told you, I'm very drawn to you. But at the same time this huge force pulls me away. The more I try to fight it, the stronger it gets." Her tears were now flowing freely.

Rogelio took his arm from around her and breathed deeply. "Please help me understand. When did you first have these conflicting emotions?"

"The first time I saw you…"

"OK. Do you have them all the time?"

"No. I felt them very strongly at Paracas, at Lake Titicaca, and at Tiajuanaco. I know it doesn't make any sense, but I'm trying the best I can to get in touch with these feelings. And put them into words."

"I understand," said Rogelio. "Kind of."

Sofía gave him a tiny peck on the cheek.

He held her hand and they sat in silence for several minutes. Finally he said, "I don't think we're going to figure this out today… or even this month. What do you say we get back on the road?"

Sofía smiled and hugged him warmly. "Good idea." She hesitated, then said softly, "Thank you for your incredible patience."

When they arrived in Ica, Elenia and Padre Anselmo greeted them enthusiastically.

Then Elenia asked, "Where's Cafre? As I recall there were three of you when you left."

After a moment she noticed the expression on their faces and became serious. "Did something happen to him?"

Rogelio explained how Cafre had tried to kill them at Lake Titicaca and how they had been strongly advised not to file a report and just explain that it was a terrible accident.

"Tell me this is a sick joke," Elenia exclaimed. "Cafre has been our friend and loyal employee for fifteen years. Dad loved him."

"We all did," Rogelio stared at the floor. "I'm sure I'll never get over how he cheated and betrayed us for years… and then was willing to kill Sofía and me to try to cover it all up."

"Cafre was a troubled soul and will need our prayers," Anselmo said quietly. "I shall say a mass in memory of him tomorrow."

Mapi's head popped around the corner from the kitchen. "What are you talking about? A mass for Cafre?"

"Mapi, it's very long story. Would it be OK if I filled you in later? I'd really love to hear about what happened to Rogelio and Sofía at Nazca and Tiajuanaco."

And so they told them about the slashed tires and snake at Nazca, Sofía's healing, what they learned from K'antu, and the fact that Rogelio could read the inscription woven into K'antu's sacred cloth and again the hieroglyphs carved into the stone portal at Tiajuanaco.

"This is extraordinary!" Anselmo exclaimed. "Rogelio has read some of the correspondence between Crespi and myself, but I haven't shared the whole story with all of you yet. Now, however, is definitely the right time."

He then proceeded to tell them in detail about his long friendship with Father Crespi, the treasures from the tunnels, the museum, the two arsons, Crespi's death, and how he himself was attacked in the sacristy.

"When I recovered, I went to the reading of Crespi's will. Indeed, no mention of my inheriting the museum was made, but it did state that there was a letter for me in a bank vault. I realized that it was a copy of the letter that was stolen from me by the unknown assailant. Father Crespi was a holy man. But he was also shrewd.

"Anyway, I've been holding on to that letter for decades, waiting for the person who could read ancient hieroglyphs. Who would have guessed that person would be right here in the Cabrera family? Here, let me show you!"

February 28, 1979

My dearest friend Pedro,

It's hard for me, indeed, to believe that we've been corresponding since we first met in 1955. And that this will be my last letter.

I know we were both devastated about the loss of the treasures and the behavior of our church. But I'm writing to give you wonderful news that will help cancel the bitter disappointment that undoubtedly lies in your heart.

Recently I've learned that there are still a hundred times more items in the tunnels than were in my collection. And even more exciting, it turns out that there's a 'library' made of metal plaques. This library has been hidden deep within the tunnels for thousands of years, waiting for the right time and the right person to find and interpret the writing. Apparently, this is what, over the millennia, has been called 'The Hall of Records.'

I believe that Moricz stumbled on those plaques but couldn't understand the hieroglyphs and, besides, he was more interested in the monetary value of the artifacts.

In case this letter gets into the wrong hands, I cannot tell you how to locate the entrance to the tunnels except to say that it's near the Caves of Tayos in Ecuador.

I think it's very possible that the same civilization that built the tunnels and hid the plaques also made the etchings on the stones. Whoever that civilization may have been, they were obviously determined to leave messages to their descendants. As I know my death is imminent, I'm entrusting to you the work of trying to find someone who can enter the tunnels, safeguard the treasures for future generations, and decipher the messages on the plaques.

I have every confidence that you will be willing to carry out this extremely important task.

Thanking you in advance and assuring you that I will be guiding and protecting you from the other side, I remain your devoted friend now and throughout eternity.

Carlo

11

DEATH IN THE TUNNELS

After doing some research on *Las Cuevas de Tayos,* Rogelio and Sofía decided it would be best to fly from Lima to Guayaquil, get any supplies they would need there, and then begin searching for the caves.

Thanks to the stories about treasure hunters, everyone in the area seemed to know about the caves, so it wasn't difficult to locate them. And just as K'antu had told them, the main entrance was blocked. They made their way to the west until they came to what appeared to be two caves with a flat surface in between.

In fact, everything was exactly as K'antu had described.

When the last rays of the sun shone on the flat surface, the two carefully made their way over the rocks to have a closer look.

"Oh my God! There it is!" Sofía breathed as she squeezed his hand. "Can you make it out?"

Rogelio studied the hieroglyphics etched in the rock.

Finally: "Yes. I got it!"

The tunnel was wider, blacker, and colder than they had anticipated. It was musty and smelled of decomposing flesh. Rogelio held his torch in one hand and took Sofía's arm with the other. "Be very, very careful. It feels like the floor is covered with something wet and slippery… maybe bat guano."

"Yech! And what are the items scattered on the ground?"

"Probably better that you don't know," Rogelio replied grimly.

Sofía was making her way gingerly, sliding her hand along the clammy granite wall for support. When she faced the wall directly the light from her miner's hat illumined a series of hieroglyphs and images of disembodied black hands. Rogelio gripped her arm tighter and could feel that that she was trembling.

As they continued downward, the ground became even more slippery. Soon they were ankle deep in water.

I should never have brought her here. What in the world was I thinking? Here's a woman probably still suffering from lupus. And I, the enlightened minister given the gift to decipher ancient codices… the one who could unlock the mysteries of the universe. The big hero! Insanity! But it's too late to turn back now. Sofía did, of course, insist on coming with me, and I've learned it's useless to argue with her.

Aloud, he asked, "Are you OK?"

"Well, I can hardly breathe."

"I know. There isn't much oxygen. We'd be smart to restrict our talking. According to the 'map' on the stone, the metal library should be less than five minutes away, straight along this corridor about 500 feet, then we make a sharp right, go through a very narrow section and it should be there in a natural cul de sac. We'll just have a quick look to see if I can read them, then we'll turn back. OK?"

"Sure." The lack of oxygen, the putrid smells, and the terror were making Sofía feel nauseous. She couldn't control the pounding in her ears. *Is that sound my heart racing?*

Or is it something else? Sofía had an eerie feeling that they were being followed.

At that moment she tripped on something and fell to the ground. When she shined her torch on the object, it proved to be a human skeleton—covered with gold dust.

"Oh God!" she screamed.

"Yes, you'd better call to your god," a voice whispered in her ear as she felt an arm grasp her around the neck from behind, pulling her up and then something sharp pressed against her back. She looked over at Rogelio. He was being assaulted in the same way.

The two men, dressed all in black including masks and gloves, threw their torches to the ground, creating ominous shadows.

Sofía noticed cruel eyes behind the mask before she was spun around and her arms pinned behind her. Her assailant put his lips close to her ear, and in a coarse whisper, said, "You shoulda known that everyone else who's tried to get in these tunnels has croaked. You seen the skeletons. What made you think you'd survive? Rather arrogant, wouldn't you say? But we are generous people. We noted that you two seem to be fond of each other, so we'll let you be close together through all of eternity." He laughed crudely.

"That one's pretty cute," the man holding Rogelio said, moving the knife from Rogelio's back to Sofía's breast. "What do you say we enjoy her a bit before we dispatch of them both?"

The other hesitated. Sofía's lungs were screaming for oxygen. Her assailant's arm was now tight around her chest. His breath, so close to her and reeking of stale beer and the stench of his body made her feel suddenly and violently ill. She started gagging.

The man loosened his grip around her neck just in time for her to vomit on him.

"*¡Pinche puta!* Fucking whore! Forget it. Let's just get the job done and get the hell out of here."

Rogelio yelled for help. The man holding him hit him hard in the face.

Quickly, the dark figures tied their victims' hands behind their backs, gagged them, bound them together belly to belly, and tossed them to the ground. Rogelio and Sofía landed in contorted positions, legs askew, as if they had been unceremoniously thrown into a heap of trash.

The would-be rapist sneared, "Don't worry, sweet lovers. You won't be left alone. Once your skeletons are clean and dry one of our guys will be back to sprinkle gold powder on them… just as we've done to all the others. So you'll look as pretty as you do now… forever."

The other one quickly drew a black hand on the tunnel wall. Then he kicked them both sharply in the back, grabbed the torches, and muttered, "Boss gonna be real glad when he hears about this."

Both men hurried away.

Sofía had never experienced such darkness. The gags prevented speaking and the ties were so tight that her hands were quickly becoming numb. She couldn't move at all. But she could feel Rogelio's body pressed to her, which was somehow comforting. She could feel him struggling to get loose. But it soon became obvious that his efforts would be fruitless.

So this is how it all ends. I really thought lupus would have the final word.

Minutes passed.

Then hours.

Rogelio was no longer struggling. In fact, he was perfectly still.

Is he dead?

At first she felt a great thirst, then hunger. The numbness moved from her hands to her whole body. She went in and out of consciousness. Finally, she let go of the will to live.

She drifted off.

Her last thoughts were *perhaps death isn't so bad after all...*

Meanwhile, Rogelio was desperately trying to think of a way to escape. But, he reasoned, even if he could find a way to release the ties, in this total darkness they would never find their way through the labyrinth of tunnels back to the cave and the entrance.

So he simply said a quick prayer to Source. Then he, too, lost consciousness.

12

THE WARI TRIBE

Had Rogelio and Sofía been conscious, they would have heard the faint sound of footsteps in a distant section of the tunnel system. Gradually it came closer, but it was muffled as if the feet were bare. Eventually there was a dim light from a torch and two shadowy figures approached the bodies.

"Jama ara lung su?" Are they breathing?

"Ish kame no. Rava lu." I don't know. I'll check.

"Ya. Ish lakana!" Yes. I think so!

If they'd been conscious, Sofía and Rogelio would have just barely been able to make out the faces of the men. They were dark with images of suns, reptiles, pyramids and stars painted on them.

With no further words, the men pulled out elaborately decorated stone knives from leather loincloths on their otherwise naked bodies. Rapidly, they severed the ties and removed the gags. Each man knelt in an apparent sign of gratitude, then lifted a limp body onto his back.

In silence the four bodies moved carefully through the labyrinth of tunnels. At times the rescuers stepped over skeletons; at times their torches reflected bizarre images of contorted figures or ancient symbols on the gray granite walls.

As they approached the tunnel's entrance, their aura of vigilance increased. They carried their burdens with extra care, walking slowly, pausing to peer into the darkness. Watching. Listening.

When they arrived at the designated spot, they stopped and tapped their knives three times on the tunnel's roof. Immediately a boulder rolled away, a vine ladder was lowered, and muscular arms reached down to help the men lift the bodies to the surface.

Hours later, Sofía opened her eyes. A woman with frightening reptiles painted on her face, but with kind, concerned eyes, was ministering to her with herbs and ointments, and, apparently, with prayers. Sofía looked over at a body laid out on a stone… sepulcher?

"Dear God! Rogelio's dead!" Sofía started to wail. But the woman simply touched Sofía's heart with one hand and her own lips with the other, gently motioning her to be silent.

Sofía's agony was more than she thought she could bear. For the first time in her life, she prayed. *If there's Anyone out there, please save Rogelio. I never thought I could feel this way about a man.*

After an interminable hour, Rogelio stirred. Then he turned to look at Sofía and smiled.

Maybe there is Someone out there. Thank you! she prayed as she turned to smile back at Rogelio.

They were both given a bitter liquid to drink. Within minutes, Sofía felt a bit stronger, and for the first time, believed that she might survive.

"What happened?" Rogelio murmured.

Again, the woman motioned silence and they both fell into a restful sleep. After several hours, they were awakened by excited voices.

Now both Sofía and Rogelio were strong enough to sit up. A small group of indigenous people was gathered around them.

A man with a headdress, apparently the chief, spoke to them.

"How are you feeling?"

"Much better, although very bruised and still exhausted," Rogelio responded. "But what happened? And who are you?"

The chief told them what he knew about what had happened. Then he explained that he would be the spokesperson for his people as he and his wife were the only ones who knew Spanish.

"You need to rest, so we're not going to ask you to do much talking right now. But I will tell you who we are if you promise to lie back, relax, and just listen."

Rogelio and Sofía were happy to comply.

"As to who we are, most people around here only know us to be 'hostile Indians' who will kill anyone who tries to enter the tunnels. In truth, we are gentle. We are the old ones, the Wari, who were here long before the arrival of the Incas. We are also known as the 'Jivas' and our language is called 'Jivaro.' Another name we go by, the 'Shuar,' simply means the 'people.' We come from beyond the seas. For thousands of years we lived peacefully, in harmony with the land, with each other, and with Source, or God, which we call the Great Central Sun. But then the Spaniards came to rape and pillage, leaving us with disease, death, and the destruction of everything we held sacred, including our most holy temples and works of art.

"At a certain point we decided to fight back. Eventually, we became so fierce that we were the only people in all the land who were able to survive the *conquistadores*."

The chief's wife, Samikai, continued, "At the time of Pizarro in the 16th century, when our men were fighting the invaders, the women were busy gathering our treasures, thousands of tons of gold and items of artistic, spiritual, monetary and historical value (we'd been trading with cultures all over the world for eons) and placing them deep in the tunnels for safe-keeping. Contrary to popular belief, the Spaniards didn't get everything.

"In fact, a certain Father Crespi, an Italian priest sent to Ecuador as a missionary, lived and worked closely with our people. We loved him and he came to admire our ways. In fact, he even made a documentary about us called The Invincibles."

"Yes, we know about Father Crespi and his treasures," Sofía said.

"Good," the chief added. "Then you understand that our dear priest was there for us—materially and spiritually—for nearly five decades until his death. The two fires that destroyed so many of the beautiful gifts we gave him were devastating to us."

"I can't even imagine," Rogelio said. "But how did all these hundreds of tunnels get here in the first place? And as huge as the system is, how did you manage to find and save us?"

"We're actually not entirely sure how the tunnels came to be. Our oral history says they were made by an Ancient Builder Race. But how were you able to get into the tunnels?"

Sofía answered. "Well, we met K'antu, a healer from Nazca. She told us we needed to use a back entrance at *Las Cuevas de los Tayos*. Then our guide at Tiajuanaco, apparently sensing that our motivations were pure, told us the same thing."

"And you were able to read the pictographs and learn about the secret entrance." The chief smiled broadly.

"Yes," Rogelio replied. "But how would you know that?"

"Our shaman has been telling us that a white man who can read the hieroglyphs would come to us soon. And here you are!"

Rogelio was feeling humble now and remained silent.

So Sofía spoke for him. "And Rogelio was also able to interpret the message carved on the Gate of the Sun at Tiajuanaco. It's really astonishing."

"It was strange," Rogelio added. "It was like a *deja vu* experience–as if somehow I had read that language before, and I could read it now."

"We wanted to go into the tunnels," Sofía explained, "not for the treasures, but because we learned that there's a metal library hidden there. We thought that if we could find it and Rogelio could interpret the symbols, they might give information that's important to mankind at this time."

"Right," Rogelio added. "But we debated about whether it was safe to enter them since they are reportedly guarded by fierce natives."

The other Waris understood this phrase and laughed out loud. The chief simply smiled and said, "Just as well that people think that way."

"You? But you were the ones who saved us," Sofía exclaimed. "Then who…?"

"Whoa," the chief exclaimed. "We're getting ahead of ourselves. So you found the entrance and entered the tunnel system?"

"Yes," said Rogelio. We knew there would be risks, but we also sensed that it was important at least to try. Now I realize how foolhardy that was."

"It was terrifying down there," Sofía added. "I could hardly breathe. But, according to the directions, we believed we had almost reached the library. Then we were attacked by two disgusting men. They tied us up and left us there to die."

"And poor Sofía was nearly raped."

"Right." She trembled at the memory. "And I remember that, just before I passed out, I felt for certain that we were going to die. In fact, I thought we had died. When I came to and found a very kind woman ministering to me, I thought maybe heaven exists after all."

"So how did you find us?" Rogelio asked.

"One of the qualities we've developed over our vast history is extra-sensory perception," the chief explained. "We had to learn to sense where our enemies were and when and how they would attack. That's one way we survived the onslaught of the Spaniards. This morning we had a premonition that good people were in the tunnels–but we didn't know exactly who or where. And we also felt that another party was there... with the intent to do harm. So we came and, thank Viracocha, found you in time."

"Do you know who our attackers were?" Rogelio asked. "And why they wanted us dead?"

"We didn't see them, but we're pretty sure they were what we would call 'those of the Black Hand.'

"Oh yes," Sofía said. "They drew an image of a black hand on the tunnel wall before they left. K'antu told us about the Black Hand. And we had already had a couple of experiences with them."

The chief added. "Sadly they've been around for millennia and have infiltrated every corner of the world–even our little remote village here."

"But why hurt us?"

"Gifted with the ability to read the contents of the library and your lack of concern for your own well-being, you were at the brink of discovering the true story of human beings. A story that they would sell their souls to prevent being revealed to the world."

"Why?"

"Because the truth would eclipse the stranglehold they've had over humanity for millennia."

Sofía was angry. "Can't they be stopped?"

The chief's wife Samikai took her hand and shook her head. "My dear, many, many people have tried to stop them. They can be held in check for a while, but they always return. You saw the skeletons covered in gold dust in the tunnels and you have first-hand experience of their brutality. We must consider our next steps very carefully. But first you two need to regain your strength."

Sofía and Rogelio stayed with the Waris for three days, recovering remarkably well under their tender and adept care.

Early on the fourth morning an abrupt beep of Rogelio's phone surprised him with a text from Elenia.

"Excuse me just a moment."

The message read, "Where have you been? Didn't get previous texts? Urgent! Come home immediately."

He tried to text her back, but the message wouldn't go through.

"I'm very sorry," he said to the chief. "We're eternally grateful to all of you and promise to help in any way we can, but I just learned that there's an emergency at home and my family desperately needs me. We'll get back to you the first possible moment. Sofi, do you think you'll be strong enough to travel by tomorrow?"

"Yes, I think so," she responded. "That message sounded pretty desperate. But I don't even know where we are."

"You're deep in the Amazon jungle. But don't worry. We'll see that you get to the airport in Cuenca so you can fly home. If you like, you can leave first thing in the morning. We appreciate the urgency of your situation back home. But please don't fail to return here when you've handled your affairs. So much depends on retrieving, translating and sharing the information on the plaques. When you do come, I'll be waiting for you."

"Don't worry. We won't disappoint you." Rogelio promised. "But I have just one question before we go. You've been guarding this Hall of Records for thousands of years, correct?"

"That's correct."

"Then why do you need us?"

"We actually know, through oral tradition, what the records say. But we can't prove anything because, unfortunately, over the millennia, we had left the plaques buried in their secret location. We've forgotten how to read the ancient script."

"Oh, I see." Rogelio sounded worried. "I sure hope I can."

"We're certain of it." The Wari chief flashed his wide mostly toothless smile.

13

BULLDOZERS AT THE MUSEUM

When Rogelio and Sofía finally arrived at the Cabrera home and museum there were police and official government cars, a blockade, several journalists with cameras, and dozens of curious neighbors. The minute Rogelio got out of the car a young man thrust a microphone in his face. "Are you Rogelio Cabrera?"

"That's right."

"So what do you think of all this?"

"All what? We just returned from out of town and I have no idea what you're talking about."

Elenia spotted them, ran over, and interrupted. "Rogelio, thank God you're here! These people want to take our home and property. They say that though our great great-grandfather homesteaded here, built the house, and then dad built the museum, that the deed has been with the bank all this time. They say that we owe mortgage payments, back interest, taxes and penalties amounting to fourteen million soles. Representatives from the bank, the mayor's office, and even the church tell us we have one week to come up with the money or they'll evict us, bulldoze the building, and seize the property."

"That's ridiculous!" Rogelio, who had been blissfully happy with Sofía a moment ago, was suddenly enraged. "We've never received any notifications or assessments or warnings."

"They say it was our responsibility to go to the bank and ask about taxes and other fees." Elenia was crying.

Rogelio saw that someone nearby had a megaphone. He asked if he could borrow it, then addressed the crowd.

"Ladies and gentlemen. Thank you for coming and for your interest in this matter. But there has obviously been a huge mistake. Please return to your homes now and give us the opportunity to resolve this misunderstanding. Thank you."

When he had finished, Sofía noticed that the first reporter reached over and clicked off his recording device, then got in his car and drove off. Slowly the authorities left and then the rest of the crowd started to disperse.

After everyone had gone, Rogelio, Sofía, Elenia, Sister Mapi, and Padre Anselmo went inside and gathered around the kitchen table. The family filled Rogelio and Sofía in on what had happened. Then Elenia said, "Rogelio, I don't think you get the gravity of this. People from the mayor's office and bankers have been hounding us almost non-stop for weeks. They're not interested in a resolution. They're only interested in taking our property. Apparently a mining company did some tests and it's very possible that we're sitting on rich veins of copper and gold… Wait. What's up with you two? You both look absolutely radiant!"

The good nun answered for them. "Isn't it obvious to everyone? We have here two people who are very much in love. When you've stopped blushing and find your composure, Rogelio, perhaps you'd be willing to tell us where you've been and what you've been up to."

"Well, my dear sisters, you're right. And we'll be happy to tell you. But it's a long and complicated story, and it must wait. Right now we've got to figure out what to do about the house."

"Could it be true that we really owe the bank all that money?"

"Is their main motivation money?"

"Or do they just want to close down the museum?"

"Maybe the church is angry at Rogelio's liberal theology. And they never did like the implications of the etchings on the stones." Sofía didn't voice her greatest fear. *Maybe a friend of Cafre got wind of his death and wants revenge.*

Could it be the Black Hand? Maybe those who attacked them in the tunnels? Rogelio asked himself.

Aloud he said, "As for taking our home and museum, those clowns have absolutely no case. This is totally trumped up and there's no way they can win." His family had never seen Reverend Rogelio so angry.

"I wouldn't be so sure," Sofía offered. "On their side they have the bank, the government, the mining company, and the church. On ours we have only the Cabrera family and a few close friends. And I didn't say anything before because I didn't want you to worry, but the fact is that I've been threatened and attacked ever since I arrived in Peru."

She described the threats and her near-death experiences. Everyone was now doubly concerned, and though they dialogued for hours, they had difficulty agreeing on a motivation, much less a solution. Finally, at three a.m. the padre went home, Sofía returned to her hotel, and the others went to bed exhausted, frustrated, and frightened.

The next morning Elenia woke up early, went out to buy a newspaper and read the headline: PROMINENT REPORTER SHOT DEAD!

She quickly scanned the article.

Last night Channel 9 investigative reporter Alberto Rivera Gomez was shot in the chest as he left for home after his late evening news broadcast. Earlier in the day he had recorded the comments of Elenia Cabrera de Martínez, current curator of the controversial Engraved Stones Museum, and her brother Rogelio Cabrera Blanco, minister of a liberal church, visiting home from Los Angeles, California. They were discussing threats by a coalition of civic leaders to foreclose on the Cabrera home due to non-payment of back taxes. Apparently Rivera had done his homework and learned that it was recently discovered that the property is sitting on rich veins of iron/oxide and copper/gold.

Mr. Rivera had just finished reporting these facts on his evening show, Transparency, when he was shot point blank and killed. As of this writing there is no trail leading to his assailant.

"Good God!" Elenia breathed.

The doorbell announced Sofía's arrival from her hotel. Rogelio greeted her with a kiss on the cheek and guided her to the kitchen where she found an extremely upset Cabrera family.

"*¡Dios mío!*" Sister Mapi crossed herself. "This is worse than I imagined. This so-called 'coalition' is simply a group of greedy cowards who are willing to murder to get their way, make millions, and destroy the truth."

"This sure looks like another stunt of the Black Hand," Rogelio said softly to Sofía.

"What are you talking about? Who are they?" Elenia asked.

So Rogelio began telling them more about the tunnels and the Waris but was interrupted by an insistent banging on the door. When they looked outside they saw three men in dark suits and sunglasses, a black Chrysler sedan with tinted windows, and a bulldozer and driver parked just outside the entrance to their property.

Sister Mapi opened the door to see Humberto Salacio, the banker with whom the family had done business for decades.

"Take your personal possessions and leave the property quietly right now!" he barked.

"Humberto!" Rogelio exclaimed. "What are you doing here?"

"Don't play stupid with me, you unholy cultist. You know very well what we're doing here. Now let's get this over with quickly and quietly." He spit a big wad of tobacco and phlegm on the ground.

"But you said yesterday that we had a week to come up with the money," Elenia cried.

"And you think we should keep our word after you instigated that lying TV program last night. Get your family out of the house! Now!

"Enrique," he shouted to the driver of the bulldozer, "Crank 'er up!"

Sofía ran out of the house into the bulldozer's path. "You'll have to run over me first!"

Rogelio ran out after her. Elenia and Mapi stood frozen in fear.

When Rogelio got to Sofía, she was tying herself to a post in front of the house.

"Now, lady," Humberto said in a whiny, cajoling voice, "let's not get melodramatic. This is not such a big deal. It will be over in a few minutes and the Cabrera family will have saved the fourteen million they owe the bank, the town will be rid of this stupid, embarrassing 'museum,' and everyone can go on with their lives. So, sweetheart, let's be reasonable."

"I repeat. You will have to roll over me first if you want to destroy this house and museum." Sofía's voice was calm, surprising even herself.

"OK!" Humberto's voice was now furious, frustrated, hysterical. "Enough of your games."

He lunged at her, trying to cut the ties with his knife. But apparently he didn't know with whom he was dealing. She scratched at his face and kicked at him. When she managed to strike hard in his private parts, he screamed in agony, exposing a set of large, uneven, yellow teeth. Then, "All right, you little banshee, have it your way. Enrique, roll it!"

Enrique's face confirmed his sheer terror. He sat, numb, behind the controls.

Rogelio put his arms around Sofía and whispered in her ear. She shook her head. Then he stepped in front of her, holding her hand and facing the bulldozer directly.

"Enrique, don't make me have to ask you again!" Humberto pulled out a handgun.

Everyone could see that the driver's whole body was shaking. He put the vehicle into first gear and slowly began moving forward.

"Stop! Stop!"

It was Padre Anselmo running towards them, his cassock flying behind him, somewhat giving the impression of wings.

He ran up to Humberto and handed him a sack. "Here's your fourteen million. Count it. And don't even consider darkening this property again."

Humberto opened the bag and glanced at the contents but didn't bother to count the money. It was obviously a huge amount of cash.

Without a word, he motioned to Enrique to turn around. Then he signaled the other two men to get in the sedan. They drove off, leaving behind a cloud of yellow gray dust and a stunned family.

Sofía sighed audibly. "Third life or death crisis in a fortnight. If I believed in guardian angels, I'd say they've been hanging around us a bit lately."

"You don't believe, my child?" the padre's question was in earnest.

"Certainly not. Nor in the church. Nor in God… at least not until a few days ago," she added sheepishly.

"Well, I must admit," the padre replied. "I've certainly had my doubts about the church recently… but never about angels or God."

"So what about the money?" Sister Mapi's smile was innocent and childlike. "Was it angels or God that produced the fourteen million soles? Or did you simply avail yourself of the church's coffers and decide to call it even?"

"Beloved Sister, you know quite well that our humble church hasn't collected that much money in its entire history. No, the money came from quite a different source."

And then he was silent, with just the slightest hint of self-satisfaction on his holy countenance.

"All right, Padre," Rogelio asked, "are you going to tell us or do we have to resort to Inquisition techniques?"

Sofía noticed that he was a pretty good actor. His sternness was a bit unsettling however.

"OK. OK. But it's a long story. Shall we all grab a cup of coffee and sit on the patio?"

When they had settled in, Padre Anselmo began his story.

"So, as some of you know, your so-called friend and loyal employee Cafre had been deceiving you for years. He had quite a racket going with Negromonte. Ishmael would come into the museum with a new supply of stones when he knew no one was around but Cafre. He would lay the stones out in two piles: one, those that were authentic; the other, those he had etched himself. Cafre paid him quite generously from the museum's funds. Then he selected the best of the authentic stones, put them in his briefcase, took them home, and proceeded to sell them on the internet to wealthy collectors. He was prepared for challenges—he'd always claimed they were all recently made innocent trinkets for tourists. After Negromonte left, he would mix the lesser quality authentic stones with the fakes and display them proudly. That's why so far tests have come back with wildly different conclusions as to the stones' age and authenticity. I'm sorry to tell you that he's been doing this since before Dr. Cabrera's death and, needless to say, he amassed a huge fortune."

"Well, I don't so feel badly, then, about Cafre's death." Mapi murmured. "But how do you know all this?"

"Don't forget, my dear, that I've been Cafre's father confessor ever since I came to Ica."

"And you never told anyone?" Sofía was incredulous.

"Sofía, my dear. We priests have pledged our souls never to repeat what we hear in the confessional—until after the confessor's death or unless someone's life is in danger. Poor Cafre. He told me everything. Even where he hid the money. I imagine he hoped that by confessing, it would assuage his guilt. But of course it never did. He was tormented until the day he died. He never enjoyed that money, and he felt that he was so deeply enmeshed in this business that he couldn't extract himself without causing more problems—and probably landing in jail."

"No wonder he wanted to kill us," Sofía whispered.

"But what about the city officials, bankers, and church officials? Won't they continue to threaten us?" asked Elenia.

"I'm quite sure you won't be hearing from them again. Remember, I'm their confessor as well. And today they've seen that I'm not the timid silent padre they thought they knew all these years. Besides, they now have plenty of money." He smiled. "I can just picture them at this moment: counting the millions, dividing it up, and very soon squabbling about percentages. That's how it is with the minions of the Black Hand."

Mapi hugged the padre. "There are no words to express our gratitude for your saving our home and museum. And apparently this property may be literally sitting on a gold mine. Looks like we'll never have to worry about money again. And, Sofía, what you did was amazing… so brave, so selfless… and quite insane."

Rogelio and Sofía were sitting a bit apart from the rest of the group not saying much.

Sofía looked over at Rogelio, "Seems I've been doing lots of things that might be considered insane lately. I shudder to think what my mother would say if she were alive and heard about all this."

Mapi smiled at her. "Well, you definitely don't much resemble the detached scientist who arrived here a few weeks ago. We'd love to learn more about your parents and your life in Spain, but I believe there are other important stories to hear today. Please tell us, my dear confirmed bachelor brother, what in the world has happened to you?"

Elenia added, "And tell us more about your life and death experience in those mysterious underground tunnels."

Rogelio blushed, cleared his throat, and told them what happened in the tunnels, about the ancient hieroglyphs that somehow he was able to read, how they were assaulted and left to die, how the Wari Indians saved them and nursed them back to health.

"Turns out the 'savage Indians' that folks around here are so frightened of are actually an ancient and very evolved tribe."

And, finally, he told them how he had fallen in love with Sofía.

"As you all know, I preach a lot about Oneness and the importance of opening our hearts. But I had constructed a wall around my own heart. I guess I wasn't going to let myself be vulnerable again after

Maria broke up with me. So I became a minister, a job that allowed me to be somewhat distant. Then to seal the contract, I moved to California. But the moment I saw Sofía I felt a magnetic attraction and all my barriers disintegrated. I know it sounds trite, but I swear that's how it happened."

Rogelio hesitated for a moment. "Problem is, Sofía has some conflicted feelings. So we're going to take this slow."

They all had a million questions.

So the family, Sofía, and Padre Anselmo shared their stories until the moon rose just where the bulldozer had been a few hours earlier.

Before they went to bed the padre commented, "I was devastated when Father Crespi died a broken man and it appeared that his phenomenal treasures would be lost to humanity forever. But now it looks like Rogelio may hold the key to solving their mystery and gaining access to way, way more than Crespi could have imagined in his wildest dreams."

14

THE PACKAGE
FROM SPAIN ARRIVES

"But how is it that you were able to read that ancient script?" Mapi asked her brother.

"I have no idea. When I looked at it, it kind of looked lit up to me and I just knew what it was saying." He paused. "Somehow it felt like this was something I knew a long time ago, had forgotten, and suddenly came back to me."

"Are you going to go back and try to find the treasures?" Elenia wanted to know.

"Well, we're actually more interested in the so-called Hall of Records. It's apparently a huge metal library written in a language no one's been able to read and hidden somewhere in the tunnels. If we can find it and I can translate it, we feel it would provide vital information for humanity."

Sofía added, "However, we've learned first hand how dangerous it will be. There are definitely people who would kill to keep that information secret."

"Right." Rogelio added. "The thing is, though, that we promised the Waris we would try. So we must. But Sofi and I are clear that not only will this be extremely dangerous; it has a very small chance of success."

"So now it's 'Sofi,'" Mapi teased.

Rogelio blushed. "I'm not afraid to tell you. Since the time I met this woman, I've been enchanted by her strength, her beauty, her courage, her intelligence, her vulnerability, her sweetness. But as I mentioned earlier, she needs some space right now…"

Sofía interrupted, "This is hard to say. It's not that I have mixed feelings about Rogelio. I love him. He taught me about faith and bravery and tenderness, the importance of relationships… and even introduced me to a God I may one day be able to believe in. But there's something that's holding me back. I wish I knew what it was."

Rogelio took her hand.

The doorbell rang.

"What now?" Mapi muttered as she waddled to the door and opened it.

"DHL. Package for Señorita Sofía Cabeza de Vaca Weissmann."

"All right! The results from the lab tests have finally arrived!" Sofía's face was flushed, but no one knew for sure whether it was because of Rogelio or the delivery.

The package contained a smaller and a larger box. Sofía's hands were shaking as she opened the smaller one. Inside were two of the stones she had sent together with a paper on the lab's letterhead. She read it aloud. "According to the latest thermo luminescent testing, these anthracite stones are considered to be millions of years old. However, the etchings carved into them are estimated to be between five and twenty years old."

No one said a word.

Sofía stared at the paper for a full minute as though it, too, were written in an unintelligible hieroglyph.

Then she opened the second package, which contained two large and four small stones. Again, she read aloud the accompanying paper. "According to the latest thermo luminescent testing, these anthracite stones are considered to be millions of years old. And there is a 99.8% probability that the etchings are at least 55,000 years old."

A cheer arose. There were high fives all around.

Elenia was all smiles. "I knew it! I just knew it!"

Rogelio grinned. But then he looked sad. "This is amazing news! I just wish dad could have been here to hear it."

"I know," Sister Mapi said. "It makes me sad, too. Especially knowing what Cafre did to him. But somehow I sense that he's aware of what's going on right now."

"I'm so thrilled for all of you… I mean all of us!" Sofía hugged Rogelio. "Now that we know that at least some of the stones are authentic it'll be fun to continue Dr. Cabrera's work of attempting to interpret them. And then of course there's the question of letting the world know."

"I say we need to consider very carefully how we do that," Anselmo cautioned. "This news changes everything. And many people won't like it at all."

"All in good time," Mapi said. "Right now I suggest we celebrate. In fact, I'm going to begin cooking right now!"

That evening Rogelio and Sofía were alone together in the museum. He took her hands in his. "Sofía, there's a part of me that understands your reticence. I can feel it deeply. But I just want you to know that, no matter what happens, I'll always love you and pray that we can be together."

"Pray?"

"Oops. Wrong language. Maybe hope."

"Or maybe know."

"You're right, of course. Would you like to talk about what may be causing your resistance?"

"To tell you the truth. No, I wouldn't. Not because I'm still being my obnoxious self, but because, truly, I have no idea what to say. So could we let it rest for a bit?"

"Sure. But I do want to thank you for making this trip even when you were feeling lousy. And I want you to know how happy we all are that the stones have once and for all, been proven authentic. This, along with you being healed and saving our home, is the best news that could happen to our family. And just imagine. Now your reputation and your career can be restored. You can probably get your university position back, or you could do more research and publish and share the truth with the world."

"Or I could become a blogger or create YouTubes," Sofía laughed. "It's nice to bask in all this good news, but you know me: ever the practical one. Just proving the age of the stones won't be as powerful as it would if we could give plausible interpretations of the etchings."

Rogelio was thoughtful. "True. And of course 55,000 years is a far cry from my dad's belief that the stones were carved by 'glyptolithic' man millions of years ago. Well, at any rate, our most urgent challenge now is how to find the plaques without getting killed. And, again, are you sure you want to take that risk?"

"Are you serious, Rogelio? The Waris saved our lives. We made a solemn promise. Besides, I'm convinced that the information on those plaques is more immense that we can begin to fathom. And apparently you're the only one who can read them. By the way, I sure hope this unique talent doesn't go to your head."

"The only thing that's gone to my head is you. Just hearing your voice and touching your skin make me dizzy. Sofía, I love you for so many reasons… which seems impossible considering the short time we've known each other. But one of the reasons is your courage. I couldn't believe you stood in front of the bulldozer, risking your life to save our home and museum. And I'm happy but extremely concerned that you're willing to risk your life to help the Waris recover the folios."

Sofía put her arms around his neck and kissed him lightly. "Of course I'm willing to risk my life. There's no choice. And besides, after all these years of being a dry scientist, I'm rather enjoying these rushes of adrenaline."

He kissed her again. This time more intensely.

There was a sharp knock on the door. "Is anyone in there?"

Rogelio's voice had just a hint of frustration. "Yes. Just a second."

"Oh sorry," Elenia said from behind the door. "I saw a light in the museum and thought to catch it before going to bed. Go ahead and finish what you were doing. See you in the morning. Good night. Dream with the angels."

"*Hasta mañana.*"

Sofía went to the guest bedroom. She lay down on the bed, trying to make sense of the day's events. Her heart whispered, "get up and go to Rogelio's room." Her head shouted, "No way."

As usual, her head won.

15

THE AYAHUASCA CEREMONY

Two days later Sofía and Rogelio arrived at *Las Cuevas de los Tayos*. Sure enough, the Wari chief was there waiting for them. After warm greetings and expressions of profuse appreciation for their having come, he spoke to them about this particular location.

"Did you know that this place has been a vortex where for centuries priests, priestesses, shamans, and others of high vibrational frequency were able to pass from the surface directly into the tunnels? Or, at times, into other dimensions?"

Even though they had experienced some logic-defying events in the past several weeks, Sofía found that she couldn't repress her skepticism. "Other dimensions?"

The chief laughed. "I'm sure that concept goes against everything you've been taught, Doctora Cabeza de Vaca. I'd love to explain in greater detail, but we don't have time right now. Let me just say that the laws of physics only work in the third dimension. When we practice ceremony we move into the fourth or fifth dimension where space, time, and 'reality' as they're commonly understood simply don't exist."

Sofía was distinctly unsatisfied with this explanation, but decided to let it go for now. She nodded and said, "OK. And please be assured that we're willing to do whatever you suggest to find and share the contents of the plaques. But where do we start?"

Rogelio added. "We've been thinking about this a lot, and we simply can't figure out how to get to the plaques and either take them out, read them there, or photograph them without being attacked. It's pretty clear that whoever the Black Hand is, they'll have their goons down there constantly guarding them."

The chief flashed a cryptic smile.

"You haven't been able to figure it out because you've been trying to figure it out."

"I beg your pardon," Sofía's expression was genuinely open and curious.

"The big questions in life," he explained, "can't be answered by logic. The big questions can only be answered by the heart and a deeper level of knowing that usually gets buried by the logical mind. That's why we're planning to go into ceremony tomorrow night. We trust that your subconscious minds, together with the wisdom keepers and the elders who have walked on, will be there to inspire and guide us. You will attend, won't you?"

"Yes, of course," Rogelio responded instinctively.

"What ceremony?" Sofía asked.

"It's called an ayahuasca ceremony. We use a very powerful medicine made from the careful blending of two plants. We'll pray that it will give us the information we need."

"OK, we'll do it." Sofía felt both frightened and emboldened.

"Excellent. Then let me explain what will happen, what you need to do to prepare, and what you can expect. We'll hold the ceremony in a location hidden in the depth of the Amazon. This is for privacy and security, naturally. It will take about a day to get there. Can you walk that long?"

"Yes, I think so…" Sofía began.

"Well, I'm not so sure," Rogelio interjected. "Sofía hasn't been well, and then there was the horrible ordeal in the tunnels."

The chief told them not to worry. "We can carry her if necessary. As I said, this is extremely strong medicine, so you must be prepared. Beginning today you must take no sugar, no coffee, no alcohol, no meat, no medications, no processed foods, and no dairy products. You must also meditate at least two hours today and begin fasting at noon tomorrow. Oh, yes, and no sex."

They both blushed.

"After you take the ayahuasca you will probably get sick. At their first ceremony most people vomit and get diarrhea. Don't be concerned; this is a necessary *purga*. It purges you of all toxicity–physical, mental, and spiritual. It's not comfortable, but it is essential for you to have a productive ceremony. Feel free to use the basin near your cot or the latrines as necessary. Are you willing to do everything I've described?"

They glanced at one another.

"Absolutely!"

"Good. We will now take you to a tent we've prepared for you where you can begin your preparations. Tomorrow at sunrise we'll begin our journey into the jungle. Apart from the dietary restrictions, we trust you will be comfortable. Please don't hesitate to ask for anything you need."

After the chief left them alone in their tent, Sofía laughed. "One double bed! I guess they believe we're married."

Rogelio took her tenderly in his arms, kissed her hair, her cheeks, her lips, and held her close for a long time. "Aren't we? At least in Spirit, which is all that really matters, right?"

"Right," she chuckled. "But we may be the first couple ever to be prohibited from sex during their honeymoon."

Rogelio kissed her again.

The next morning they walked several hours until they were deep in the jungle. Whether it was the anticipation, the strict preparation, or the coca leaves they were given to chew, Sofía didn't know. But she was able to make the trek with relatively little difficulty.

By the time they had gathered for the ceremony, though, Sofía noticed that her stomach was in knots, her heart was beating wildly, and her palms felt like the tunnel walls. She tried to remain calm and looked around. About a hundred Waris sat around a fire in concentric circles. The men were wearing intricately embroidered tunics of red and black over loose white pants. Just as they were when the two Waris first rescued Sofía and Rogelio in the tunnels, the men's faces were elaborately painted. The women wore white blouses over long embroidered skirts and their black hair hung in braids down to their waists.

The chief motioned for Rogelio and Sofía to sit down next to him. Then he addressed those gathered.

"As you know, our prophecies have been fulfilled. The person who can read the sacred folios has been brought to us. However, when he and his wife were exploring the tunnels, they were viciously attacked by members of what we think are the Black Hand. They were assaulted, tied up, and left to die. Fortunately, we found them in time. They are here with us tonight and have graciously agreed to join us in ceremony that we may all connect with Source and with Truth.

"As we move into meditation we ask you to hold the intention that whatever needs to be known will be brought to consciousness."

The shaman then stepped forward, lit a large bundle of copal, placed it in the fire, and began singing *icaros*. Everyone except Rogelio and Sofía joined him. The volume gradually rose to a crescendo and then, just as gradually, faded out.

After several minutes of silence, the shaman spoke: "We trust that you, Mama Aya, Ancestors, Guides, and the Great Central Sun will hear our sacred song and be moved to heal our hearts and minds and take us from confusion to clarity. Take us, Mother/Father God, into that great place, the Nagual—that place that encompasses all that cannot be named. Take us to the void… so that we might return to the Tonal with the answers we seek."

He then proceeded to mix the ayahuasca concoction, offering slightly different amounts to each participant.

It was a greenish-gray liquid with an acrid smell. Sofía took her small amount gingerly. Its taste was reminiscent of licorice, though much more bitter. She lay down on her mat… and waited.

For about twenty minutes nothing happened. Then it felt as though snakes were crawling inside her. At first it wasn't uncomfortable, just an odd, tingling sensation. Then there was a swell of energy like an internal whirlwind. She began to feel dizzy. Her stomach started doing somersaults. Though she tried to suppress the urge, she found that she had to make use of the small basin that had been placed by her mat.

Ah, that's better, she thought.

But then she began to feel sharp cramps in her stomach. *This will pass,* she thought. *Just breathe into it.* But it didn't pass. It got worse. She rushed to one of the makeshift latrines at the edge of the wooded area. And not a second too soon. Considering she had hardly eaten anything, she found it astounding how much came out.

The fire had gone out. It was dark except for the faint light of the new moon mostly covered in clouds and Sofia worried that she would return to the wrong mat. But she did find her own spot and was pleased that someone had provided a small pillow and a blanket.

171

I wonder if this is going to get worse. She could hear others vomiting, moaning, and walking to the latrine. *Could the Waris, with all their experience in using ayahuasca, also be having this extreme discomfort? I wonder how Rogelio's doing...*

The nausea and diarrhea continued. Sofía now felt too weak to get up again to go to the latrine. So she lay down on her mat and tried to clear her mind. But it was difficult to focus. Strange visions appeared before her closed eyes—geometric shapes in changing colors, bouncing lights, buzzing sounds. Then everything was spinning. This lasted about an hour.

I can't calm my mind. Every cell in my body is in raging pain. Seems like the ayahuasca is doing nothing but making me violently sick. They did warn us that it doesn't offer answers to everyone. But why didn't they warn us that we could have such a terrible reaction? Obviously, no novice would participate in the ceremony. Well, maybe something is happening to Rogelio. I'll just have to lie here and wait till it's over.

Again, the urge to vomit hit. Again, she had to use the basin. Again, she lay back down. Finally, she drifted off to a restless sleep. When she awoke several hours later, it was still dark. She observed her body.

Ah, thank God! I feel much better.

She lay for a few more minutes, paying attention to her breathing. And her stomach. Her breathing was slow and relaxed. And her stomach now seemed to be fine. She tried sitting up. She felt pretty good, maybe a little light-headed but actually quite good. The sleep had been refreshing. But now she had to go to the bathroom again. It had turned cooler, so she wrapped her blanket around her as she headed to the latrine.

Now the clouds had cleared and brilliant stars lit a giant ceiba tree. As she walked, Sofía remembered reading that this tree was sacred to the natives of this land. She could see why. Its gnarled trunk seemed to reach out in a gesture of offering and the branches stretched to the heavens.

Perhaps trees really do have a consciousness of sorts. Could it be possible that they gladly offer their shade, their fruits, their wood, to help people as that children's book I once read said... what was it called? Ah yes, The Giving Tree. I loved that book as a child... but then as I got older I decided to become a scientist. I wonder what happened to change me from a dreamer to a realist? Was it something my parents did or said? I can't remember... I'm glad I'm a scientist, though. I'm glad that my improved method of thermo luminescence has proven that the Ica Stones... many of them anyway... are authentic. Sofía smiled to herself.

Hmm, seems I should have reached the latrine by now. Oh well, maybe not. But if I'm honest, I must admit to myself that I'm happier about the Cabrera family being happy than I am about saving my reputation... oh, look at the way the moon reflects on those tropical plants... they're so big... but of course they would be. There's so much rain and such fertile soil here in the jungle. Ah, the Cabrera family. They're all so earnest... and so sweet. And Rogelio! It makes me shiver just thinking of him... it's odd that I didn't notice how handsome he is when I first met him... but then I was in such a negative place. I love his passion for the concept of Oneness... though I can't say I really understand it... I'll have to ask him about it again soon. And he's so protective of me. Oh my God. When he stopped the car on the way back from Tiajuanaco and kissed me... and the way he touches my hair. Today he said that we are already married. Oh, such bliss. I can taste his kisses even now. I can feel the warmth and strength of his body against mine...

When Sofía looked ahead, she saw in the distance the shadow of a figure slowly moving toward her.

Oh my God! Have our captors found us again?

Then he was right in front of her, reaching for her. "Oh, it's you," she breathed.

"Yes, it's me." He held her close. Then, "I've come for you. We must hurry."

"Why hurry? I'm so happy walking here in the jungle. And now I'm especially happy that you, my love, are here with me."

"But don't forget, *wale iho.* This is an important night. We have promises to keep."

"Yes, you're right. We must fulfill our obligation. The citizens are waiting for us. We must hold ceremony for the final time."

"OK. I think we're almost there."

The two continued walking through the jungle. The moon and stars were again covered in clouds. Shadowy images moved in and out of view.

"What's that?" she asked a bit nervously.

"I'm not sure, but I feel confident they are allies. Are you fearful, my love?"

"No. Not with you next to me. Look just over the ridge. I think they're up there… Can you see the fire?"

"Yes. Let's hurry."

When they arrived to where the citizens were gathered, the two greeted the others solemnly, *"Sala man ja,"* then joined them in the circle. The intoxicating scent of copal and frankincense filled the night air. In the background they could barely make out the temple with its mystical symbols etched on the door. In the center of the circle to one side was the fire. To the other side, placed on a cloth woven of golden threads, was the Solar Disc.

All the citizens of Raj Haroon, including the children and the elders, sat in perfect stillness. Then, when the moon was directly overhead, the great priest Amaru stood and gave the signal. In less than a heartbeat, music filled the air. There were twenty reed flutes, thirteen drums, six ragdons, and a whistling vessel. A moment later the music was joined by song:

Shama 'an lu.
Sama ama lu.
Jaya
salamajaree.
Lee sol zaru
Acharaya lu.
Raj Haroon.
Sama ama lu.
Shama 'an lu.

The verse was repeated three times. Then Amaru stood, removed the Solar Disc, and spoke these words: *"Jaya sumat lu."*

"So be it."

Without so much as a murmur, the crowd stood up and, in a huge procession, left the circle and disappeared.

When Sofía awoke, the sun shining through the trees created a dappled pattern on the ground. She shivered then looked around. Nothing was there. No Rogelio, no other blankets, pillows or latrines. She felt light-headed and slightly disoriented. Then she heard Rogelio's voice and felt his kiss on her brow.

"Good morning, *mi amor.*"

"Good morning. What happened? I don't know whether I just had the most amazing experience, or whether I had the most amazing dream."

"La vida es sueño," replied Rogelio, quoting Pedro Calderón de la Vaca. "Life is a dream."

16

THE CITY OF LIGHT

Samikai came over to Sofía's cot and put her hand on her forehead. "How do you feel, my dear?"

"Wonderful. There's an energy surging through me. I feel healthy, happy, safe. My mind is clear. It's like all the weight of the past, all the sorrows, all the worry, and, yes, all the bitterness and distrust have simply melted away."

The chief appeared next to his wife and took Sofía's hand. "We told you this was strong medicine. When the conditions are right, the ayahuasca is able to bring people back to their original state of grace. Those snakes you felt inside you were actually eating negative energies, leaving you clear and whole. That's why you had diarrhea and vomiting. All that negativity had to go somewhere."

Rogelio said, "I feel great as well. It's like magic."

"It *is* magic. A magic that our people have relied on for centuries. We're so glad that both of you feel well. Can you tell us what you saw and heard?"

Sofía told them what she had experienced.

"But, you know, it didn't feel like a dream or hallucination. It felt as though I were really living (or remembering) events."

Samikai asked her gently, "Can you give us more details?"

Sofía paused for a few moments and then continued. Her voice was desolate and her eyes filled with tears.

"Yes. The ceremony was the last time we were all together. We prayed for safety. Then I was on a ship…" She sobbed.

"The explosion occurred sooner than we'd anticipated. I was pregnant and afraid, but I didn't give up hope. When we arrived at Itzla, we carved a giant tree of life on the rocky coast to serve as a kind of lighthouse in case, by some miracle, the other ships arrived safely. They never did, of course. I never saw my beloved Zamayo again."

Rogelio put his hand on hers. "You were so brave in those last days…"

Then he sighed. "The ayahuasca opened memories for me as well. Pleija and I attended the ceremony and then we had to part. When I boarded the last ship, I had a premonition that we wouldn't make it. And I carried guilt for having said, originally, that I wanted to die because I was ready to return to the Light."

Sofía hesitated. Then she became very animated.

"Does the effect of ayahuasca last until the next day?"

"Yes, it can," the chief replied.

"Well, I feel I'm experiencing more flashes of insight. In that life I loved Zamayo so deeply that the intense loss burned into my soul. As a result, I believe I didn't dare to love again through many lifetimes."

Sofía laughed and interrupted herself. "Oh my goodness, what would my colleagues say if they heard me talking about many lifetimes? Anyway, I couldn't possibly risk enduring that much pain ever again. Ah, I get it now! I'm sure that's why, even though I'm so drawn to Rogelio and truly do love him, something very strong was holding me back."

Samikai asked her softly, "Do you still feel that resistance?"

Sofía took Rogelio's hand. "No. Somehow reliving those last days during the ceremony dissolved the sadness and the fear."

"Beautiful!" Samikai looked almost as happy as Rogelio and Sofía.

The chief continued, "So, Rogelio, now you understand the reason behind your being able to decipher the hieroglyphs, right?"

Rogelio nodded. "It's beginning to make sense. Your tribe descended from the people who first came here. And you took on the sacred task of guarding the tunnels, occasionally offering gifts to Father Crespi—though there are still thousands more treasure hidden there. And even more importantly, you've kept the plaques of the Hall of Records safe. Am I correct?"

The chief grinned. "We had a hunch that you two are the ones we've been expecting. But we needed to have the ayahuasca ceremony so that we could be sure… and so that you could remember. By the way, do these words mean anything to you?

Shama 'an lu.
Sama ama lu.
Jaya
salamajaree.
Lee sol zaru
Acharaya lu.
Raj Haroon.
Sama ama lu.
Shama 'an lu.

Sofía and Rogelio smiled and answered as one voice:

*"I will remember you.
I will always love you.
I hold the light of love of the
Sun in my heart.
No matter what happens.
Even if we should separate.
Even if we leave our blessed Motherland
I will always love you.
I will always remember."*

The chief and his wife broke out in joyful laughter.

"The plaques aren't in the tunnels anymore, are they?" Sofía asked suddenly.

"My goodness. Your intuitive powers are blossoming beautifully. Actually, you're right. After your attack, we had to move them. They're now part of a larger library that contains ancient records and modern information. If you're willing to go back to the tunnels, they'll lead you to that library. Getting to them won't be dangerous this time as my wife and I will accompany you and we'll be protected by our fiercest warriors." He grinned and his eyes danced. "Even the toughest of the Black Hands are terrified of dying a slow agonizing death by our poison arrows and then having their skulls shrunk!"

"What?!" Sofía gasped.

The chief laughed again. "Oh, we don't do that now. But that reputation lives on and keeps even the darkest of the evil ones far away. So are you willing?"

"Of course."

The chief heard the fear in their voices and silently applauded their courage.

Preparations were made. When the appointed day arrived and the chief and his wife together with the entourage of warriors came to pick them up, they were visibly excited. Rogelio and Sofía, on the other hand, were visibly nervous.

"Look at the war paint on those guys. It's terrifying!" Sofía whispered to Rogelio. But Samikai overheard and assured them this was just an extra insurance policy.

Six of the warriors, followed by the chief and his wife, followed by Sofía and Rogelio, followed by six more warriors, walked silently through the jungle to the same spot where Rogelio and Sofía had been lifted out of the tunnels. Silently the sixteen climbed down the rope ladder back into the pitch black, clammy tunnel system.

This time they had torches instead of miners' helmets, which cast eerie shadows on the gold dust covered skeletons.

Sofía shuddered but forced herself along the same path they had taken earlier that nearly led to their deaths. But this time they went much farther, entering labyrinths and then continuing on through more tunnels. Finally, they came to a tiny enclave. The chief motioned the warriors to wait there. Then he held his torch along the wall until he came to an extremely faded image of a red hand painted on the stone. He put his hand on that spot, and, slowly, a section of the tunnel wall slid back to reveal an opening large enough for a person to walk through. The four of them went through the opening and soon came upon perfectly chiseled large stone steps. They walked down those steps to another flight. And another. And yet another.

"Are you OK?" the chief asked, mostly to Sofía.

"Oh yes. Normally I would have been exhausted with such an exertion. But I can't believe the energy I have."

181

"Good. We don't have far to go now."

They came to a modern looking 'elevator.' When they were all inside the chief pushed a button. They waited a moment, then he pushed another button, the door opened and they exited.

"You are now ten kilometers below the earth's surface," the chief announced.

"But don't worry," his wife added. "There's plenty of oxygen here, so you'll be fine."

In front of them was an ornate door carved of a dark wood with embedded sapphires forming a spiral. The handle was made of gold and shaped to resemble the sun with an indentation in the center. Samikai removed the pendant she was wearing around her neck and placed it on the indentation, where it fit perfectly. The door swung open to reveal an exquisite garden with flowers of every imaginable shape. The colors were of hues not seen on the earth's surface and of brilliant intensity. The air held a subtle scent of cinnamon and lavender. There were ponds with streams of water shooting straight up to the sky. Yes, the sky. Even though they were thousands of feet underground, the atmosphere mirrored the earth's surface. There were white clouds, foliage, mountains, oceans. But everything seemed clearer, fresher, more alive. Tiny particles of what appeared to be gold dust sparkled in the sunshine.

"Wow!' Sofía breathed. "Is this real or another ayahuasca dream?"

"It's real all right," the chief responded, picking a succulent-looking unidentifiable fruit and offering it to Sofía. Immediately another one appeared on the tree to take its place. "When you becomes accustomed, I think you'll…"

Just then a child of about eight with violet eyes and long, curly strawberry blond hair covering an elongated head came running up to them.

"Zamayo and Pleija! It's you. I know it. I recognize you from the painting in the temple! Please stay right here. I'm going to get my mother!"

Sofía and Rogelio couldn't have moved if they'd wanted to.

Soon the girl returned with her mother, a tall, lithe woman with long auburn hair and an almost bluish translucent cast to her skin. She wore a white toga, a crystal on her forehead, and an amulet around her neck similar to that of Samikai.

Without showing a lot of surprise, the woman greeted the chief and his wife warmly. *"Shala 'am,* my beloved friends." Then she saw Rogelio and Sofía.

"In the name of the Mother/Father God, Karamí was right!" Then, taking their hands and giving them a look of almost otherworldly love, she greeted them, *"Shala 'am."* And then, "Where are my manners? Of course you don't know our language. We're so used to communicating telepathically, you see, that we have to stop and think before we speak."

Rogelio responded, *"Shala 'am.* Actually, I do kind of know your language, but we'd be much more comfortable communicating in Spanish."

"Excelente. A thousand welcomes. Please let's sit on this bench and we can all introduce ourselves."

"First of all, do you know where you are?" she asked.

"We have no idea," answered Rogelio. "Our Wari friends asked us if we'd come with them. And here we are."

"Well, you are in The City of Light, also known as New Lemuria. We're in the inner earth complex known as Agartha. And my name is Shelaya. I am a descendent of Pleija and Zamayo, the heroes who left Lemuria just before it sank. Tragically Zamayo's ship didn't make it, but Pleija helped lead the people first to what is now Peru, and then underground, where we have lived safely and happily now for thousands of years as you would count time."

"This is all so incredibly strange…" Sofía's voice drifted off.

Shelaya's whole countenance glowed. "I can only imagine how this must sound to you. But you see, we know who you are as we can read each other's life streams. Since you occupied the bodies of Pleija and Zamayo thousands of years ago, you still carry a striking resemblance to them and of course in this lifetime you have a magnetic attraction to each other.

"There are many other parallels. Rogelio, you teach people about Oneness and the interconnectedness of all people; Zamayo taught his people about the Law of One. He taught them to love one another just as Jesus did many years later and just as you are doing today. But always there were the Sons of Belial, who didn't have much use for the concept. They were much more interested in amassing wealth, power and control. Sadly, that's what happened to the Atlanteans all those years ago and of course is happening again today on the surface of the earth. So we decided to create this underground city where we could be safe to carry on our lifestyle of joy and peace and harmony. But before we came here, we left messages on the surface."

Sofía was getting very excited now. "Rogelio, maybe that's why you were born into the legacy of the Ica stones! Shelaya, was it your ancestors who carved the stones found near Ica in order to give future generations a sense of their lives?"

"Yes, of course. And there are hundreds of other hints to convince people that Lemuria is historical fact and not just a legend or a fairy tale. When we arrived in Itzla we realized that the natives had lost most ancient knowledge. So we taught people about the true purpose of the pyramids and also about astronomy, agriculture, healthcare, the arts, and, most importantly, spirituality.

"But I'm getting ahead of myself. Let me just say how excited we are to meet you. You see, we've been waiting a long, long time for you to finally come and there's so much to share. Please sit down and relax. I'm sure you could use some refreshments after your journey."

Shelaya touched her amulet and a tray of aromatic teas, freshly baked cookies, and a vast assortment of fruits appeared.

After Rogelio, Sofía, and the Waris had partaken of the delicious snack they were offered, Shelaya asked them if they'd like a tour.

Samikai responded, "Why don't you go ahead. We're very familiar with the City of Light. We'd like to stay here and visit with some friends that we haven't seen in ages."

"Very well. We'll meet you back here."

"Pleija and Zamayo... Sorry, I mean Sofía and Rogelio, please follow me."

As they walked, Shelaya explained. "This City has five layers. We're on level one where most of our citizens live."

Sofía and Rogelio looked around and noted that they were now in an area that looked like a series of caverns with ledges where buildings seemed to be tucked into the very walls. A soft glow permeated the entire area.

As if to answer their unasked questions, Shelaya said, "Look over this way and note the light emanating from the capstone of that pyramid. That's plasma, which, together with the inner sun, provides all the light we need. Directly under that light is our main temple, called Ma-Ra. It's made of jade and is dedicated to Amara, the Lemurian priestess who along with her consort Amaru led the people to these lands. Here the priests and priestesses maintain the eternal flame and hold ceremony. I'm sorry I can't show it to you as only the initiated are allowed to enter."

"Why is that?" Sofía asked.

"Because the frequencies inside are so high that they would blow the circuits of anyone who wasn't prepared. But I'd love to show you one of our homes. Let's walk along this path. Every family's home is designed around sacred geometry and they all have a circular component, though there is endless variety in the final outcome. You see, we very much enjoy using our creativity in everything we do here."

"How is sacred geometry used in the designs?" Rogelio asked.

"Excellent question," Shelaya replied. "We've been studying both mathematics and the natural world for eons. And we've learned that every natural thing in existence conforms to a set of ratios and repeating patterns. We've found that when we incorporate those patterns into our temples and homes, the result is not only aesthetic beauty, but an environment that enhances our vitality and strengthens our connection to the Divine. The house up ahead on our left happens to be my family's."

"It's lovely. But it has no windows!" Sofía remarked.

Shelaya smiled. "That's because it's made of a special crystalline matter which makes it appear opaque from the outside so the inhabitants can have their privacy. From the inside, however, it appears as a glass house with a 360-degree view. When we get to the library you'll see that some of the 'books' are made of a similar crystal, which also stores information."

Rogelio spoke softly. "Just like how crystals store information in our computers on the surface."

"Right." Shelaya continued, "There's much more to show you and you'll have time later to enjoy a more detailed look at the homes. But now I'd like to move us along to the second level. Please step onto this moving sidewalk. From there we'll catch an elevator which will take us up to the area of production, manufacturing, and education."

When they arrived they learned that there were two types of production and manufacturing.

"Most everything that has already been invented and produced or grown is simply copied as needed by replicators. Over here you'll see the area where new items or concepts are invented. Those people look like they're just daydreaming, but they're actually brilliant scientists who are imagining what might make our lives better or richer. After they come up with an idea they make sketches, then go to laboratories where they experiment with a variety of materials to determine the best approach.

"Now let's get on this vehicle that will remind you of a sled. It's fueled by electro magnetic energy and will take us to the area where our children are educated."

When they arrived, Rogelio and Sofía were surprised to see, not classrooms with a teacher lecturing in the front, but clusters of students working on projects together.

"Since we believe that educating our youth is the most important job there is, our facilitators are all Melchizadek priests who have achieved great wisdom and compassion. The children learn through play, cooperation, the arts, and by being encouraged to follow their own natural passions. One of our goals is to encourage lifelong learning.

"Something you'll find interesting is that every child is equipped with a computer. But it's very different from the computers you use on the surface. These are powered by amino acids, which of course are alive, and they're all connected to Source and to the Akashic records. So the information the children get is complete, accurate, and of the highest vibration.

"Now please follow me as we proceed up to the next level. I think you'll find this fascinating as well. Here is where we produce our food. Our citizens don't eat meat and we use a sophisticated hydroponic system to grow a wide variety of fruits, vegetables, nuts and grains. In fact, our system is so efficient that in just seven acres we're able to produce enough food to feed our population of one and a half million. What you see up ahead may look simply like lovely waterfalls, but it's also the way the water picks up nutrients as it passes over stones and crystals. And as it moves, it's aerated and purified before it reaches the plants."

"My goodness. All these fields of crops, vineyards, and fruit trees look extremely healthy," Sofía commented. But I still don't understand how you can feed so many people in just seven acres."

Shelaya smiled. "Well, as I mentioned, we use replicators to duplicate a wide variety of foods. Also, our people don't need to eat much. They mostly take energy from the air they breathe, from the time spent meditating in the temple, and from crystals."

On the fourth level they saw a gorgeous park-like setting with small lakes, fountains, flowers, and a blue sky with just a few wispy white clouds. The people were obviously enjoying each other's company under the warmth of the sun.

The fifth level was apparently left to let nature take over. Here the ambient temperature was cooler than on the fourth level. There were trees as big as redwoods, large lakes, mountains, and a wide variety of plants and animals. As they stopped to admire a colorful bird that resembled the quetzal of Costa Rica, they heard a roar behind them and turned to see a saber-toothed tiger.

"Oh my God!" Sofía screamed.

"Don't worry," Selaya laughed. "None of the animals here would hurt anyone. We even have animals that have become extinct on the surface ages ago, like some dinosaurs including pterodactyls. But they're now all vegetarians and at any rate they tend to keep to themselves on several acres on the northeast portion of this level. One thing you might find interesting. We respect the intelligence of animals here. In fact, we often communicate with them and benefit from their wisdom.

"Now I'm going to leave you alone to take in this place on your own time and in your own way. There's much that can be known beyond what you can experience with your outer senses. Just wander around and enjoy."

Rogelio and Sofía sat on a bench and took in this City of Light. They noticed that the aromas changed. Sometimes the breeze was scented with oranges or cloves; other times it carried the scent of jasmine or hyacinth. Likewise, the sky gradually changed from blue to lavender, to orange. And the background sounds seemed to reflect their moods. At first they heard children laughing, then crickets chirping, then a violin concerto.

"I believe we are in Paradise," Rogelio remarked. Sofía agreed. But after a while that seemed all too brief to them, Shelaya returned and announced that it was time for lunch.

"What do you think?" she inquired.

"It's beyond amazing," exclaimed Rogelio. "I wish we could stay here forever."

Shelaya changed the subject. "Let's return to the first level and see if we can find the chief and his wife. I'd like to have all of you sit down with some members of our pod over lunch so we can tell you a little more about our history. After that, you can refresh yourselves in the fountains."

Over lunch Sofía and Rogelio learned that there are 120 different civilizations living in the inner earth. The citizens are not all humanoid and their societies differ quite widely. But they have a federation and are always able to come to agreements about whatever issue may come up. The current topic of concern is whether to make their existence known to surface populations.

"Unfortunately, not all the civilizations in the inner earth are of the light. But we can talk more about that later.

"Lemuria was established four and a half million years ago and the people lived in peace and harmony until about 50,000 years ago when an experiment by Atlantis went disastrously wrong and the entire continent sank. By the way, that immense continent included what is now Hawaii, Easter Islands, Fiji, Australia, New Zealand, the Indian Ocean, Indonesia, and Madagascar.

"The sinking of Lemuria was an unspeakable loss and still pains us all these millennia later," Shelaya went on. "The catastrophe came quicker than they had anticipated so most people weren't able to leave in time and 300 million people perished. Only about 25,000 people made it to what is now Peru."

Shelaya's profound sadness brought tears to Sofía.

"Well, let me continue. Zamayo's beloved Pleija, as I mentioned, did make it. After her group landed, they made friends with the natives, taught them many ways to improve their lives, and lived in harmony with them for centuries.

"However, eventually some of the Sons of Belial, the dark forces from Atlantis and elsewhere, decided to revamp their efforts to try to take over the earth. The Lemurian immigrants didn't want to resist, so they decided, after much deliberation, to resettle here in the inner earth. Thankfully, the ancient civilizations of the Agarthan network welcomed them, and they created this community based on the principles that their ancestors enjoyed on their home continent."

After some discussion, it was decided that Rogelio and Sofía would stay in the City of Light for eight days so they could get to know the people and their customs. They greatly enjoyed the diet of fresh fruits, vegetables, nuts, and sweets. They took part in their ceremonies. They danced, sang, and played with the children. They were given lessons in telepathic communication and levitation. They were blissfully happy.

17

THE HALL OF RECORDS

During the indescribably rich, inspiring, and joyful week spent in the City of Light, Rogelio and Sofía continued to ask their hosts about the mysteries that had baffled them for the past month: What's the real story behind some of the images on the Ica Stones? The Crespi treasures? The Pisco holes? Tiajuanaco? The Solar Disc? The Sons of Belial and the Sons of the Law of One?

But every time they hinted or asked outright, they received the same answer: "All will be revealed in good time."

Rogelio sensed that that meant when he would be allowed entrance to their Hall of Records and tasked with the job of translating the different languages and hieroglyphics into a modern day language that people could understand.

Finally near the end of the seventh day, they were summoned by the governing council which announced that it was time to enter the Hall of Records.

"We had to be certain that you are who we thought, that you are of the highest integrity, and that you do, indeed, have the ability to read ancient scripts. We are now satisfied. So let us proceed."

The council priest, Shelaya, the Waris, Rogelio and Sofía took the 'elevator' to the lower level. Then they followed an elaborate staircase down, down to what appeared to be a highly secured underground chamber. They walked through a hundred-cubit corridor. Shelaya touched her amulet, a flash of light appeared, and they found themselves in a completely different world. The wall, floors, and ceiling of this vast room were of a pure white marble that emitted a translucent glow. Along the walls were shelves that held records that were apparently arranged chronologically. First they passed stone tablets, then rolled scrolls, then metal plaques hanging from a rod, then parchment folded accordion style, then old leather bound books, and, finally, modern books with ISBN numbers that looked, as Sofía remarked, as though they might have been delivered yesterday. At the far end were rows and rows of computers that appeared to be made of crystal, quartz and glass. They seemed somehow to be alive.

On finally seeing the Hall of Records, Rogelio was speechless. Then he managed to say, "May we ask a couple of questions?"

"Of course."

"Well, first, are the metal plaques the same ones that were hidden in the tunnels and guarded by the Waris for centuries??

Shelaya's eyes twinkled. "Yes."

"OK. Secondly, we thought these records were thousands of years old. How is it that there are also modern books here?"

Shelaya smiled. "This library is alive. It holds ancient and modern information which we're able to obtain through our highly developed technology."

"I see," responded Rogelio. "My last question is this: Are you saying that you want me to translate all of this? The library is huge!"

The priest grinned. "No, of course not. Who knows what the future will bring. But right now we'd just like to show you a sample from a few chapters of our history. That way you can increasingly trust your powers to read different scripts, learn some quite surprising facts about the universe, and begin translating them into Spanish and English."

Rogelio exhaled, grinned, and said simply. "OK. I'm game."

"Good." The council priest pulled out a scroll at the beginning of the vast rows of records, handed it to Rogelio, and asked him what it said.

Sofía couldn't contain herself and interrupted, "Oh my Gosh! That script looks like ancient Norse runes."

Shelaya said, "That's right. It's because it's written in the Language of Light. It's a language we still use, and it's the precursor to Sumerian, Phoenician, Sanskrit, and Hebrew—all languages with powerful energetic properties. Rogelio, will you please see if you can read and translate this for us."

At first Rogelio hesitated and stumbled a bit. But soon he gained confidence and his voice was low and strong.

"Millions of years ago, there was a race called the 'Guardians' or 'Elders.' They were extremely advanced spiritually and technologically and protected this part of our galaxy. No other race would dream of countering them. These Elders have long since left our frequency, but they left a force field of protection.

"When the surface population completes the third of its 25,900-year cycles, the Guardians will return to once again protect against the dark forces. These Guardians are known by various names, including 'Blue Avians,' 'Quetzalcoatl,' and 'Ancient Builder Race.'"

The Waris faces lit up. The priest showed no surprise.

But Sofía was clearly impressed. "How did you do that, Rogelio?"

"You know," he replied. "I really can't say. It's kind of like it came to me on two levels. On the one hand, the script felt very familiar,

as though I were reading Spanish or English. But on another level…
well… it's hard to put into words. It just felt like a pure and clear
knowing. Kind of like a message coming directly into my heart area.
Does that make any sense?"

"It makes perfect sense," the priest said. "And by the way, your
translation was totally accurate. If I may, I'd like to explain what you've
been experiencing. Our language isn't just a series of symbolic marks
representing meaning. The sound and shape themselves are their own
meaning. In a sense, 'the medium really is the message.' This Language
of Light, or Ur language, is the primal seed language. It's a natural
language because the alphabet comes from our very nervous system,
mimicking the waveform properties of light and sound. The shapes
affect our very DNA, so that's why the message went directly to your
heart chakra and to your higher consciousness. Do you understand?"

Rogelio nodded. "Yes. I think so."

The chief added. "You may be interested in knowing that the Huari
culture (another spelling for ours) flourished near Lake Titicaca at the
same time as the Tiajuanaco culture, about 50,000 years ago."

The priest replaced the scroll, walked a few paces, pulled out a
stone with etching on it, and handed it to Rogelio. "If you would be
so kind, may I ask you to translate this."

After just a moment's hesitation, Rogelio read.

"For millions of years various planets and star systems in this galaxy
have been inhabited and then abandoned. This includes Mars, Venus,
Orion (later related to the Aryans), Sirius, and the Pleiades. There was
much travel among them and also much warfare. Eventually, one of the
lords of the Pleiades star system named Atlas decided he was tired of
all the bloodshed and decided to scour the galaxy for a planet that was
uninhabited and where he could start anew. After hundreds of years of
traveling through the galaxy, he found the beautiful blue sphere known

as earth and determined that this would be the ideal spot for his experiment in living harmoniously while allowing the people free will. So he returned to the Pleiades, gathered hundreds of ships and thousands of people, including his beloved daughter, Pleija, and settled on a continent that would later be called Lemuria. There life flourished, for they had all the knowledge and technology necessary plus the appreciation of and connection to Divinity, to nature, and to each other.

"For hundreds of thousands of years the Lemurians lived in consumate joy. They developed such a perfect society that it is still known as the Garden of Eden in mythologies throughout the world. The people were very spiritual—they could move from third to fifth dimension and back, they carefully tended their 'garden,' they respected all life, and they continued to love and praise Source.

"However, some of the citizens tired of this idyllic way of life and again developed a fierce desire to explore. So they traveled to a new continent which they named Atlantis in memory of their original founder. Eventually, many of those who settled Atlantis decided that, since they were superior to the natives already living there, they should rule not only Atlantis, but all of earth. Their experiments with vril and nuclear energies eventually resulted in Lemuria's destruction.

"Many Lemurians who escaped to what was later called the Americas eventually moved to the inner earth where they remain to this day. More wars and natural disasters resulted, after many more thousands of years, in the sinking of Atlantis."

"That is a perfect, precise translation, Rogelio." Shelaya smiled. "I know it takes a great deal of concentration to read this script and then translate to Spanish. So I suggest we take a little rest and then we can continue."

Again, the touch of her amulet brought a tray of tantalizingly delicious food and drink.

As they were enjoying their snack, Rogelio commented. "You know, this is fascinating to me in so many ways. For example, when I was studying for the ministry, I took a course in Comparative Religions and learned that in 1912, Dr. Paul Schliemann, the man who discovered that Troy was a real place and not a myth, found hidden texts in a Buddhist temple. They were 4000 years old, part of a series of Lhasa records, and they referred to Lemuria as 'Ra Ma.' I wonder if that's related to Arama."

"Or perhaps," Sofía offered, "to the 'Ra' of 'The Law of One.' And speaking of that teaching and its emphasis on harmony and service to others, I find it troubling that our history is so full of stories of war, greed, and a desire to conquer and control. Has it always been that way? Are we doomed to continue to relive that story line forever?"

"That's an excellent question," Samikai answered. "There definitely have been peaceful societies throughout the galaxies, but, sadly, those who refused to fight back have often been destroyed. How many people today, for example, even remember the Cathars and the Essenes from this planet's history—much less planets that have been totally destroyed—such as Maldek? That's why we Waris have, reluctantly, decided to become 'fierce.' We're actually not fierce at all. In fact, throughout our long history we've been pacifists. But when we saw how the Spanish invaders cruelly destroyed layer upon layer of magnificent civilizations, we realized we had to be tough. We needed to preserve, not only our own communities, but those of our inner earth family."

"It's all starting to make sense, now," Rogelio said. "But where did it all begin? Are humans innately contentious as a species–or did something happen to us?"

"Well," Shelaya answered, "we believe that something happened eons ago. Most cultures throughout the world have a story about a

'Fall.' We believe that it started with the Anunnaki. These were off-planet beings who resembled reptilians and who had a great deal of power. At first they were benevolent to people on the earth and were seen as gods. In fact, the name given to them comes from the words for heaven, 'anu,' and earth, 'ki.' So their name is often translated as 'those who from heaven to earth came.' We feel, though, that a better definition is 'royal seed.' No one is sure about who the Anunnaki really were or where they came from. But it does seem to be fact that they were among the progenitors of the humanoid race. Even the Christian Bible refers to the Nephilim, half gods whose fathers were gods and mothers, humans. We believe the Anunnaki were those very Nephilim.

"These Anunnaki guided humans along their evolutionary path for millions of years. But legend has it that thousands of years ago there were two brothers called Enki and Enlil who broke ranks from the prevailing belief system in Oneness with the Creator/Source/Great Central Sun. They decided they were as powerful as Source and they should conquer and be worshipped. So they and many of their followers came to earth and copulated with human women in order to create a slave race that could be made to do menial and dangerous work, including mining for gold.

"These practices led to a division on earth and elsewhere. Those who continued to love and know oneness with the Creator became known as the Sons of the Law of One and their passion was service to others. Those who followed Enki and Enlil became known as the Sons of Belial and their passion was service to self. Not in all cases, but generally, the Lemurians followed the Law of One and the Atlanteans, the Sons of Belial."

"So are the Sons of Belial other names for the Illuminati, worshippers of Lucifer, the dark cabal, the reptilians, and the syndicate?" Rogelio wanted to know. "Also, I seem to remember that in the Dead

Seas Scrolls there is a reference to 'Angels of Light' and 'Angels of Darkness.'"

"You're right," Shelaya responded. "Although in truth it's much more complicated than that, and we don't have time to get into all the details right now. If you end up reading all the records you'll have every bit of information you want."

Sofía was visibly excited. "Did these two groups, by chance, leave any identifying signature?" she asked.

The Wari chief smiled. "What would your guess be?"

"Well, I'm thinking about the images of a red hand and a black hand…"

"Precisely," the chief answered. "We know you've already experienced the image of a red hand on the wall of the Chauvet Cave and here in inner earth, and a black hand on the signature of the note you received, on your car, and again in the tunnels."

"But how could you…?"

The chief laughed. "After all you've experienced, you still don't fully understand the powers of a shaman. At any rate, you may be interested to know that images of a red hand have been found on cave walls all over Europe, in Indonesia, in cave dwellings in North and South America, and on the walls of Mayan temples in the Yucatan. In truth, the Order of the Red Hand has worked throughout earth's history to preserve ancient wisdom and to assist humans in their struggle to return to the light. You won't find as many images of the black hand, of course, because they know they can better achieve their nefarious goals by working in secret. They don't want to 'tip their hand.'"

Sofía smiled at him. "You're pretty funny."

"Thanks, but I'm trying to be serious."

Rogelio, too, was pensive. "I've been perplexed by some of the images on the Ica stones for decades. First, almost every stone contains a depiction of a serpent. And, even more confounding are the images of dinosaurs interacting with humans, reptilian-looking creatures inside the belly of women, people holding what appear to be baby dinosaurs, and even giant penises ejaculating into a jar. This begins to make some sense."

Shelaya added, "And that isn't the only place where depictions of dinosaurs can be seen interacting with humans, although most renderings have been destroyed or hidden away from public viewing. In 1944, Waldemar Julsrud, a German traveling in Acamparo, Mexico, came across thousands of strange items, including statues of reptilian type beings copulating with women!"

"You mean humans really did interact with dinosaurs?" Sofía asked.

"Yes, but not in a recent time cycle."

"So you're saying that the forces for the dark and the forces for the light started hundreds of thousands or even millions of years ago and they're still battling to this day?" Rogelio asked.

"You've seen it from your own experience, right?" the Wari chief responded.

Shelaya interjected. "I suggest we return to the Hall of Records. They will answer many of your questions. By the way, Sofía, I have the strong opinion that you, too, would be able to read and translate them. Would you be willing to give it a try?"

Sofía hesitated. Then her eyes lit up and she nodded. "Sure. Why not?"

"Wonderful," Shelaya replied. "Let's move on to the next section then."

As they walked, Shelaya told them that the next topic she'd like to show them covers the suppression of information by the Sons of Belial.

"This topic is huge, but we'll just look at a few facts to give you an overview. Be prepared for a shock when you learn about deliberately withheld facts and inventions that could have totally transformed the lives of people on the surface. In this first section, the information hasn't necessarily been suppressed, just called a 'hoax' or basically ignored," she explained.

When they arrived at the next grouping of plaques, Sofía was delighted to realize that after some focused concentration she could, indeed, read them.

Suppressed Information in Ancient Times

- 1000-year-old Sanskrit texts such as the Mahabharata from India mention the use of flying machines called 'vimanas,' nuclear generators, and powerful concentrated light beams.

- Using the power from the sun, the stars, and concentrating this energy in structures such as pyramids for a variety of practical uses has been known and practiced for thousands of years.

- Genetic manipulation of humans has been documented in texts and depicted in such ancient artifacts as the so-called 'Ica stones.'

- The importance of the pineal gland was known by the ancients and that is why we still see images of a pine cone (its symbol) depicted in art and architecture all over the world, including the Vatican. For thousands of years it was known that the pineal gland, part of the endocrine system, has rods and cones just as does the retina of the eye and contains floating crystals. It was designed to be a receptor. In the past, people enjoyed telepathic communication, enhanced intuition, and connection to higher dimensions. Descartes called the pineal gland the seat of the soul. It is also associated with increased serotonin (pleasure producing), melatonin (regulating sleep patterns), and neurotransmitters. Today, however, for a variety of reasons, including flouride in our water, toothpaste, and consuming non-organic vegetables and fruits, the gland has shrunken to a fraction of its original size and in most people is virtually useless. Incidentally, elevated flouride levels have been linked to lower IQ in children, ADD, Parkinson's disease, and Alzheimer's.

- The Dead Sea Scrolls, written over 2000 years ago but not discovered until the 1940's, have been altered to exclude certain information deemed classified. In 1993, Dr. Frank Stranges made a presentation to the Aetherius Society regarding galactic activity such as Ezekiel's UFO journey and the prophet Daniel's experience in the cosmos, the shielding of Noah's Ark, and other advanced technology of the ancient world. He was threatened many times and was killed by blood poisoning in 2008, just prior to the release of a DVD, The Mysteries of the Dead Sea Scrolls.

SUPPRESSED INFORMATION IN MODERN TIMES

- In the 1920's and 1930's Nikola Tesla, arguably the greatest inventor of all time, developed wireless electricity and was backed by the millionaire J.P. Morgan. When Morgan, owner of copper mines, realized that this new free energy could greatly diminish the need for copper, he not only withdrew financial support, he methodically destroyed Tesla's career. Thomas Edison, his great rival, completed the destruction of Tesla, who died a penniless and unknown man.

- In the 1930's Dr. Wilhelm Reich noticed that all beings share an energetic connection. Even though it had, so far, been impossible to measure, Reich called it orgone energy (also known as 'ether' or 'scalar energy') and he realized that both gravity and electromagnetic energy are related to orgone. Then realizing that orgone energy was actually responsible for the biological pulsation of all life on earth, he invented instruments that could funnel and direct that energy. Eventually Reich was able to use this energy to heal most diseases and he consistently produced rain in drought-ridden areas. He continued his brilliant work for four decades and was decorated in six countries. However, the United States mounted a hysterical campaign against him. They put him in prison where he died. They destroyed all his research. They banned the word 'orgone' from the annals of history. Even though Dr. Reich had achieved so much with it, the FDA claimed orgone didn't exist!

- In 1934 Royal Rife invented the Rife Beam, which in a controlled 90-day study witnessed by doctors and researchers, cured 100% of cancer patients using magnetic energies. The medical profession, pharmaceutical companies, research organizations, and hospitals were not happy with this invention. Rife's equipment was vandalized. There were arsons. Those who had witnessed the study swore they hadn't. Medical journals refused to publish his work. After 50 years of meticulous research and phenomenal contributions to medicine, Rife died virtually unknown, alone and despairing.

- In 1946 John Roy Robert Searl invented a method of producing energy by generating continual motion through the use of magnetized rollers and rings. Known as the 'Searl Effect,' 'Quantum Energy Field of Space' or 'Zero Point Energy,' it provided an unlimited and constant source of energy. However, scientists rejected Searl and his invention, saying that what he had accomplished was impossible. Working in England in the 1960's, he built free-energy electricity generators that doubled as anti-gravity machines. He was thrown in jail on the charge that he was stealing electricity from the grid. He was, in fact, running his home on his energy generator. When he was arrested, all his research was confiscated. Emerging from jail penniless, John found it difficult to secure the necessary funds, materials, tools, and talent to reproduce what he had developed.

Sofía stopped translating for a moment to interject a comment. "It reminds me of a quote by the British satirist, Jonathan Swift, 'When a true genius appears in the world you may know him by this sign: All the dunces are in confederacy against him.'"

Shelaya chuckled. "Fair enough. But this story, at least, has a happy ending. At 84, Searl has gathered the funds and talent and continues to refine free-energy generators. In fact, Hollywood is considering making a movie of his life.

"But let's go on. I need to warn you, though, the rest of the stories' endings are not so sanguine."

Sofía continued translating.

- In 1979 Archie Blue of New Zealand invented a car that could run on water. The petroleum giants made sure that car never got to market.

- In 1996 Stanley Meyer also invented a car that could run on water. He was poisoned to death and his car and research destroyed.

- In 1997 Dr. Gary Schwarz, along with 10,000 others in Arizona, witnessed orbs (light spheres that are believed to have an off-planet origin). The media denied this ever happened. Dr. Schwarz, who received his PhD from Harvard and is now a professor of psychology and neurophysiology at the University of Arizona, has been an outspoken defender of consciousness after death. He has been ridiculed mercilessly by colleagues and the press alike, but he continues to write books and speak at international forums.

- Dr. Ralph Moss is a researcher who has written ten books on the politics of cancer. He has found that many viable alternatives to surgery, chemotherapy or radiation have been methodically ridiculed or ignored by the 107 billion dollar cancer industry. As an example, the chairman of the board of Bristol Myers, the main company that produces anti-cancer drugs, also happens to be on the board of Memorial Sloan Ketterling Cancer Center, and is on the board of the New York Times newspaper. Dr. Moss has been called a quack and a liar by this powerful cartel even though he has cited thousands of cases where cancers were cured without the harmful, sometimes deadly, side effects of costly and intrusive approaches.

"So hard to believe," Rogelio exclaimed.

"I know," Shelaya nodded. "But it's true. And even more astounding is that these examples represent only a small number of this kind of deceit perpetrated on the surface population."

18

GOLD

The following day Shelaya, Sofía, Rogelio and the Waris again walked past countless scrolls, books, manuscripts, and metal plaques. Finally they came to a set of sheets that appeared to be made of gold.

"I think you'll find this section equally fascinating. And, yes," Shelaya said, reading their thoughts, "these are all made of the purest gold. We like to make our records as alive as possible. In other words, we like to experience our history sometimes rather than just reading about it."

She pulled out one of the leaves, about three feet high and two feet wide, and set it against the wall. At first it just appeared to be a blank sheet. But when Shelaya touched it with her amulet, hieroglyphic images appeared and Shelaya again asked Rogelio to translate.

"One of the most important, powerful, and sacred items at the time of Lemuria was the Solar Disc. It was a huge convex disc made of a special kind of metal that made it appear almost translucent. Gold was thought to be a gift of the gods, and the disc was considered the most precious object on earth as its high vibrational quality helped people connect directly to their inherent godlike nature.

"Before the sinking of Lemuria, the Solar Disc was held in the Illumination Temple by ropes of pure gold over an altar of emerald green jade. There it resided for thousands of years, capturing powers from the sun and offering longevity, health, wisdom, spiritual growth, and psychic powers to the Lemurian citizens.

"When the priests divined that Lemuria would be destroyed and Amaru lead a group of pilgrims to what later became known as Peru and Bolivia, they took the disc to the Lake Titicaca area for safekeeping and to enhance the lives of the natives there. They taught those natives how to approach the disc, open themselves, and receive sacred wisdom directly from Universal Mind Source. They also taught them how to use it as a cosmic computer.

"Over the years the Lemurians taught the various tribes, in addition to the mysteries of the Solar Disc, the basics of building a great civilization—on physical, emotional, and spiritual levels. These tribes eventually merged to become the great Inca culture and they called themselves 'The Children of the Sun.' Their capitol was Koricancha, or Garden of Gold, in Cuzco. It was also known as Amarucancha or 'Place of the Serpents,' named after their founder. For the name 'Amaru' meant cosmic energy symbolized by the serpent. The 'garden' was located right next to the Temple of the Sun and it contained magnificent solid gold, life-sized figures of people, animals, plants and flowers. At a certain point Amaru determined that the Solar Disc should be located here so they brought it from Titicaca and hung it over the entrance to the temple.

"The 'great *conquistadores*' destroyed the temple. Then they looted the magnificent garden, melted the gold, and put it on a ship headed back to Spain. Ironically, the ship was attacked by pirates, sank, and all the gold ended up at the bottom of the sea. When tourists visit the current church called Santo Domingo, built over the remains of the temple, they can still see the hooks that once held the golden ropes.

"Luckily, the priests had presaged this horrific destruction and were able to take the Solar Disc back to Titicaca and again hide it in the Eternal Etheric City under the lake."

Turning to Shelaya, Sofía asked. "So is the Solar Disc still in the Etheric City? I guess that means invisible..."

"My dear, you're in the Etheric City and the reason you and Rogelio can see and experience it is that you've sufficiently raised your vibrational levels. People keep hoping to find the disc inside or near the physical lake, but it's here, in the fifth dimension, in this City of Light. We've learned that this is the only place where it can be safe from those of the Sons of Belial who would like to use its powers for personal aggrandizement, greed, and control. They would use it to enslave others and probably force them to mine for more gold."

"But wouldn't it be important for the disc to once again be available to help the people?" Rogelio asked.

Shelaya smiled again. "Now perhaps you can see why our Wari friends and our entire community are so excited that you two have arrived. Our traditions teach us that life moves in cycles—actually cycles within cycles. As you know, there are 25,900-year cycles and here we count 500-year cycles that we call a Pachakuti. For the Inca, in fact for all the peoples of Meso and South America, the last 500 years have been ones of misery. But now we are in the tenth Pachakuti, when it is predicted that the numbers of the Sons of the Law of One will greatly outnumber the Sons of Belial and it will soon be safe to reactivate the Solar Disc and make it available to help the people. We dream of the day when it will once again be a source of information, a way to increase vitality and lifespan, a healing device, a connection to the stars, a way to raise vibrations, and a way to augment psychic powers."

Shelaya paused. Then she said, "This would be a good time for a break."

Over another delicious snack of foods that were totally new to Rogelio and Sofía, Shelaya continued.

"Now I want to tell you (actually remind you) of another way in which gold has enhanced the lives of people in quite remarkable ways."

Sofía asked "What is it?"

Shelaya answered, "'What is it.'"

Sofía repeated "What is it?" and received the same response.

Rogelio and Sofía looked totally flummoxed. Shelaya laughed. "That's actually one name for it: 'What is it?' To quote the Book of Exodus, 'the Israelites called it *manna* because they knew not what it was.'

"It's a powder that was well known to ancient initiates. In Babylonia, they called it 'an-na,' the ancient Mesopotamians called it 'shem-an-na,' the Egyptians called it '*mfktz*,' the Greeks called it '*soma*,' the Alexandrians simply called it a gift from paradise, European chemists like Nicolas Flamel called it the 'philosophers stone.' It's also known as the 'red lion,' but most people today who are aware of it simply refer to it as 'white powder gold.'

"But let's return to the scrolls where you'll get more information. Rogelio, would you like to translate again?"

After they walked back to the library, Rogelio was handed a leather bound book with parchment pages. This time the text was in an ancient script that Rogelio didn't recognize at first, but after a few moments it became clear to him. He began:

"There is a mysterious substance that has intrigued scholars, scientists, and philosophers for thousands of years. It can convey powers of healing, wisdom, teleportation, psychic abilities, and longevity. It has anti-gravity properties and can defy the laws of time and space. It generally appears as a white powder, though sometimes it's red. It's depicted at times in a cone shape, and is often referred to as 'light' or 'bread.'

"The tomb of the Egyptian King Unas makes reference to this white powder. It describes the place where the King now lives forever with the Gods–an ethereal, otherworldly dimension called the Field of *Mfkzt* or the Realm of the Blessed.

"In 1450 BCE, the pharaoh Tuthmosis III, together with 39 members of the High Council, founded his metallurgical fraternity of Master Craftsmen in Karnak. They were called the Great White Brotherhood–a name that, it was said, came from their preoccupation with a mysterious white powder of projection which they called 'white bread.'

"The Old Testament of the Bible speaks of Moses, the Ark of the Covenant and shrines on Mount Horeb all make reference to *mfkzt*.

"There is a parable about Alexander the Great's journey to Paradise and his encounter with a 'paradise stone' that had numerous magical properties. When it was heated and transposed to a powder 'even a feather could tip the scales against it!'

"It appears again in the story of Moses and the Israelites at Sinai, when Moses is disturbed to find that his brother Aaron has collected the gold rings from the Israelites and forged from them a golden calf as an idol of worship. The account relates that Moses took the golden calf, burned it with fire, transposed it into a powder, mixed it with water, and fed it to the Israelites."

"Now let's move to a modern description of this white powder," Shelaya suggested.

She invited them to move along the very long corridor of manuscripts until they came to the computers. She touched one with her amulet, it turned itself on and opened to a section called A Parallel Dimension: The Hudson Files. She asked Rogelio to translate.

"An Arizona cotton farmer named David Hudson was having difficulties with his high sodium soil so in 1976 he decided to inject it with sulfuric acid to break down the hard surface. One particular constituent of the soil, however, had a most unusual quality. When heat-dried in the Arizona sun, it would flare into a great blaze of white light and then totally disappear. Under spectroscopic analysis, however, the substance registered as 'pure nothing!'

"David sent samples for testing at Cornell University, Oxford's Harwell Laboratories, and the Soviet Academy of Sciences, and it consistently tested as 'nothing.' Eventually they figured out that the substance was composed entirely of platinum group metals including platinum, iridium, ruthenium, and rhodium—but in a form hitherto unknown to science.

"Scientists found that when heated to a certain point, it would turn to a white powder and its weight would drop to 56% of its starting weight. When cooled, it went to 400% of its starting weight. But when heated again, it dropped to less than nothing! The pan actually weighed more when the substance was removed. It was eventually determined to be anti-gravity classified as 'exotic matter' and capable of bending space/time.

"Hal Puthoff, Director of the Institute for Advanced Studies in Austin, Texas, theorized that when the substance weighed less than nothing it would resonate in a different dimension and become invisible. And that is exactly what happened.

"Hudson and Puthoff experimented by trying to move the substance with a spatula when it was invisible. But when they adjusted the temperature and it again became visible, it reappeared where it had been originally. It hadn't just become invisible; it had totally disappeared!

GOLD

"The Platinum Metals Review has featured regular articles concerning the use of platinum, iridium, and ruthenium in the treatment of cancers, which are caused by the abnormal and uncontrolled division of body cells. When a DNA state is altered (as in the case of a cancer) the application of a platinum compound will resonate with the deformed cell, causing the DNA to relax and correct itself.

"Researchers further determined that when monatomic ruthenium resonates with DNA, it dismantles the short-length helix associated with disease and rebuilds it again correctly. Such treatment, of course, involves no surgery; it does not destroy surrounding tissue with radiation nor damage the immune system, as do chemotherapy and radiation.

"In summary, extensive written records prove that the secrets of white powder gold, or manna, or mfkzt were known to our ancestors many thousands of years ago. *They* surmised that there were superconductors inherent in the human body that were the elements of individual consciousness which they called the 'light body' or *'ka.'* Initiates considered gold to be condensed light. They also knew that both the physical body and the light body had to be fed if mortals were to gain extraordinary powers. For eons, this 'food' was only given to kings. But it is written in the Akashic records that there will come a time when it will be made available to all human beings. At that time, the prophecies will be fulfilled and 'men will become as gods.'

"In May of 1994 the mathematician Miguel Alcubierre announced in the Journal of Classical and Quantum Gravity that: "It is now known that it is possible to modify space-time in a way that would allow a spaceship to travel at an arbitrarily large speed by a purely local expansion of the space-time behind the spaceship and an opposite contraction in front of it."

Shelaya added, "In the time of Lemuria a person would imbibe the white powder gold and then adjust the Solar Disc to a certain angle to the sun, looking at the sun, not directly, but reflected by the Disc.

"It was known that both iridium and rhodium have anti-aging properties, while ruthenium and platinum compounds interact with the DNA and the cellular body. Also that gold and the platinum metals, in their monatomic high-spin state, can activate the endocrinal glandular system in a way that heightens awareness, perception and intuition to extraordinary levels. In this regard, it is considered that the high-spin powder of gold has a distinct effect upon the pineal gland, increasing melatonin production. Likewise, the monatomic powder of iridium has an effect on the serotonin production of the pituitary gland, and would appear to reactivate the body's 'junk DNA,' along with the under-used and unused parts of the brain.

"There are stories in the Christian Bible," she continued, "of Methuselah and other figures living hundreds of years. Could it be because of this white powder? This mysterious powder is also referenced in The Keys of Enoch, in novels such as The Red Lion, The Devil's Elixir, and in Plato's writings."

Sofía asked if this white powder is used here in the City of Light.

"Absolutely."

"But what happened to David Hudson?" Rogelio wanted to know. "Why aren't his discoveries well known and why isn't the substance available to people on the surface?"

"Well," Shelaya explained, "the truth is, no one knows. Hudson built a plant to manufacture the powder and make it available to the public. But he was continually harassed, refused the necessary permits, and then the plant mysteriously burned down.

"After that, he disappeared. There are rumors that he died in a car accident and the government confiscated all his research and patents for 'national security reasons.' All that's known for sure is that Hudson, just like his healing powder, has vanished."

"How tragic," Sofía murmured.

"But we do have a surprise for you." Shelaya smiled demurely.

19

THE REPTILIANS

Shelaya asked Sofía, Rogelio, the Wari chief and Samikai to follow her up the marble steps into the central sanctuary of the temple.

When they arrived, Sofía gasped her astonishment. There were thirteen priests and priestesses, dressed in white robes adorned with colorful serpentine symbols at the hem. She and Rogelio looked at each other, both experiencing a sense of familiarity. They realized they had been in an Illumination Temple almost precisely like this one and sensed that today they were about to re-enact a sacred ceremony from so many thousands of years ago.

The room was lined with mother of pearl, which reflected images of flowers made of a kaleidoscope of liquid lights. Harp music and the scent of cloves, lemon, and lavender filled the air. On the wall was a *bas-relief* of a tree of life fashioned of ebony, gold, and emeralds.

Shelaya reached behind one of the fountains of light and brought out an obsidian and gold inlaid box. She opened it to reveal a white powder.

"Ah," Rogelio said. "This is it?"

Shelaya nodded, inviting everyone to meditate silently on these syllables of the Language of Light: AMMA RA HAR LOT NOK LAR. Then she offered a small spoonful to each person in the circle.

Suddenly there was a crash behind the door and six hooded figures burst in.

"So sorry!" one of them shouted. "Are we interrupting something?"

The Wari Chief and Shelaya glanced at each other.

"How did you get in here?" he asked.

"Well, since we're neighbors, we thought we'd drop by to say hello."

Shelaya quickly explained to the others that these entities were from a civilization that also dwelled in the inner earth, but until now they had kept totally to themselves.

"That's right," the apparent spokesperson said. "But that doesn't mean that we haven't been monitoring you. And let me just say that our leaders are not at all happy about this business of translating the information on the plaques. In a word, sharing that information is simply not going to happen. But don't be alarmed. We're not going to hurt you. We're here to negotiate. Ooh… Is that white powder gold in the box? We call it 'manna from hell.' Our favorite! Would you mind sharing?"

Shelaya answered for the group. "Of course not. Please sit down."

She passed around the box with the precious powder and a small spoon. But instead of tasting it carefully as the others had done, the intruders each scooped out a heaping spoonful and gulped it down.

"Now," asked Shelaya calmly. "What can we do for you gentlemen?"

A second entity answered. "Well, here's the thing. As you know, it would be the end of us if the information on your plaques were to get out to the public. We've done to the people what we had to. Their numbers and their abilities had to be kept in check or there would have been chaos over the entire planet. In a word, we have contributed to

216

the survival of the world. Now we simply wish to survive." He added, almost as an afterthought, "Just as everyone does."

He leered awkwardly at Shelaya, flashing extraordinarily large incisors. "Oh, before I continue, would you mind passing the powder again?"

As Shelaya did, she glanced surreptitiously at the Chief, who nodded ever so slightly.

The first entity spoke again. "We will never, ever allow this information to get out. We haven't in thousands of years and, as you can guess, we will do whatever it takes to prevent it. But, I repeat, we don't want to harm you."

His speech was starting to slur and he was becoming quite difficult to understand. "So here is our very generous proposal: As you know, we have perfected the sublime technology of nanites. Into these microscopically small robots we are now able to insert batrachotoxin and we've also perfected the art of causing these robots to multiply faster than the speed of sound. You know about batrachotoxin, do you not?"

"Yes, of course," Sofía replied. "It's an extremely poisonous substance that comes from dart frogs. Their secretion, an airborne toxin, attacks the nerves of humans, eventually causing paralysis and then a slow and exceedingly painful death. And there's no known cure. It's called a 'dart frog' because the Emberá tribe of Colombia smears their blowgun darts with it when hunting or warring, insuring that their victims won't survive."

"Precisely," the spokesperson slurred. "This lady is very smart. But I still think it's a shame we didn't kill her directly when we had the chance. Anyway… what was I saying? Ah, yes. We'll keep the batrachotoxin under wrap as long as you do the same with the information on the plaques. But once we see any hint of its being made public, we will release the poison.

"Sadly, that would be the beginning of the end of you homo sapiens. Do I make myself clear?"

The others in his group nodded gleefully.

"As you will surely agree," he continued, "that is a very fair agreement. We'll give you a moment to think about it while we have another tiny taste of your delicious powder."

This time when Shelaya handed him the box, he pulled a flask of what smelled like wine from under his robe and poured it into the powder. The mixture produced a red bubbly substance and the visitors greedily swallowed it, fighting over the last drop.

All was still for a minute or so. And then something horrific started happening to these creatures. Several fell to the floor and began crawling, writhing over each other, a greenish-brown substance drooling down their mouths. The spokesperson's skin began turning into yellowish scales. His eyes, too, turned a yellow-orange and the pupils were now vertical slits. A low guttural sound came from several of the men. Some tried to stand but kept falling over each other. Their fingers turned into four sharp talons. But the worst was the most putrid smell emitting from their bodies.

Sofía feared she would pass out.

Rogelio, too, looked stunned and as though he might faint. He reached over and took Sofía's hand. She squeezed his, then glanced at Shelaya, the Chief, and his wife, and the priests. They all looked concerned but not totally shocked.

When these reptilian hybrids (for that is what they were) were totally out of control, the Chief nodded to Shelaya, who stood up, walked to a side door, and opened it. Inside was a room with open containers of fresh blood. When these tormented creatures saw them they howled and rushed into that room and began devouring the blood as if their lives depended on it.

Shelaya quietly closed the door to the room.

"We've had experience with these fellows before," she explained. "They're not, however, the ones we fear. They're simply goons of Pindar and the cabal. These guys have taken in so much of the white powder with wine, and now with blood, that they will soon self-destruct."

And, indeed, the noises coming from the room (actually, the trap) did sound like a doomsday scenario. There were screeches, the sound of objects crashing to the ground, gnashing of teeth, and blood curdling howls. After a while it became silent.

"What happened to them?" Sofía was almost afraid to ask.

"They have expired." The chief was succinct.

"You mean they're dead?" Sofía looked terrified.

"Don't be too alarmed," Samikai said. "These creatures have no soul, no compassion—in fact, the only emotions they're capable of are hatred, fear, lust, and greed. They can appear to be human, but their true nature is reptilian, programmed by their masters to do evil."

"Their masters?" Rogelio was confused.

"Yes," Shelaya explained. "The dark ones who control most of the world. As we've mentioned before, they're the reason we had to move to the inner earth thousands of years ago."

"And they're also called the Black Hand—the ones who've been threatening us?" Sofía asked.

"Yes, I'm sure of it," answered Shelaya. "But more often the ones with the power prefer to work in anonymity, allowing their puppets to do the dirty work... and take the risks.

"That's why we're not concerned too much about our recent visitors. They, and thousands like them, are relatively harmless. But what we do need to worry about is the threat from those who pull the strings. I am under no illusion that they would hesitate in releasing the batrachotoxin if we don't bow to their demands."

Sofía commented, "I haven't said anything up till now, but I've always thought the cabal was simply a conspiracy theory."

"As do many people," Shelaya replied. "I think you need another history lesson. Let's return to the Hall of Records and have a look at the section on the Illuminati."

20

THE ILLUMINATI

The vast section covering the Illuminati was written in script on rolled leather scrolls.

Shelaya explained to them that it would take months to read all that was recorded about the cabal. "So let's just read the summary. That will be sufficient to give you an idea of what we're up against."

She pulled out and unrolled the first scroll. "This is divided into eight sections. Will you please begin, Rogelio."

Rogelio carefully unrolled the first scroll and began.

1 Definition and Purpose

The Illuminati is a group that practices a form of faith known as 'enlightenment,' which is actually Luciferian. (The root of the word 'Lucifer' is, of course, light.) They teach their children that they are special, destined to be leaders and, by following specific protocol, eventually become enlightened. They tell them that their 'religion' can be traced back to the ancient mystery traditions of Babylon, Egypt, and

Celtic Druidism. Ultimate world government is their goal; their grand design is to rid the entire world of Christianity and bring it under the 'illuminated dictatorship of Lucifer.'

2 History

It is widely believed that Adam Weishaupt created the Illuminati in the eighteenth century in Germany. However, he was just a figurehead of the powerful financiers whose tradition goes back to the Templar Knights in the Middle Ages. In 1770 Mayer Amschel Rothschild consolidated and named the Illuminati with instructions that it was to remain, under pain of death, completely secret.

However, in 1871 a bizarre accident revealed the truth. Guiseppe Mazzini, the Pindar (meaning 'Pinnacle of the Draco') at the time wrote a letter describing the group's goals and strategies and sent it to a meeting by courier. But in a seeming act of divine intervention, lightning struck the courier, killing him instantly. The document was seized and handed over to the Bavarian government. Unfortunately, however, the information was so outrageous that most refused to take it seriously and ignored it.

3 Strategies

- Use violence and terrorism to achieve control of the masses.

- Any and all means are justified; having a moral code leaves a politician vulnerable.

- Remain invisible until the very moment when we have gained such strength that no cunning or force can undermine us.

- Use mob psychology. Without absolute despotism one cannot rule efficiently.

- Advocate the use of alcoholic liquors, drugs, moral corruption and all forms of vice, used systematically by 'agenteurs' to corrupt the youth.

- Seize property by any means to secure submission and sovereignty.

- Foment and fund wars, but direct the peace conferences so that neither of the combatants gains territory. Both sides will suffer further debt and therefore fall more deeply into our control.

- Choose candidates for public office who will be servile and obedient to our commands. Thus, they may be readily used as pawns in our game.

- Use the press for propaganda to control all outlets of public information while remaining in the shadows, clear of blame.

- Make the masses believe they have been the prey of criminals, terrorists, or evil countries. Then restore order to appear as the saviors.

- Create financial panics and use hunger to subjugate the masses.

- A Reign of Terror is the most economical way to bring about speedy subjection.

- Masquerade as political, financial, and economic advisers to carry out our mandates without fear of exposing the secret power behind national and international affairs.

- When a child of our 'family' is deemed a suitable candidate, begin forming her from infancy to be an unquestioning cabal member. Mental and physical torture, mind control, and terror are the most effective means to accomplish our goals.

Basically, their belief is that all the pain, torment, and cruel 'training' will lead to enlightenment. Many illuminists, including the infamous Mengele, believed themselves to be gods. This, in addition to mind control, promises of wealth and fame, and black magic, a la Aleister Crowley, encourages them to literally make a 'pact with the devil.'

4 Steps to 'Enlightenment'

There are twelve steps that must be rigorously followed. Training should begin as early as possible, ideally even before birth.

The child is conditioned to [1] never ask, [2] never want, and [3] never need, through horrific experiences and 'teaching' sessions.

These are designed to break down their will and sense of self and teach them to look to others for cues as to what they should want.

The next three steps involve a breaking away from emotional relationship with others.

[4] To hurt is love [5] To care brings pain, and [6] Betrayal is the greatest good.

The next three steps instill deep loyalty to their owners with the directives to [7] never disobey, [8] never question and [9] protect the triad (the three adults the child is enmeshed with through a trauma bond).

This is the point where most of the assassin training and suicide programming are added.

Steps (10-12) involve intense training in one of the six specialty branches.

5 The Specialty Branches

Depending on children's personality and talents, they are eventually assigned to one of six branches: Military, Media, Leadership, Scholarship, Sciences, or Spirituality.

[For more detailed information on the above, including the relationship between the Illuminati and Freemasons, please refer to the book "Breaking the Chain" by a woman who calls herself Svali. She was able to break her intense programming, escape, and tell her story. For more detailed information, please go to the free online book by David Wilcock called *Financial Tyranny*.]

Rogelio and Sofía were stunned at this information. He had a hard time accepting it. She, however, sensed that it had to be true.

As they were walking back from the Hall of Records, Shelaya received a thought message on her smart glass pad.

WE SENT YOU REPRESENTATIVES TO NEGOTIATE PEACEFULLY. YOU MURDERED THEM. NOW WE HAVE NO CHOICE BUT TO UP THE STAKES. YOU HAVE A FORTNIGHT TO PROMISE NEVER TO RELEASE THE CONTENTS OF THE PLAQUES. SINCE YOU ARE INCAPABLE OF LYING YOU WILL COMPLY OR WE WILL RELEASE THE POISON THAT WILL CAUSE THE DEMISE OF THE HUMAN RACE. EVEN IF OUR OWN PEOPLE BECOME CONTAMINATED AND DIE AS WELL, IT WILL BE WORTH IT. WE WOULD RATHER GO DOWN IN GLORY THAN FACE THE HUMILIATION AND PUNISHMENT OF OUR ILLUSTRIOUS BLOODLINE.

PINDAR, LIZARD KING OF THE GLOBAL ELITE (DO NOT CALL US THE CABAL!)

"Whoa!" Rogelio spoke into the silence. "What do we do now?"

They discussed their options long into the night and finally determined it would be imprudent to come to a decision immediately. The Waris would go back to their people on the surface and discuss this with the elders and their shaman. Rogelio and Sofía would continue the task of translating the plaques, and Shelaya would speak to the governing council of the City of Light. They would meet again just shy of a fortnight to determine their best course of action.

For the next fourteen days Sofía and Rogelio worked all day on their translations and then joined the citizens for dinner and evening conversation. During those evening discussions they learned more details about the story of Pleija and Zamayo, of the Garden of Eden that had been Lemuria, and the tragedy of a paradise lost.

In that time Sofía was feeling more and more the presence of Pleija—what her life had been like, the terror of the premonition of the disaster, the moment she became pregnant, the time on the ship when she was worried to the point of illness about her beloved Zamayo. She had never recovered fully after learning of Zamayo's death. But she did feel proud of her courage when she gave birth to their daughter and then carried on working to teach the natives of Itzla how to improve their lives. More than anything, though, she felt the excruciating loss.

Was the tragedy of Lemuria to be repeated? The thought was too painful to contemplate.

One night Sofía couldn't sleep. *Who were these so-called Global Elites? They sounded so similar to the leaders of Atlantis who believed that they were divinely decreed to rule over the rest of the world.*

She felt a pain——but this time it wasn't in her body. It was emotional. When she paid attention, she realized it was a pain she hadn't felt before. It seemed to come from sadness and sweetness at the same time. A new kind of love was welling up in her… but also a deep confusion. She knew this love was even deeper than the love she felt for Rogelio. That love was glorious. But this was even deeper and sweet/sad. The only word she could think of to describe it was the Portuguese *saudade*—a tenderness, a nostalgia for something lost, that couldn't quite be recalled, but that could never be regained. She felt that a small knife was permanently wedged in her heart. Her breathing was ragged.

So is this our lot as humans? Did we come to earth to suffer… and to experience occasional happiness just to motivate us to keep going? Or perhaps it was original sin. If there is a god of love and mercy, why would he allow so much suffering? No. It can't be a god's fault. It must be humans. Somewhere along the path, we must have lost our way.

I, for example, have spent most of my life stuffing down feelings to protect myself. How ironic to realize that no one is responsible for the pain and illness I've experienced except myself.

If I look at the people I've met since I came to Peru and sense who is really happy, I think of K'antu, Rogelio, his sisters, the Waris, and, of course, all these people living in the City of Light. Have they just been lucky enough to escape suffering? No. They've suffered profoundly. But what do they have in common?

They've been able to forgive. And to love. And to serve.

As loathsome as the cabal is, could it still be possible to forgive… even love… them?

And what about Oneness? Rogelio teaches that we're all, not just sisters and brothers, but literally One. What does that mean? Perhaps we're all different facets of one diamond that is both Source and reflections expressing themselves infinitely.

So if we continue to hate and feel the need to punish transgressions, won't that just breed more hate and separation? Look at K'antu and what she suffered. And Christ. And Gandhi. And the Lemurians. And countless others. They all lost everything. And they forgave. And they found peace.

If they could do it, why can't we?

Perhaps it was a result of the ayahuasca experience. Or perhaps it was the white powder she had imbibed. Or perhaps Sofia had truly learned unconditional love and forgiveness.

At any rate, she was inspired. Sofía began to compose a letter.

The next morning the Waris arrived and everyone met to decide what to do. It was clear immediately that none of them had gotten much rest over the past fortnight. Nor had anyone else come up with a solution.

"I fear," the Wari chief's wife began, "that they have us in their grip. They know that we would never allow harm to come to the people. It seems we have no choice but to acquiesce."

"I'm afraid you're right," Shelaya said. "I've become exasperated trying to come up with a solution. Apparently there is none. I guess they win again. The people will never know the truth and the Illuminati will continue to control, impoverish, and destroy them."

"May I ask a question?" Sofía ventured.

"Of course."

"You all believe in the Law of One. Correct?"

"Yes."

"And in forgiveness?"

"Right."

"Well, what if we take a different tack. Instead of confronting them, how about if we let go, act as though we really are One, find it in our hearts to forgive, and then send them a letter to that effect."

Rogelio looked at her with immense love and respect. "You are incredible and you never cease to amaze me. I hardly recognize the woman I met on the bus a short time ago."

She winked at him. "It seems like ages, though, doesn't it? Truth is, I've had a pretty good teacher. So here's a rough draft of a letter I wrote."

Shelaya and the Waris looked a bit skeptical but nodded for her to continue.

Dear Pindar, Lizard King of the Global Elite,

We have received your message and threat of annihilation of human beings on the surface of this planet.

We must begin by saying that you are seen, known, understood... and loved. Just as you are, right here and right now, you are loved.

You didn't expect this, did you? You expected rage at the horrors you've perpetrated over the millennia. We're quite aware of who you are and what you've done. We know that you were behind the sinking of Lemuria and Atlantis. You have inflicted untold suffering of innocents and protected the guilty. You have incited wars, funded both sides, and felt no compassion for those whose lives were destroyed. You have murdered presidents, popes, philosophers and scientists. You've pulled the strings of those in positions of power in religion, industry, finance, the media, education, politics, entertainment, and the military. At every turn you have encouraged fear and discord and buried the light.

Recently you have tried to eliminate Rogelio and Sofía, have whisked away the artifacts collected by Father Crespi, and have tried to convince people that the Ica stones are a hoax. And now you threaten to destroy humanity if the truth of the Hall of Records is made public.

We know that you've operated out of fear and greed and your lust for power has no limits. We know that you're furious at the thought of being outed now that you're so close to your ultimate goal of world domination.

And still we love you.

In spite of all you've done, we have compassion for you because we understand that all is One. You are no different from us. You have simply walked a different path and that path has led you to where you are today, just as everyone's has.

So before we answer your threat we'd like to suggest to you a new way of looking at things. The way we see it, you really had no choice. You were born into a family of 'blue bloods' who taught you that you were special, that you were a descendent of gods, and that your destiny, your birthright, and your responsibility were to accumulate vast wealth and wield total power over humanity.

There are, however, a few things that you must understand. This is not a random universe. There is order beneath the seeming chaos and there is a Divine Plan. Yes, Divine. We know you think you are a demigod, but there is something far more powerful than you. It is called by various names: Source, the Field, God, Oneness, Love, and Light. There is an irreversible plan and there are cycles. The cycle of your time to control is coming to an end. Humanity is awakening. It is divinely ordained.

As new cycles are beginning, you stand at a crossroad. You have a choice to continue as you have, realizing that you will lose. You will be ground down, and no dark god will come to save you. Or you can accept that sooner or later you will rise spiritually and the wisest course of action would be to do so now. You could use your ancient knowledge and administrative skills to benefit mankind. It could be glorious. You could help bring light. You could reunite with the family of mankind and once again be happy!

This decision is important—much more important than worrying about whether the information on the plaques will get out to surface humanity.

So we ask you to listen to your heart and your higher mind and consider this carefully. We understand that you're probably thinking: Those guys must be crazy to suggest this!

If all that our family bloodline has done over the centuries were known to humanity, they would be enraged. They would imprison, torture, or murder us.

And that is a very reasonable assumption. So we wish to help. We will begin a campaign to educate the surface people. We'll tell them that you did what was required. You took charge in a dark period on earth, the Age of Forgetting. You had contracted for this work a long, long time ago. We'll show the people that you are not demons; actually not that different from them. We'll ask them if they would have behaved differently had they been born into the families that you were. There are many light workers (teachers and spiritual leaders) in contact with us. We will encourage them to step up their teaching of forgiveness and love.

Your lives could become beautiful. No more secrets, no more lies, no more ugly incidents. No more guilt, hatred, or fear.

As we leave you to your choices, we close on the same note that we opened: Know that you are our brothers and sisters and that we love you.

Respectfully,
Citizens of the City of Light

Everyone agreed that this idea was inspired and that they should try it.

The chief laughed and said, "Wish I'd come up with it!"

That evening Sofía and Rogelio were together. He didn't say anything at first, but his eyes watered. He held her close then breathed into her hair. "You are extraordinary."

The letter was sent. They all waited nervously for an answer.

None arrived.

21

THE SMART GLASS PAD

Each day that passed waiting for Pindar's response added to Sofía's anguish. She had taken a huge risk suggesting they reach out to the "Grand Master" in a spirit of love and forgiveness. Some in the Council had advised that this approach was pure folly.

"These entities," they said, "don't understand anything but force and sadistic gamesmanship." They reminded Sofía how Pindar had insisted on being addressed as 'Grand Master of the Global Elite.'

"They do see themselves as gods and regard humans as ignorant, not fully formed, and they believe the qualities of love and forgiveness are distinct signs of weakness."

"True," Rogelio pointed out. "However, no one has been able to come up with a better solution to our dilemma."

On the tenth day of waiting, Sofía and Rogelio were alone together in the Hall of Records. She cried and he held her tight.

"I'm afraid that letter was a huge mistake," she sobbed. "Every day that goes by makes it seem more likely that they're either ignoring us or already preparing to unleash the poison. Can it be possible that for a second time we'll fail to save our people from disaster?"

Rogelio's voice was deep and calm. "Sweetheart, as Pleija you didn't fail anyone. You were a courageous leader who, in spite of impossible odds and unfathomable sorrow, managed to lead the Lemurians to safety and rebuild lives here in Peru. And I believe you're going to do it again."

"It's just that now that I've found you again I couldn't bear to lose you." Sofía pressed her face against his.

"You know" he said, "nearly 50,000 years have passed since the catastrophe. I just can't believe that destiny would allow for another destruction. But all I can think of right now is how ecstatic I am to have spent these last weeks with you…"

Rogelio stepped back, put his hand on her cheek, and looked deeply, lovingly at her.

"You have the most beautiful eyes. Ever since that first day on the bus I've been enchanted and intrigued with their color. And now I'm remembering something. As Pleija, you were admired for many things—not the least for those liquid eyes that betrayed every emotion and whose colors reflected the changing sea just under the Maoi statues." Rogelio's voice became husky. "Oh, my God, how I want to make love with you right now!"

Sofía looked up at him, her lashes moist, her body trembling slightly.

He took her hands in his and said gently, "My darling. Are you still feeling resistance?"

She paused for a long moment. Then she said softly, "No. Not at all. It's just been such an emotional time. And… and… I guess I'm overwhelmed by everything that's happened in the last few weeks… and by my feelings for you."

And then, just as he had thousands of years earlier, Rogelio took off his jacket and laid it carefully on the floor. There, in the midst of all the knowledge and memories and wisdom of the world, they re-consummated their love.

The next day at breakfast Sofía thought Shelaya was looking at them a bit strangely. A subtle Mona Lisa smile lit her beautiful face.

"I know you two are distraught that we haven't heard back from Pindar. But please try to relax and trust. What you've contributed so far is phenomenal and we are all grateful beyond words."

Sofía and Rogelio smiled at her, and then at each other.

"And so we want to gift you with something we think you'll enjoy." She reached into a fold in her white and gold robe and produced a smart glass pad. "This is for you to keep. We don't idolize technology as much as some of our neighbors here do, but we thoroughly enjoy playing with these pads and learning from them." She chuckled. "We actually find them to be slightly magical! Look, you just hold it, think any question you'd like, and it answers in words or pictures." She handed it to Sofía. "Try it."

Sofía found herself trembling a bit as she took the pad and formed a question in her mind. *What's the true story behind the Ica Stones?*

In quick succession there appeared images of many of the stones, followed by spoken words. "The authentic stones—for all of them are not—were carved by the natives of Itzla after the arrival of the Lemurians, who taught them a brief history of the human race. The natives feared there would be another cataclysm and they wanted to preserve this history for posterity. They etched over 50,000 of them, organized them into specific categories, then buried them in caves, riverbeds, and tombs all over the Nazca Valley. It is, indeed, unfortunate that the stones aren't all in one place, making it difficult to decipher contiguous messages. And then, of course, the mixture of faked etchings with authentic ones has further confused the matter.

"We know you are wondering how there could possibly have been interactions between humans and dinosaurs.

"If you look carefully at the stones depicting dinosaurs, you'll see that some of them show humans riding them or otherwise interacting—sometimes killing them. On others you'll see images of baby dinosaurs inside a woman's womb, a reptilian holding up a human baby, or entities with giant penises ejaculating into a jar.

"The fact is that dinosaurs had not yet become extinct on Lemuria when it perished. So when the survivors told the natives of Itzla about their life, they naturally told about the dinosaurs, which the natives dutifully etched on the stones.

"Now dinosaurs also existed on Atlantis. And the people there were very interested in genetic experiments. They mixed seeds of different species, often ending up with bizarre creatures. Most of these died, but some survived and they became the animals of mythology."

"I wonder if they're talking about Greek mythology," Sofía mused.

"Absolutely," Shelaya responded. "You see, Atlantis wasn't that far from present day Greece. The Greek poet Homer and various Roman writers immortalized these creatures in their stories. Today people think that the minotaur, pegasus, chimera, harpy, siren, and cyclops are simply wild inventions of extremely imaginative writers, but, just like the dinosaurs, who were also subject to genetic experimentation, at one time they all existed."

"Whew!" Rogelio whistled. "Amazing! And it all makes perfect sense. May I try asking a question?"

Sofía handed him the smart glass pad and he formed the question in his mind.

There immediately appeared on the screen images of elongated heads and then the giant *candelabro* that they had seen on the coast of Paracas. Sofía blushed to remember how obnoxious she had been on that trip.

The images were followed by these words: "Those skeletons are the remains of Lemurians. At the height of the Lemurian culture, all the people had larger skulls with a greater brain capacity—and many had red hair, which still exists on some of the remains. If you do some research, you'll find skulls of elongated heads in North America, Egypt, and Africa—and of course right here in the City of Light.

"Incidentally, you'll also find entire skeletons of entities that were up to 36 feet tall. These are from the Ancient Builder Race, progenitors of the Lemurians. That's why places like Tiajuanaco are built in such gigantic proportions.

"This area was home to many different races over the millennia. Archaeologists have also discovered skeletons of humanoid beings that were only two feet tall.

"What many have been calling a *candelabro* is not a candelabra. It's a 'tree of life,' a symbol of hope and the continuity of life for the Lemurians. It was to be a kind of lighthouse in case any of the other ships survived and were looking for the scout ship. Of course, none did."

Rogelio put his arm around Sofía' waist. "I'm so sorry our ship didn't make it and you had to face your pregnancy and all the hardships of your new life alone."

Sofía's big turquoise eyes watered as she looked at him. "I was never alone. You were always with me."

A somber silence followed for a few moments. Then Shelaya asked, "Did you know that the baby you carried while traveling to Itzla is my ancestor? And I must tell you that every generation from your seed has had extraordinary leadership qualities, a fine mind, and great creativity."

"Actually," Sofía smiled. "That would be Zamayo's and my seed."

"Yes. Give me some credit here," Rogelio feigned a hurt look.

"Right. And I must say that our oral history is filled with your story. For eons we've been sad that future generations never got to meet Zamayo.

"Now, do you have other questions for the smart glass?"

Rogelio grinned. "Yes. Hundreds. But that would probably take a lifetime (that is, my lifetime) to get to them all. But there is one that's been nagging at me lately. May I?"

Rogelio took the pad and mentally formed his question.

Instantaneously, images of the Nazca lines appeared, together with these words: "First, it's important to point out that such geo-glyphs are found all over the world—in Saudi Arabia, Syria, Jordan, Russia, England, Chile, and Germany to name a few places. And in every country thoughtful people are perplexed. The guidebooks will say inaccurate things like they are runways for spaceships. When did a spaceship need a runway?! Or they were lines to walk on as a ritual, like a labyrinth. They'll say the Nazca lines were etched by the natives around 300 A.D. At that time the people could barely eke out a living. So they spent their time and energy creating perfectly straight lines that went on for miles over mountains and valleys and can only be seen from the air? Some guides will say that they're underground sources of water. How many rivers have you seen that run for miles stick straight, then cross each other to form trapezoids? When visitors ask about the images of animals, especially those that are extinct or are only found thousands of miles away, they just shrug their shoulders.

"Please remember that on the side of the hill, apart from the others, stands an image that depicts an astronaut, complete with helmet, goggles, and boots. When the locals are asked who made these lines, they point to the skies or mountain tops and say 'apu,' which means both 'mountain tops' and 'sky gods.' Similarly, when local Bedouins are asked who made the glyphs in the Middle East, they respond, 'The Old Ones.'

"The fact is, the planet earth was seeded by star people. Your DNA, for example, has been proven not to come from the earth."

"So all these geo-glyphs were made by visitors from other planets?" Rogelio mused aloud.

"You got it!!" a delighted Shelaya said.

"But why?" Sofía asked. "What do they mean?"

"You've heard all the theories, right?"

"Yes, but none of them is very satisfying, especially when you add in the random lines and circles found in other parts of the world," Sofía replied.

"Our ancestors and space brothers understood that everything is energy. So the straight lines are an indication of where the so-called synchronic or ley lines are located. These lines crisscross the planet and even go up into the skies. They were put there to help earth dwellers access that energy.

"The images of animals, created much later, were basically a message to let folks know that they weren't abandoned, that their space brothers were kind of winking at them, saying 'Hi. We're still here. Open to us and we can help you.'"

Sofía asked for the pad to be handed back to her and formed her next question.

Immediately this message flashed on the screen.

"Caral is the oldest settlement in the Americas. It's an example of an early society that lived in a way that's very similar to the way the Lemurians lived. Archaeologists found no instruments of warfare or struggle. What they found were flutes and other musical instruments, artwork, structures used for rituals and communal gatherings, and indications of global trade. In other words, your people need to know that war isn't inevitable. In fact, it's an activity that's limited to places of lower consciousness. In much of the galaxy and in specific places on earth in specific time periods, peace has reigned."

22
DESTINY

After waiting a fortnight without a reply, Rogelio and Sofía, the Waris, and the citizens of the City of Light decided that it was useless to continue to expect an answer from Pindar.

"As always, the cabal has a stranglehold on the surface population," Shelaya sighed. "I suppose it was naive of us to hope that they would change and at least agree to talk to us."

"Right." Samikai added, "They simply don't hold the consciousness of love and forgiveness. So how could we expect them to understand that we do?"

"What now?" Rogelio wondered out loud.

"Well," Shelaya answered, "if you're willing to continue working on the translations, we'd be eternally grateful. And we love having you here."

After exchanging a quick glance with Rogelio, Sofía answered, "We'd be delighted. It's fascinating to learn about the true history of our planet and remembering our lives as Pleija and Zamayo. Maybe we'll even gain some insights into where we as a civilization may be going."

The chief smiled and winked. "Be sure, then, to have a look at the section about prophecies."

Rogelio returned his grin. "OK, then, it's set. But we're a little concerned about our friends and family on the surface. For sure they'll be worried about us and wondering why we've been gone so long."

"Oh dear," Shelaya offered. "There are so many things we haven't had a chance to share with you yet. One of them is about time. You see time doesn't really exist. It's just an artificial construct that people on the surface have devised to try to make sense of and to try to take control their lives. We can easily stretch out or contract the appearance of time. So your friends and family won't sense that you've been gone a long time at all. However, if you would like, you can both compose texts to folks in Madrid, Los Angeles, and Ica just to say 'Hello. Thinking of you. All is well,' and we can send them via our smart glass pad."

So it was agreed. Sofía and Rogelio loved just being together without all the surface distractions. They became closer and closer and were increasingly fascinated by what they learned from the plaques.

Intrigued by what the chief had said about prophecies, they asked the council permission to work on that section. Here is what they learned:

What people in the lower dimensions perceive as time happens, not in a linear fashion, but in small and large cycles, one of which is the precession of the equinox, a 25,900-year cycle.

The ending of a great cycle occurred when Lemuria sank, approximately 52,000 years ago, and the ending of the next great cycle occurred at the major sinking of Atlantis, approximately 25,000 years ago. Great spiritual teachers such as Amaru Meru, Sananda, also known as Jesus the Christ, Buddha, and others appeared at the beginning of smaller cycles.

"Now you happen to be at the end of several cycles: Two turnings of the great cycle of 25,900 years, a 6,000 year cycle marking the shift from masculine to feminine energies, and a 2160 year astrological cycle, now moving from Pisces to Aquarius.

"So you can see that, as you read this, the planet is at a pivotal point. People must either choose to be Children of the Law of One or Sons of Belial—a simple choice between unity and separation. In other words, they can choose to live in love or in fear.

"Soon the surface population will have rediscovered space travel and will have established colonies on your moon, on Mars, and inside the moons of Jupiter and Saturn—although the vast majority of your citizens will be unaware of all this. Sadly, you will have also created a race of slaves just as the Atlanteans did with their so-called 'things' to do mining and other labor intensive, backbreaking and demeaning work. This time, however, the 'slaves' won't even realize they're slaves because of the insidious way the Black Hand has control over their lives.

"At that point in time, the situation on earth will be much like it was when the leaders of Atlantis (mostly governed by the Sons of Belial) determined that they should control, not only earth, but the entire solar system. Again, there will be boundless greed, selfishness, and cruelty. Obscene amounts of wealth will be in the hands of a very few while billions of others suffer from famine, disease, nuclear and chemical warfare, homelessness, extreme poverty, and hopelessness.

"Unless enough people consciously choose to work for the light, earth will likely self-destruct, leaving only a handful of people to stumble over a cold, dark, inhospitable landscape, faced with the daunting task of starting all over again as cavemen.

"Well, that was depressing," Sofía sighed. In their blissful state of living in the City of Light and their growing love, she and Rogelio had pushed to the back of their consciousness all the negativity they had experienced since her arrival in Peru.

"Right," Rogelio replied. "And I think it's time we look carefully at what's happened to you and try to figure out what caused it."

"OK. First there was the betrayal by my colleagues at Chauvet Cave. What caused that?"

"I think they were threatened by you. What do you sense was their main motivation?"

"A strong sense of competiveness, maybe caused by jealousy. And fear."

"I agree. Next, the bomb placed by your seat on the bus from Lima. Obviously someone didn't want the truth about the stones to get out. Motivation?"

"Fear of losing their ability to manipulate our understanding of our true history."

"Then there are the archaeologists, anthropologists, and historians who've found every reason in the world to dismiss the legitimacy and importance of the stones. If it were known that our history is much longer and richer than we ever imagined and all their books and research and reputations had to be discarded, how would they react? Motivation?"

"Fear that everything they've taught and learned and worked for would be thrown into the dustbin of history. This would cast doubt on everything, including their very identity."

"The goons who smashed our car and smeared a symbol of the Black Hand, obviously following orders from above. Motivation?"

"Fear, anger and frustration."

"Cafre's deception of your family?"

"Greed. Based on fear, I suppose."

"The Vatican who confiscated Father Crespi's treasures?"

"Definitely fear and pride."

'The thugs who attacked us in the tunnels and later turned up at the white powder gold ceremony?"

"Fear and gluttony."

"The clowns who showed up at our home and museum and threatened to bulldoze them?"

"Fear of their 'owners' wrath and pride, I suppose."

"All those throughout the course of history who have suppressed inventions that could have helped mankind?"

"Greed, stemming from fear and intellectual laziness."

"In other words, the cabal, which makes up less than 1% of the world's population, couldn't have maintained their stranglehold over the population if it weren't for our fear. And at the risk of offending you with religion, I'd like to suggest that all fear is related to one of the seven deadly sins: avarice, envy, wrath, sloth, gluttony, lust, and hubris."

Sofía smiled at him. "Your references to religion don't offend me anymore. In fact, I find it quite charming. Well, that was very enlightening, but shall we get back to the scrolls?"

As they were walking to the next section, they heard a tremendous rumbling of the earth above them, then a shaking. Items started falling to the ground. Shelaya rushed into the area of the Hall of Records where Rogelio and Sofía were working.

"Are you OK?" she shouted.

"Yes, I think so."

"Follow me!" she commanded.

The three of them ran to an elevator which took them down a long, long way. They could see crushed, cracked rocks, then an area where the rock had been completely vaporized. When the elevator's door opened, they found themselves in a large room that resembled a giant bunker. Most of the other citizens were already there.

"What in the world…?" Rogelio started to ask.

"We don't know yet. But we suspect that some surface group was stupidly conducting an underground nuclear test. Just a second, I'll check my smart glass pad for news."

Apparently Bolivia had illegally decided to develop a nuclear program with help from Russia, North Korea, and Venezuela and they chose this area, away from their own country's borders, to test it.

After several hours it was deemed safe for all the citizens to return to their homes and workplaces and begin the process of cleaning up. No one had been hurt, but they were seriously shaken up over the possibility that any country that wished to could test an atom bomb, start another world war, and destroy communities in the inner world as well as the surface. So the Council, Shelaya, the Waris, Sofía and Rogelio and decided to contact Pindar again. This time the note was succinct and to the point:

SURELY THE GLOBAL ELITE MUST REALIZE THAT ALLOWING FOR (OR EVEN ENCOURAGING) NUCLEAR WAR IS GLOBAL SUICIDE. WE KNOW YOU'VE PROFITED FROM WARS FOR MILLENNIA, BUT THIS COULD BE THE END OF ALL OF US.

Again, there was no answer.

Again they convened. An ominous silence filled the room. Finally Samikai spoke up.

"I have an idea. It's a long shot but obviously we don't have another solution. And it carries a big risk. It would require Sofía and Rogelio to return to the surface and begin a campaign to teach The Law of One. If they can get across to the people the idea that, in essence, we're all one, that we must forgive, that there is no such thing as death and therefore nothing to fear, we may have a chance to save humanity."

"How would that save humanity?" Sofía asked.

"Because the Illuminati rely on fear and divisiveness and anger. Once the people have a sense of unity rather than competition they may well be able to work together and quickly find an antidote to the poison."

The Wari chief added, "I agree. The people are ready. They're tired of fighting, tired of suffering, tired of oppression under cruel, greedy, oligarchs. Since the precepts of Oneness go back to the time Lemuria flourished, there is still a soul memory in many people. Also, the major world religions have as their core principles the same seven tenets as the Law of One."

"Which are?" Sofía asked.

Rogelio answered. "If I may, I'd like to answer that. I've been studying this my whole adult life. I believe the basic tenets are these:

1   Spirit, by whatever name, exists.

2   Spirit, although existing 'out there,' is also found 'in here,' or revealed within to the open heart and mind.

3   Most of us don't realize this Spirit within, however, because we're living in a world of sin, separation, or duality—that is, we're living in a fallen, illusory, or fragmented state.

4   There is a way out of this fallen state (of sin, illusion, and disharmony). There is a path to our liberation.

5   If we follow this path to its conclusion, the result is a *rebirth* or enlightenment, a direct experience of Spirit within and without, a supreme liberation.

6   Achieving this liberation marks the end of sin and suffering.

7   True enlightenment manifests in social action, mercy, and compassion toward of all sentient beings.

And so it was that, under the wise tutelage of Shelaya, Rogelio and Sofía began studying The Law of One.

"You must understand," Shelaya began, "that The Law of One is an ancient Truth that goes back 75,000 years even though it wasn't presented to your current civilization until 1981. And even then, very few people had access to it. At that time an entity known as RA spoke to a woman named Carla Rueckert and her colleagues, Don Elkins and James McCarty, wrote down the words verbatim. Eventually they produced a five-volume book called *The Law of One by RA, A Humble Messenger*. I'll give you copies of the book for you to study at your leisure, but I wanted to give you an overview first."

"So who is this fellow RA?" Sofía's voice carried just a hint of sarcasm.

Shelaya laughed. "You still hold a shadow of skepticism. But that's OK because it will help you relate better to those on the surface who respond to this teaching with doubt—or even outright rejection.

"RA is not a person. RA is a highly evolved group consciousness that originally came from Venus. It is of the seventh density (dimension) who came to earth several times to attempt to teach people about love, light, unity, and service to others. We'll get into more details when we delve into the teachings. But I wanted to give you some background first.

"The seed syllable RA comes from the first language known as the Universal Language of Spirit or the Language of Light. This language was used on earth eons ago, but has mostly been lost to time. More than descriptive, it's evocative and creative, intended to touch the vast and omnipresent reality of Spirit. Each syllable of the language carries a particular vibrational energy. As an expression of light/love, which is the central tenet of the Law of One, RA evokes the Divine attribute of the radiance of the Great Central Sun. You've heard of RA in other contexts, have you not?"

"Yes, of course," Rogelio replied. "RA was the sun god, the greatest of Egyptian gods."

"Right." Shelaya beamed. "That's because RA imparted this wisdom to the Egyptians 5,000 years ago. At first they accepted it and lived by its strictures. But, sadly, the Truths were then distorted and used for selfish gain among the rulers."

"You mentioned," Rogelio added, "that RA has attempted to share the Truth several times on planet earth. Was it ever successful?"

Shelaya again smiled at Rogelio. What do you think?"

Rogelio mirrored her smile. "Well, it seems pretty clear that your way of living here in the City of Light reflects those principles."

"Precisely," she exclaimed. "We've held them sacred ever since our ancestors left Lemuria. I know you two have gradually been remembering your lives as Pleija and Zamayo. Do you recall the name of your leader at that time?"

Rogelio's response was immediate. "ARaMu Meru."

"Ah, yes. I'm remembering now!" Sofía added.

"And have you thought about the etymology of his name?

'A' means to come into the physical, to manifest.

'Ra' refers to RA, the group consciousness from Venus.

'Mu,' of course, is another name for Lemuria.

'Meru' refers to 'serpent wisdom,' the understanding that everything is energy. The snake represents kundalini or life force."

"This is getting very exciting!" Rogelio exclaimed. "Several of the stones in my dad's collection represent just that!"

"Definitely something to think about," Shelaya commented. "Well, at any rate, you should know that, although few people remember ARaMu today, his teachings of the Law of One spanned from Lemuria to South America and then to much of the rest of the world. Today many places still carry his name and energy. For example, Mount Meru is a sacred mountain in Buddhist, Jain, and Hindu cosmology and is considered to be the center of all physical, metaphysical, and spiritual universes; mountain peaks in Angkor Wat in Cambodia and also in the Himalayas in India are called Meru; the ancient Sumerian culture is believed to come from the prefix 'su' meaning excellent, and 'meru;' and the Lemurian language is called Solara Meru, referencing both the sun and serpent energies."

"I'm just remembering," Rogelio added, "there's a tribe in southern California called the Chumash. They speak of the 'first people' from a land called 'Mu' and many of their villages have names ending in 'Mu.'"

"That's outstanding," Sofía commented. "But I always thought this legendary figure was named Amaru Meru."

"It's an alternative form," Shelaya explained. "You can imagine that, after thousands of years and spanning thousands of miles, variations of the name would evolve. Sofía, are you familiar with the mystical portal called Amaru Meru near Lake Titicaca?"

"No. I'm afraid not."

Rogelio jumped in. "I was going to take her there when we were in the area, but at that point I was desperately trying to get her to like me and she was desperately clinging to her belief that if you can't measure something it doesn't exist. So I figured that if I showed her the portal and told her the legend of Amaru Meru, she'd be on the first plane back to Spain."

Sofía laughed and took his hand. "You judge me harshly, my dear. Anyway, what's the legend?"

"It's not a legend," Shelaya explained. "It's historical fact. When our ancestors were preparing to leave Lemuria, Amaru was charged with taking the Solar Disc to the new land and keeping it safe. Which he did. At first it was hung at the Illumination Temple that they built in what later was called Cuzco. People had access to it to improve their lives in all kinds of ways. But then when the Spaniards came to steal, rape, and pillage, he decided it wasn't safe there… and apparently neither was he. So he took it to the inter dimensional portal known an Hayu Marca (also called Amaru Meru) and handed the disc to a shaman who was guarding the entrance. That shaman hid the disc under the lake.

"Amaru?"

"He walked straight through the solid stone and disappeared."

"Whew," Sofía exclaimed. "I can see why he was revered as a god and why his name's still all over the planet."

"But of course he wasn't a god," Shelaya explained. "He was simply a person of such high frequency that he could do things that seemed like magic. And this is the reason why The Law of One is so important. It helps people raise their frequency so that they can reclaim their God-given powers and re-create the paradise that once was."

This understanding motivated Sofía and Rogelio to double their efforts to learn the principles of The Law of One.

After a month of study with the text and Shelaya's guidance, they felt ready. So on the summer solstice Sofía and Rogelio sadly bid their friends in the City of Light goodbye and proceeded to the surface to begin teaching the basic concepts of the Law of One.

23

THE LAW OF ONE

Below are the teachings that Sofía and Rogelio shared with the surface population by means of lectures, webinars, booklets, and videos.

"The Law of One simply states that all things are one, that all beings are one. There is no polarity, no right or wrong, no disharmony, but only identity. All is one, and that one is love/light, light/love, the Infinite Creator. Each entity (mind/body/spirit complex) is a unique portion of that Creator.

"The universe is infinite. There is no end to your selves, to your journey of seeking, or to your perceptions of the creations.

"Love may be seen as the type of energy of an extremely high order. All love emanates from the Oneness/the Creator.

"The group known as RA came to earth many times to teach the Law of One. They wanted to impress upon those who wished to learn that in unity all paradoxes are resolved. All that is broken is healed. All that is forgotten is brought to light.

"Following is a list of their visits:

75,000 BCE – They helped the Martians come to Earth after their planet was destroyed.

58,000 BCE – Help was given to the citizens of Lemuria, who accepted the Law of One and lived by its precepts.

13,000 BCE – Help was offered to Atlantis.

11,000 BCE – The next attempt was to help the Egyptians and to some in South America.

7,500 BCE – Help was offered again to certain populations in South America.

2,300 BCE – There were more attempts to aid those in Egypt.

"Each time RA offered the same Truth: 'You are all players upon a stage. The stage changes. The acts ring down. The lights come up once again. And throughout this lifetime and the following and the following there is the undergirding majesty of the One Infinite Creator. All is well. Nothing is lost. Go forth rejoicing in the love and the light, the peace and the power of the One Infinite Creator.

"Students asked why, in each incarnation, entities forget what they had learned previously. RA answered with a metaphor of a poker game. If a player could see all the hands he would then know the game. It is but child's play to gamble, for it is no risk. The other hands are known. The possibilities are known and the hand will be played correctly but with no interest and no learning.

"Outside of time/space (in between incarnations), the hands of all are open to the eye. The thoughts, the feelings, the troubles, all these may be seen. There is no deception and no desire for deception. Thus much may be accomplished in harmony but the mind/body/spirit gains little polarity from this interaction.

"Let us re-examine this metaphor and multiply it into the longest poker game you can imagine, a lifetime. The cards are love, fear, dislike, limitation, unhappiness, pleasure, illness, loss, natural disaster, etc. They are dealt and re-dealt and re-dealt continuously. You may, during this incarnation begin—and we stress begin—to know your own cards. You may begin to find the love within you. You may begin to balance your pleasure, your limitations, etc. However, your only indication of others' cards is to look into their eyes.

"You cannot remember your hand, their hands, perhaps even the rules of the game. This game can only be won by those who lose their cards in the melting influence of love; can only be won by those who lay their pleasures, their limitations, their all upon the table face up and say inwardly: 'All, all of you players, each other-self, whatever your hand, I love you.' This is the game: to know, to accept, to forgive, to balance, and to open the self in love. This cannot be done without the forgetting, for it would carry no weight in the life of the mind/body/spirit beingness totality."

"Wanderers are a special group of people. Though they go through the same forgetting process as everyone else at birth and experience the same confusion, they have actually accomplished a union with light/love/oneness in a previous incarnation. They may not know why, but they came to earth with an overpowering desire to use their talents to serve their sisters and brothers who are suffering."

SUGGESTED EXERCISES FOR THE ACCELERATION TOWARD LIVING THE LAW OF ONE

Exercise One. The moment contains love. That is the lesson/goal of this density. The exercise is to consciously be that love.

Exercise Two. The universe is one being. When a mind/body/spirit complex views another mind/body/spirit complex, see the Creator.

Exercise Three. Look in a mirror. See the Creator.

Exercise Four. Gaze at the creations produced by every person. See the Creator.

These exercises are deepened through meditation, contemplation, or prayer. Otherwise, "the data will not sink down into the roots of the tree of mind, thus enabling and ennobling the body and touching the spirit."

That which is infinite cannot be many, for many-ness is a finite concept. In an infinite Creator there is only unity.

In truth there is no right or wrong. There is no polarity, for all will be reconciled at some point in your dance through the mind/body/spirit complex (lifetimes). You have chosen this belief in polarity instead of understanding the complete unity of thought that binds all things together.

You are unity. You are infinity.
You are love/light, light/love.
You are.
This is The Law of One.

24

THE POISONOUS DART FROG

Pindar unexpectedly burst into the chambers of the City of Light.

"OK," he screamed. "We warned you. You have acted in blatant disregard for our agreement and now we will carry out our end of the bargain. Now we must release the poison."

"What do you mean?" Shelaya asked.

"Don't play dumb with me. We know that Rogelio and Sofía are on the surface sharing the information on the plaques. It's all over the internet. Soon the whole world will know about the history of the world and our part in it."

"We have not released any information," Shelaya said calmly. "Sofía and Rogelio returned to the surface for a totally different purpose."

"You lie!" Pindar's rage was terrifying. "Then how did it get out?"

"Well. There are many possibilities. Surely you know that this isn't the only Hall of Records on the planet. There is another copy in Sumer and another under the paw of the Sphinx in Egypt. Additionally, pieces of this information have been uncovered by archeologists, by the American National Security Agency, by whistleblowers, and by intuitives from every corner of the world. Your 'global elite' buddies certainly must have known that the information would be leaked sooner or later."

Pindar's fury seemed to increase the scaly appearance of his skin. As he spun around toward the door, Shelaya said calmly, "Before you go we'd like you to have this. Please take it back to your people and show them the contents." She handed Pindar a small device as he slammed out the door.

"What was that?" The Wari chief asked.

"It's a flash memory-based digital magazine that contains a movie of the worst of human suffering over the millennia. It shows the unspeakable agony of billions of people caused by the dark cabal. If Pindar and his people have even an iota of compassion, they may be moved to see up close and personal the misery caused by their unquenchable quest for power. I don't hold out much hope for success, but seemed like it was worth a try."

Several months went by. Sofía and Rogelio continued teaching. Life in the City of Light went on although everyone was noticeably tense.

One day they received a message from Pindar on the smart glass pad. "We have viewed your ridiculous movie. Can't you see that to us, it would by like your watching the scurrying around of mindless cockroaches? It means nothing. Therefore, we hereby give notice that we are preparing to release the toxin. In fact, just so you know, we are currently preparing the nanites and breeding sufficient number of frogs to produce enough secretion to stamp out the scourge of life on this planet."

Shelaya was desperate and wrote, "You would destroy your own followers as well in the process?" The smart glass pad was silent.

But later it lit up with a message from Sofía and Rogelio. "How are the negotiations going?"

"Not well at all," Shelaya wrote back. "Pindar says they're in the process of preparing the nanites and batrachotoxin and will release them as soon as they're ready. How are you doing?"

Shelaya and the council members waited a long time before they received an answer. "People are responding extremely well to our teachings. But to what avail...?"

25

DESPERATE DECISION

When they returned to the surface, Sofía and Rogelio decided to live temporarily in Rogelio's home in Los Angeles. They felt that they could more effectively broadcast the Law of One's message from a large U.S. metropolis, and Rogelio didn't want his family in Ica to worry unnecessarily by knowing what they were doing and why.

After receiving Shelaya's message they were paralyzed with shock. Then they fell into each other's arms.

They clung to each other, speechless, for long moments.

"So it comes to this," Rogelio finally spoke. "We lose Lemuria and each other. Two major cycles of time pass. We finally remember. We find each other again, only to lose, not only each other this time, but all of life on planet earth."

"I'm not sure my heart can take it. It may simply stop right now." Sofía whispered.

"We could return to the City of Light. We'd be safe there," Rogelio ventured.

"And you know we won't do that," she smiled weakly through her tears.

At that very moment the smart glass pad lit up with a message from Shelaya. "You have both been brave and smart and dedicated through this whole ordeal. But it's clear there's nothing more to do. We beg you to come back now before it's too late."

They replied immediately. "We can't. We're making great progress. It's obvious that the world is now ready to learn about The Law of One. People are tired of the fighting, suffering, lies, and oppression. The teachings are spreading quickly. If we can't save lives, at least we can bring comfort to the people's hearts. Perhaps their deaths will be easier. Perhaps their souls will have taken a step forward in preparation for their next lives. So we plan to stay here and continue teaching for as long as we can."

That night their passion was even more intense than it had been thousands of years earlier, the last time Pleija and Zamayo were together and when she became pregnant.

Later that night as Sofía lay peacefully in his arms, Rogelio said to her, "You know, in all the turmoil, we've never discussed the birthmarks that we both have. Have you been able to figure out what they mean?"

Sofía clung to him as she sighed, "No."

"I finally figured out the symbols."

"The circle with the dot in the middle and the upside down N?"

"Right. Basically they say: Do not grieve. Everything lost comes round in another form."

Sofía and Rogelio continued their teaching for three more months, creating webinars that went viral worldwide.

26

THE END OF THE WORLD

Meanwhile Pindar called together the 300 most powerful Illuminati families and the most elite scientists at their secure quarters at Bohemian Grove in California. There he explained the plan. Some cabal members were ordered to set up a lab, others to perfect the nanite technology, and others to travel to Colombia and coerce the natives there to help them collect 50 dart frogs.

It took two months for the plan to materialize as the technology was tricky, the natives were at first reluctant to comply, and some of the most elite cabal members simply rebelled, saying this plan was total insanity.

"How are we going to control a planet that has no inhabitants?"

"We aren't. When we release the poison you'll be directed to a safe place—either in the inner earth or on another planetary system. Isn't it clear that we're living our last few months of existence on the surface of this planet? Our future work will be elsewhere."

Those illuminists who continued to argue with Pindar were eliminated in the most inhumane ways.

Another two months went by.

Rogelio and Sofía continued to spread the word about the Law of One.

The Illuminati continued to work on their plan to poison the planet.

Eventually those who had gone to Colombia returned with their deadly cargo.

Meanwhile, the biologists in the group had set up an elaborate breeding program for the frogs.

In another three months everything was in place. The nanite technology was perfected. The breeding had begun. The plan was to go through four cycles (of three months each) from egg to tadpole to frog. Since dart frogs lay hundreds of eggs, the experts calculated that it would take about a year to have the required number. Then they devised a variety of torture techniques—many of which they had already used on humans—to create great stress and causing the hapless frogs to secrete their fatal fluids.

Living in close quarters for so long was creating tensions among many of the illuminists. After all, they were accustomed to living in luxury with slaves available to fulfill their every fantasy. There were already hostile feelings among the various factions and the diabolical plan that Pindar had devised was asking even the most hardened of them to take a second look at what they'd committed to. But keeping in mind what had happened to those who objected, most remained belligerently silent.

Rogelio and Sofía continued to teach about oneness, forgiveness, and love.

The citizens of the City of Light were not at all optimistic about the planet's future, but they continued to pray and send loving energies to all involved.

Finally the day arrived when the nanites with the poison were to be released.

Pindar organized a bloody ritual to commemorate the occasion. Then, using drones, they dropped the nanites on every region in the world.

After Operation Amphibian, as it was named, was launched, Pindar sat back and chortled. He couldn't remember feeling so content in his long, long life. All he had to do now was wait. Civilization on earth would vanish and with it the threat that he and his cohorts would be punished, humiliated, tortured, and probably killed for their vicious crimes against humanity.

He sent a gleeful, taunting message to Shelaya.

He waited.

He watched the news closely.

But after a week there were no reports of an epidemic—in fact, no unusual outbreaks of disease at all.

However, after eight days Pindar's own team began to get desperately ill and die.

One day later the Great Pindar, Lizard King of the Global Elite, ruler over all the earth since time out of mind, took his last breath.

EPILOGUE

What the Illuminati had failed to take into consideration, and what the Emberá natives astutely didn't mention, is that the dart frog is only poisonous in the wild. There it feeds on a beetle that combines with its own DNA to create the toxic secretion. In captivity it is harmless. So for the first generation of frogs, the stress of being captured and transported had caused the deadly secretions to be emitted. Those who were sent to Colombia to collect them brought the toxin back to the Bohemian Woods and inadvertently shared it with all in the compound. The secretion of the frogs' progeny that was dumped onto the populace did no damage whatsoever.

Although the inner circle of the cabal (the Black Hand) had virtually eliminated themselves, there were still thousands of people who considered themselves part of the elite because of their bloodlines and training. These people were in leadership positions in finance, religion, politics, education, healthcare and science. It seemed that they would not give up their wealth and power easily.

Rogelio, Sofía, and the Waris returned to the City of Light to confer with Shelaya and the Council members about how to address this problem. They decided that they would send the announcement of the deaths of Pindar and his inner circle along with a version of Sofía's letter and the video to major world leaders. They also posted copies on the internet, in newspapers, and on television and radio. This was followed by announcements that there would be a peace and reconciliation forum for all those who came forward, admitted what they had done, and released classified documents.

Surprisingly, most did come forward—enough so that the systems that kept the populace in a stranglehold were dismantled. Those cabal leaders who had done the most damage were required to do public service and undergo rehabilitation therapy.

As a consequence, the following years brought huge changes to the people. In another decade poverty and all the miseries it brought were gradually eliminated.

Gold worth hundreds of billions of dollars that had been stolen and hidden by the cabal was redistributed to the populace.

Papers on suppressed inventions enabled people to build sources of free energy and invent transportation systems that were fast, quiet, and pollution free. They developed efficient ways to produce nutritious food, created techniques for healing every disease known to mankind, cleaned the environment, balanced the climate, and began using replicators to duplicate everything needed by the happy and grateful surface population.

Pyramids, stone circles, and energy hot spots were reactivated and once again utilized for anti-aging and rejuvenation.

Ancient healing technologies such as the use of plasma, sound, light, color, herbs, and the power of intent were 'remembered' and used widely.

The Ica Stone museum was enlarged and, thanks to the book that Sofía wrote giving her interpretations of the etchings, enjoyed great popularity and welcomed hundreds of thousands of visitors.

The Nazca lines were reopened so that people could walk in the positive energies and be uplifted. Civilizations from the City of Light, as well as those from other star systems visited the surface population often, teaching and sharing the secrets of their advanced societies.

Under a more compassionate pope, Father Crespi's treasures were returned to Cuenca and the museum was reopened under the direction of Padre Anselmo, who decided he wanted to spend his final years with Crespi's treasures and ministering to the natives of Cuenca. Prominently displayed in the museum's window was the statue that

Crespi had saved and hidden in the basement of his church. It portrayed a reptilian that held an uncanny similarity to Pindar.

It would serve as a reminder to the people of the Reptilian Illuminati who had wreaked such misery on the surface population for millennia, but from now on, thanks to the efforts of many brave souls, would only remain a distant memory.

At Tiajuanaco, the local Aymara people saw Amaru appear and disappear through the portal of Haya Marca. "He must return home to the realm of the gods," they said. "But then he returns, as he always has, to bring peace and prosperity to the people."

The Solar Disc? With great ceremony the citizens of the City of Light returned it to the surface and taught the people how to use it. Then, to everyone's astonishment, they used their replicators to make copies so that every community on the planet that wanted a solar disc could have one.

The Waris returned to their old ways. Freed from the task of guarding the tunnels, they reveled in their joyful connections with Gaia, with each other, with their music and dance, their rituals and their stories. And one of the stories most enjoyed by the young ones was that of two white people who participated in an ayahuasca ceremony, learned who they had been, translated the ancient texts, and changed everything.

As for Sofía and Rogelio, they had a beautiful wedding ceremony in the Illumination Temple. They spent their honeymoon on Easter Island, where a guide pointed out a recently excavated Maoi with the image of a sailing ship etched onto it.

They worked as sacred activists on the surface for ten years, helping to bring about what many called the Return of the Golden Age.

They named their first daughter Pleija.

Then they returned to the City of Light and lived in joy with their soul brethren whom they had been missing without ever realizing it... for so very, very long.